The War Everlasting had consisted of a thousand battles

But rarely had the Executioner been pushed so hard, bludgeoned and bruised and battered like he had this time.

But he pushed himself. He had become too personally invested in what started out as a favor for Aaron Kurtzman.

The reason? The nature of the crime struck a powerful chord in Bolan. He had seen war. He knew men who were captured by the enemy.

It was to a nation's shame that it failed to bring back its prisoners of war. But for a man of power to deliberately abandon his nation's soldiers to the enemy was so dishonorable to those men that it was a personal affront to Bolan.

That was why he had fought and fought and struggled to keep going despite the pleas of his body to rest.

Bolan the Patriot had been incapable of permitting the stain to linger uncleansed.

MACK BOLAN ®
The Executioner

The Executioner

Don Pendleton's

MERCY MISSION

A GOLD EAGLE BOOK FROM

W☉RLDWIDE®

TORONTO • NEW YORK • LONDON
AMSTERDAM • PARIS • SYDNEY • HAMBURG
STOCKHOLM • ATHENS • TOKYO • MILAN
MADRID • WARSAW • BUDAPEST • AUCKLAND

First edition May 2004
ISBN 0-373-64306-3

Special thanks and acknowledgment to
Tim Somheil for his contribution to this work.

MERCY MISSION

Nothing can excuse a general who takes advantage of the knowledge acquired in the service of his country, to deliver up her frontier and her towns to foreigners. This is a crime reprobated by every principle of religion, morality and honor.

—Napoleon I

There is no greater crime than when men of power buy amnesty for themselves. I am here to deliver justice to those men. I am here to make them pay.

—Mack Bolan

THE
MACK BOLAN®
LEGEND

Nothing less than a war could have fashioned the destiny of the man called Mack Bolan. Bolan earned the Executioner title in the jungle hell of Vietnam.

But this soldier also wore another name—Sergeant Mercy. He was so tagged because of the compassion he showed to wounded comrades-in-arms and Vietnamese civilians.

Mack Bolan's second tour of duty ended prematurely when he was given emergency leave to return home and bury his family, victims of the Mob. Then he declared a one-man war against the Mafia.

He confronted the Families head-on from coast to coast, and soon a hope of victory began to appear. But Bolan had broken society's every rule. That same society started gunning for this elusive warrior—to no avail.

So Bolan was offered amnesty to work within the system against terrorism. This time, as an employee of Uncle Sam, Bolan became Colonel John Phoenix. With a command center at Stony Man Farm in Virginia, he and his new allies—Able Team and Phoenix Force—waged relentless war on a new adversary: the KGB.

But when his one true love, April Rose, died at the hands of the Soviet terror machine, Bolan severed all ties with Establishment authority.

Now, after a lengthy lone-wolf struggle and much soul-searching, the Executioner has agreed to enter an "arm's-length" alliance with his government once more, reserving the right to pursue personal missions in his Everlasting War.

1

The big man in the wheelchair stared at the phone, then allowed his eyes to wander to one of the flat-screen computer monitors. Several windows on the display silently tracked the progress of various high-level global spiders. The spiders, the man's creations, were cybernetic monsters—among the most sophisticated network cataloging and analysis applications ever invented. They hacked indiscriminately into high-level secure systems the world over. The man in the wheelchair wasn't interested in their progress. He was looking at the tiny blue numerals in the top right corner of the screen: 12:23 a.m.

Just four hours to go.

Seven more minutes was all he could give it, and then he was going to have to start involving the others. That would launch all of them on a course of action he would prefer to avoid if at all possible.

This was a matter that had to be handled quietly, ideally by someone who could and would ignore the repercussions.

The big man wasn't the nervous type—not by a long shot— but when the phone chimed he jumped. The phone was in his hand before the ring was complete.

The voice on the line said only, "It's me."

"Striker, thank God," the man in the wheelchair said. "You still in the vicinity?"

"I just checked into a hotel in Providence," the caller said. "What's wrong, Bear?"

"I need you to handle something. If you will."

"Of course. Just tell me what," the caller said.

"I'll explain while you drive. There's just four hours to go."

The man on the other end of the line did not ask, "Four hours until what?" Instead, without hesitation, he said, "I'll check out and call you from the car. What's my destination?"

"Head west. Pennsylvania."

"I'll call you back in five."

As the line went dead, the man in the wheelchair felt eyes on his back. He spun and found himself being scrutinized by a beautiful blond woman with intelligent eyes, dressed in jeans and a casual shirt. She was leaning on the door frame.

They were old friends, and the silence communicated volumes. The big man said, "Don't even ask. Please."

The beautiful blonde nodded and left.

AT 4:39 A.M. the south gate of the Fairchilde Federal Penitentiary opened. An extended Chevrolet delivery van rolled through, and the driver waved to the guard at the post. The gates slid shut as the van drove slowly along the access road. The land outside the prison was pancake flat and was lit up like a night baseball game. Finally the van pulled onto the highway, leaving the penitentiary behind it.

The driver had his window open, straining to hear some sound of alarm from the prison, but there was only the rush of wind.

"Anything?" he asked.

"Nothing," said the hawk-nosed giant in the passenger seat, who was poking his head out the window to look for pursuit while monitoring an emergency radio scanner with a plug in one ear.

"We pulled it off," the driver said, his excitement growing. "Congratulations, Khalid. You're a free man!"

Khalid al-Jabir crouched in the back with a broad grin on his face. "Congratulations go to you. That was a fine piece of planning and your timing was perfection," he replied.

The driver beamed. Once it was known he was the man behind the breakout he would achieve an instant high level of esteem. He would reap the benefits from this success for years to come.

Then he glimpsed something on the road, like a wood plank, suddenly visible out of the blackness. It was too late to swerve around it. The van went right over it and all four tires burst noisily.

The driver swore and wrestled for control of the van while the others shouted in alarm, not understanding what had happened. The van loped sloppily across the four empty lanes, then swerved across the other way.

"Use the brakes, you idiot!" snapped the man in the back.

The driver didn't have time to defend his driving skills. "I am!" he cried.

He dragged on the steering wheel as the shoulder loomed but couldn't steer the van away from it. The ruined, soggy tire rubber rolled into the gravel, and what little control the driver had was lost. Still traveling more than thirty miles per hour, the van felt as if it were sliding on polished ice. Its rear swung into a ditch and one of the rims found a shallow drainage depression, not even six inches deep, but deep enough to grab the rim and not let go. The inertia lifted the van's outermost rims off the ground, while the front rim dug into the gravel and for a half second the big, ungraceful truck was pivoting on the one rim. Then gravity took it, pulled it over, and the passenger side of the van slammed into the opposite earthen wall of the drainage ditch with a bone-jarring crunch of metal.

An instant later came silence and darkness so abrupt that the driver thought he was dead until the pain told him otherwise.

The van was lifeless, lights out, the engine stalled. There were no highway lights here. No nearby glow of a town. Even the crickets had stopped chirping. Then he heard a groan from the back seat.

"Are you injured, Khalid?"

"I don't know," was the terse response.

The man in the passenger seat was slumped against the door, where the window was now filled with grass and weeds and broken glass. When the passenger turned to look at the driver zombielike, his face was a mass of blood and torn flesh. "What happened?" he slurred, mouth hanging open.

"A trap," the driver said.

"What?" the man in the back seat demanded.

"Someone put a piece of wood in the road with nails to blow the tires. There was no time to go around it."

"Let's go!" al-Jabir ordered. The driver heard him climbing over the empty pallets, then one rear door opened.

"Come on," the driver urged as he unlatched the seat belt that held him dangling at a strange angle. He crawled through the rear after al-Jabir, not giving voice to his doubts that the man in the passenger seat was capable of even standing, let alone extracting himself from the wreck. But the passenger followed him and a minute later they were all clambering up the drainage ditch, where they marched through a dark field of wildflowers.

"If it was a trap, then where are the police?" al-Jabir asked, panting.

"I do not know," the driver whispered. "It is strange."

"Are you sure you didn't drive into a pothole?" demanded the bloody passenger, who acted oblivious to his wounds but strained to keep up with the fast pace set by al-Jabir.

"No pothole will flatten four tires at one time," the driver retorted. "Look, we're just a mile from the rendezvous point."

He ignored the pain in his shoulder. He knew if he started thinking about it he would feel its full intensity. Broken shoulder, maybe. The ground sloped away, the going was easy and the fugitive al-Jabir matched him step for step.

The driver and al-Jabir marched through a weed-filled depression in the field, then the driver glanced over his shoulder to check his lagging partner. He was just in time to see the man plod into the depression. For a moment the man was hidden from view by the tall plants and ground-hugging darkness.

Then the moment turned into seconds.

"Os?" the driver called.

Al-Jabir halted. "What's the problem?"

"Osman collapsed. I'll help him."

"We can't afford a delay. If he's too weak to continue…" Khalid al-Jabir shrugged.

"I understand."

The driver hurried back and descended into the depression. It was dark, but he thought he could make out a flat place in the waist-high field grass. He crouched and felt in the grass. No Osman.

The driver was suddenly angry. Where was the man? Had he trooped off in the wrong direction? Why had everything gone so wrong? Dammit, his shoulder hurt!

And why hadn't he brought a flashlight? He couldn't see a thing. But who would have thought he would need a flashlight, of all things, for this job?

"Osman!" he whispered.

The man was a friend, but that wouldn't stop him from abandoning him here to fend for himself. The risk was too great to al-Jabir.

There was something on his hands where he had touched the flattened grass. He sniffed his hand and smelled blood. He thought he saw a spot where the grass was drenched.

Osman hadn't been bleeding that much. Had he?

Then something materialized out of the blackness where there had been nothing before. It was inhuman, a walking nightmare—nothing else could have come through the night so silently, passing among the plants without moving them. The thing was somehow blacker than the darkness, a phantom that absorbed light. Every one of the supernatural night creatures in his grand-uncle's folk tales came true in this thing that came at him now.

In his moment of terror, the driver saw Osman sprawled at the feet of the phantom, his neck opened from ear to ear. *The phantom had begun to feed.*

The driver opened his mouth to scream and raised his handgun, his last wish to be the instrument of his own death rather than allow his soul and body to be consumed by this American specter.

The phantom reached for him like the flitting of a shadow and the same blade that killed Osman sliced the driver's neck wide-open, cutting off the scream.

The driver's last heartbeat of life was spent trying to reconcile superstition and reality. If it moved like a spirit it had to be a spirit. But why would a spirit use a mundane steel blade for killing?

KHALID AL-JABIR BECAME suspicious. Something was wrong, and all that fool had brought him was a handgun to defend himself! He aimed at the place where the two men had vanished, holding the weapon in both hands.

A sound came from the dark place, almost like a whisper, strange yet familiar. Al-Jabir felt his blood grow cold when it came to him: it was the wet wheeze of breath from a freshly cut throat.

The murderer cursed silently. He was alone, he was pursued! Two men dead in two minutes!

Al-Jabir ran.

THE SPECTER USED UP precious seconds retrieving the wallets belonging to the dead men, then crept out of the depression in time to see the fleeing figure of Khalid al-Jabir. The specter raced after the fugitive, taking care on the uneven ground. Al-Jabir was a gaunt, long-legged giant who ate up the distance and was lucky or skilled enough to avoid a twisted ankle.

But his luck didn't last.

AL-JABIR SAW THE CAR, tucked out of sight of the highway behind the shelter of a small copse of roadside trees. He poured on the speed, ignoring the needlelike sting of the grass that whipped against his arms. He yanked at the door, snatching the key from under the seat and stabbing it into the ignition. When he cranked the key hard he heard an ominous silence.

Someone swept out of the trees, and al-Jabir understood the trap in an instant. The car's battery was disconnected. Another figure moved in from the rear, coming to the passenger door. They were just waiting for him.

"Don't move! Hands on the wheel!" The first man had a shotgun aimed through the open window and moved sideways to take a safe position over al-Jabir's left shoulder.

Al-Jabir came up with a plan and knew it had to go into effect instantly, before the second man had him fully in view and before the shotgunner was unreachable.

"Okay! Okay!" al-Jabir said, but then he twisted in his seat, yanked up his feet and propelled them against the unlatched passenger door. It slammed into the shotgunner's groin and abdomen. The shotgunner went flying. Al-Jabir twisted and thrust a hand at the rear window, triggering the Glock at the second ambusher. There was an explosion of glass, and the figure disappeared from view.

"Son of a bitch!" the shotgunner exclaimed. Al-Jabir sought him in the blackness, but the man was behind a tree, still armed. "Team Beta, I have a man down! Get over here!" the shotgunner cried.

Al-Jabir scrambled out the passenger door and fired twice at the trees for cover, then bolted away as a pair of headlights appeared, barreling in his direction. He ran back into the field and felt the headlights sweep across his body with spotlight intensity as the vehicle swerved off the road, tires skidding on the gravel. He heard its engine power it into the field, following hard on his churning heels, and al-Jabir wondered if he'd find a place to lose the thing on terrain like this.

A small tree less than six feet to his left dissolved into confetti under a burst of murderous machine-gun fire.

What was *that?* Al-Jabir had enough experience with man-portable machine guns to know that wasn't one. He also knew they hadn't missed. If they wanted him dead, it would have taken a simple sweep of the landscape to cut him down.

"Stop and drop the weapon." The order came through a bullhorn and echoed into the night.

Al-Jabir froze, the scraps of green leaves still fluttering around his ankles, and he let the Glock fall from his sweaty hand.

2

Something wasn't right.

The man in the shadows knew it when he came upon the altercation at the parked getaway car. The men who tried to arrest al-Jabir didn't act like cops. The armored SUV that brought the fugitive to the ground, a customized Ford Excursion, definitely was not standard law-enforcement equipment. So who were they? Why were they here? What were their motives?

He held back, monitoring the situation. He would let the behavior of the newcomers tell him what action to take, if any. If these were agents from a legitimate government agency, then they were welcome to al-Jabir. Let them have the job of returning the fugitive to his cell in the federal penitentiary.

But the man in the shadows doubted that was their intention.

Mack Bolan had lived through the hells of war, and the purgatory of more battlefields than he cared to remember. His skills were honed to an uncanny level, but it was his warrior instinct telling him now that things were even stranger than they looked.

And they became stranger still.

Khalid al-Jabir was surrounded by three armed men in dark clothing. One of them was the ambusher with the shotgun, the others sported Vektor CR21 assault rifles, and they all kept a healthy cushion of space between themselves and their prisoner. They did not identify themselves. There was no reading of rights. They didn't even seem anxious to get him into handcuffs. Al-

Jabir just stood there with his hands on his head, the discarded Glock inches from his feet.

"Where are the others?" asked the shotgunner, a man with a heavy build and a bad case of nerves. He looked like an agitated gorilla, pacing, scratching, gesticulating, incapable of standing still.

"What others?" Al-Jabir feigned ignorance.

"The ones who sprung you! Don't play games," growled the shotgunner.

"You are the one playing games. You killed those men."

"Oh really? When did we do that, amigo?"

"Only just five minutes ago. Back that way." Al-Jabir jerked his head slightly back the way he had come.

Bolan crept through the grass, trying to get close as the heads of two of the men converged. One was Shotgun, who came across as the leader.

They were in black sweatshirts and sweatpants with black deck shoes—outfits that looked like they were just bought off the rack. The shirts swelled over body armor but the pants clung to their legs. No leg armor. Potentially useful information.

They never took their eyes off al-Jabir as Bolan moved close enough to hear their quiet exchange.

"He either killed them himself or they got lucky and got away when we moved in on Khalid at the car," Shotgun said. "It would be a stroke of luck if he did them."

"Yeah, well, here's another possibility," the taller, leaner man said. "The others are still in the vicinity. We go hiking around out there, and we'll be totally exposed."

Shotgun shook his head. "Not at all. We have night vision. They don't. They would have seen no need for it on this jailbreak job."

"That's assuming they didn't plan on pulling the car off to the side of the road and hiking the last mile. I'm not convinced it was a genuine breakdown."

Shotgun rocked from one foot to the other, nodding. "We'll take the SUV and we'll all go on thermal, no lights. You drive. Jay will stay at the gun and I'll walk our friend to the corpses,

if there are any. Jay'll see any warm living bodies before they
can reach us, and he'll swat 'em."

"You sure it's worth the risk?" The other man sounded
skeptical.

"Hell, yeah. It makes the hit a lot easier to explain, and that
means less likelihood of a full investigation. You gotta know it'll
be the Bureau looking into it."

"I don't like it."

"I don't care," Shotgun retorted. "We're doing it."

MACK BOLAN WRESTLED with a list of unusual facts, but every
logical structure he tried to make with them collapsed in a mess.

He had been given a full briefing on al-Jabir. Who he was,
why he was in jail, who he *really* was and why he was important. Aaron Kurtzman, a cybernetic scavenger without peer, had
assembled a few meager scraps of information to come up with
the background information. One of those scraps was a code
name used by a U.S. cell to identify its leader.

Kurtzman's network-roaming spiders had come up with an
unexpected reference to the code name. The system automatically alerted him, and he read the hacked communiqué with
growing dread. He had immediately tried to reach Mack Bolan,
the one man who might actually be able to do something about
the situation.

That was eight hours ago. Bolan had been…indisposed, and
was unable to respond at once. When his business in Rhode Island
was completed, he learned Kurtzman was eager to talk to him. The
Stony Man cybernetics master had given him all the details on a
jailbreak about to happen, but Kurtzman's briefing included nothing about an interested third party. Bolan needed to know more.

He wasn't going to let them cut down al-Jabir in cold blood,
which was what it sounded like they were planning. Not that al-
Jabir didn't deserve to die. It was just that the Iraqi killer had information that Mack Bolan wanted—before he was sent to hell.

BOLAN MOVED like a shadow after the dangerous caravan that
rolled off into the night. First was al-Jabir, hands on his head. It

now made sense to Bolan why he wasn't cuffed. They planned to murder him alongside the bodies of his companions and set it up to look like a fatal fallout occurred among the members of the terrorist cell. Wrists abraded by struggling in handcuffs would be a sign that there was more to the story. Shotgun wanted a nice, neat murder scene, one that would satisfy the FBI with minimal investigation.

Behind the fugitive walked Shotgun himself, with the big combat 12-gauge pointed unerringly at the sweat-drenched back of his captive. The weapon was the only part of him that stayed still—he was always scratching, wetting his lips, nodding to himself, flipping his bangs off his forehead. He walked just ahead of the Excursion, which had custom exterior styling that did away with any and all brightwork and replaced it with an almost matte black finish. The paint made a token effort at disguising the custom armor body panels. The tires were heavy-duty run-flats. The glass was dark and doubtless bullet resistant.

The SUV's most extravagant nonstandard equipment was the oversize moon roof, which slid back to allow a .50-caliber belt-fed machine gun to be elevated out and manned by a gunner standing on footrests. The man Shotgun had called Jay stood there now, protruding from the roof from the waist up.

If al-Jabir had any thoughts of making a run for freedom, he changed his mind when he got a good look at his escort. The combat shotgun wasn't three yards behind him. It couldn't miss, and even if it somehow did, the torrential fire from the machine gun would defoliate the land until it found him and cut him in two.

Bolan knew precisely where the bodies lay and knew the procession would reach them in minutes, even at their measured pace. He did not have long to act, but he wasn't even sure what to do.

Doubt was an odd sensation for a man like Bolan. He was a veteran of countless interdictions, and was guided by an innate ability to read the hearts of men—at least well enough to identify those worthy of his justice. He was absolutely confident that all of these men were murderers. He wouldn't hesitate to wipe them out, every one of them, if the situation required it.

But the stakes were bigger than these four men, and Bolan wanted to know how much bigger. Aaron Kurtzman would want to know too. Bolan was thinking about how to most effectively stir things up. Then Kurtzman could track the disturbance all the way to its source. Then, maybe Bolan would find an opportunity to cut the head off the snake.

But there was an even more important concern, and as much as it went against his nature he had to make saving the life of Khalid al-Jabir his top priority.

Al-Jabir knew he would be a dead man as soon as they reached the bodies of his companions, and he was looking for any chance to try to escape, no matter how risky. Al-Jabir had nothing to lose. Bolan knew the fugitive had probably decided that the depression where the bodies lay would offer him the best chance—a place where he just might have enough cover to avoid the gunfire that would come chasing after him the moment he bolted.

Bolan's biggest risk came from the machine gunner, who was perched high and wore thermal night-vision goggles that would have made the Executioner stand out in the cool night air. But the machine gunner's attention was on his prisoner. He never even considered that attackers might come from the rear. Bolan reached the rear bumper unseen and got a handhold, then walked along with the vehicle waiting for the right moment.

It came seconds later when a rear tire rolled over and crushed a bush with a small bounce. Simultaneously Bolan put his body weight on the big Ford's seven thousand pounds. The driver never felt the difference. The gunner never sensed the presence of the Executioner and couldn't quite believe it when somebody spoke right behind him. "Hey."

Jay's head whipped around in time to receive the butt of a heavy black handgun in the temple.

Bolan caught the slumping body, relieved it quickly of its eyewear and propped the body on the machine gun, then slithered off the platform into the back seat of the Excursion.

"What the hell are you doing?" the driver demanded, glancing in the rearview mirror. "Cap'll ream your ass."

Bolan inserted the cold steel muzzle of the Israeli-made Desert Eagle in the man's neck. "Not if I ream his first."

"Who the hell are you?" The driver was disdainful, without a hint of fear in his voice.

"That's my question for you," Bolan said. "You a Company outfit?"

"Listen, asshole, I ain't answering none of your fu—" The next sound he made was a combination gag and choke when the cold edge of a heavy blade pressed against his throat. The pressure was strong enough to close his windpipe, and the driver stiffened from the keen edge creasing his skin. He was fully aware that his slightest movement would send it slicing through the flesh.

The driver lost his attitude.

"Who?" Bolan said, and released the pressure just enough to allow a squeak of air to pass through the man's neck.

"Army. Staff of General Juvenal."

"Let me guess—you're his personal chauffeur, and the clown with the 12-gauge is his secretary."

"More or less," croaked the driver. Bolan could feel the man's tension under the knife, his body held as motionless as possible while continuing to make the small adjustments to the steering wheel to keep the Excursion rolling over the uneven terrain.

"Juvenal sent you?" Bolan adjusted the pressure.

"Not officially," whispered the driver.

"So what are you unofficially supposed to be doing?" Bolan asked. "Assassinating Khalid al-Jabir?"

"Yes!" wheezed the driver, sounding desperate as he fought the rising panic that came from getting not quite enough air to live on.

"Because he knows about the Seven Scorpions," Bolan stated.

The driver's eyes went wide in the rearview mirror, sufficiently shocked to momentarily forget about the gun pressing into his skull and the knife edge drawing blood against his throat.

"Seven Scorpions?" The driver's stammering made him sound unconvincing.

"The prisoners."

"What prisoners?"

Bolan glared into the mirror. "You're a bad liar. Thanks for the confirmation. Maybe I'll let General Juvenal know it was you who implicated him."

The driver's eyes swam in lunatic circles, and his lips pursed to optimize his intake of each tiny breath. Bolan watched the panic bubble swell, then burst. The driver twisted his neck and jerked aside to free it from the blade while twisting the wheel. Bolan's iron grip on the blade held fast, and the result was suicide—the driver sliced his own throat. Bolan leaped for the steering wheel as the driver went limp, whipping it back on course.

Shotgun was staring at the misbehaving SUV, and it was quite possible that with all the lights off he would be able to glimpse the events going on inside the vehicle—enough to know something was going wrong. They went from bad to worse as al-Jabir took the opportunity to make a break for it.

Bolan saw it happen as if in slow motion. The fugitive launched himself into a run. Shotgun spun and raised his weapon to shoot the fleeing man in the back. Bolan had just one course of action, and it was not good enough. But he did it anyway. He yanked the wheel, aiming the big Ford at Shotgun, and extended his reach to shove the limp body of the driver onto the floor, hoping his foot still somehow managed to stay on the accelerator pedal.

The long shot failed. The Ford did lurch forward unexpectedly and bore down on its target, but by then the combat shotgun had fired into the night.

Bolan saw al-Jabir vanish into the small depression where the bodies of his comrades lay. The darkness and confusion made it impossible to judge if the man dropped in the instant before or after the 12-gauge blast.

There was a crunch when the armored front end of the SUV bounced the shotgunner into the night, flopping him into the weeds like a squashed raccoon. Bolan twisted himself into the front seat, manhandled the driver unceremoniously out the door and accelerated toward the weedy depression where al-Jabir had dropped. He flipped on the high beams and braked hard, tearing up the earth under the heavy tons of steel and struggling to control the big vehicle before it went into the hole.

But his concentration was on what was revealed by the lights—and the gamble paid off. Al-Jabir was crouched in the weeds, blinded by the sudden intensity of light and scrambling away from the locomotive-like thunder of the 300-horsepower V-10 that sounded entirely out of control.

Al-Jabir was tearing out of the pit when the Excursion halted with its front wheels just over the rim. Bolan dragged it into reverse as the weight of the 6.8-liter engine became too much and the ground crumbled under the front wheels. The tires spun and caught, displacing several cubic yards of sandy soil before dragging the SUV to freedom. Bolan steered it around the pit, pursuing al-Jabir.

There he was, sprinting cross-country. The high beams showed sparse prairie grass and scrubby bushes, but nothing that would hide the fugitive for the next hundred yards. Bolan bore down on him, forcing him to leap out of the path of the huge SUV. By the time the Executioner had maneuvered the Excursion through a trench-digging 360, al-Jabir was on his feet and running in the opposite direction. Bolan's tactic didn't change. He drove at the fugitive's back until the man dodged again, this time with less agility.

By the time Bolan had the vehicle turned al-Jabir was on the hoof again, but his weariness was showing. The soldier bore down on his heels and al-Jabir found a burst of energy, suddenly making a last-second sprint for the cover of the trees.

Bolan tapped the gas and the Excursion slammed into the fugitive, swatting him to the ground, only for him to stagger drunkenly to his feet. His face was a mask of dirt, and blood splattered from his panting lips. Bolan saw his prey broadcast his next move with his eyes.

Al-Jabir bolted toward the SUV, intending to run alongside and behind it and get a good head start while Bolan wasted precious seconds making the turnaround. But the soldier did not let it happen. The moment al-Jabir shot toward him the Excursion veered, and they intersected like a baseball bat meeting a rotten tomato.

Bolan cut the lights and slid out, covering al-Jabir with the business end of the big Desert Eagle. The fugitive had the eyes-wide, bitter look of a man who had been defeated despite exhaustive effort. He panted and tried to see the shadowed face of the man who had run him to ground.

"Just shoot. I don't deserve to be toyed with like a rat."

Bolan grimaced. "There's nothing you don't deserve."

Al-Jabir never saw the foot that lashed out at his face and drove him into semiconsciousness, and before he overcame the stunning blow he was trussed up, his wrists bound behind his back in disposable handcuffs, while plastic cords looped around his neck and through the cuffs. His body was lifted off the ground as if without effort. When he tried to stand up straight, he found himself struggling to balance the pain in his arms and throat.

"My arms are going to break!" he complained. Then al-Jabir saw something curious. The man who had taken him prisoner was backing away and peering into the darkness.

Al-Jabir abruptly pictured the one with the combat shotgun, who had nearly blasted his skull from his shoulders. The man had been knocked off his feet by the front end of the SUV, but that didn't mean he was dead. Al-Jabir tried to bolt for the protection of the SUV, but out of the night came a shotgun blast and a hot swarm of pellets tore into his flesh, sending him sprawling to the earth one more time.

Al-Jabir was in hell, and in hell he was a mongrel dog who got smacked down again and again. And always there was pain.

BOLAN TARGETED the blast and triggered the Desert Eagle twice, riding out the recoil of the .44 Magnum rounds. After the echoes of the shots receded in his head there was only the rumble of the idling SUV.

The 12-gauge blasts had been a long way off. Bolan knew his return fire had probably not scored. Crabbing through the grass in near silence, he dragged on the night-vision goggles appropriated from the machine gunner. He scanned the cool night, looking for warm spots, and found one.

It was moving in his direction, and if the man possessed his own night-vision goggles he'd see his enemy soon enough, too. Bolan went flat and counted off fifty seconds, which he judged would give his adversary enough time to get very close. At forty-eight seconds he heard footsteps in the prairie grass, not five yards away.

Bolan stood, and his night-vision display came to life with the sickly image of a green ghost squatting nearby, holding a brilliantly glowing hot shotgun barrel.

The green ghost of Shotgun spun to face Bolan, finding in his own display the abrupt appearance of body heat where there had been none before. He tried to aim his weapon at the Executioner, but Bolan already had him in the sights of the Desert Eagle. The big handgun spoke once, twice.

Bolan pushed off the night-vision goggles. Shotgun was a corpse, slumped lifeless in the prairie grass.

AL-JABIR WAS a bleeding, sweating, filthy mess, with multiple abrasions and bruises and probably some broken bones and a concussion. But he was alive. Bolan hoisted him into the SUV, using more plastic handcuffs to bind his ankles around the extendible machine-gun mount.

There was nothing left now except for janitorial work. Bolan's cleanup included unceremoniously heaving the .50-caliber machine gun and machine gunner into the grass, after binding the unconscious Jay to the weapon with high-tensile wire. This *after* he took the gunner's fingerprints using packaged ink packets he carried for the purpose. The PDA and scanner in his car would make quick work of scanning the prints and getting them to Kurtzman at the Farm. He hurriedly took prints off all the other corpses, then left the scene and put distance between himself and the Fairchilde Federal Penitentiary.

It was time he got some answers.

3

Aaron Kurtzman heard the familiar voice of Mack Bolan say "It's me."

"How'd it go, Striker?"

"I have al-Jabir and he's alive. More or less. But it was messy, Bear."

"How messy?"

"You tell me how messy after you ID the third party who came on the scene. I'm sending you prints now."

The computer and phone communications systems Aaron Kurtzman had assembled for his field teams were powerful devices that exploited the best of military and commercial technology. A phone call originating from these customized devices automatically appropriated any and all portable communications resources needed to handle data flow. When Bolan called Kurtzman, his mobile satellite phone also opened a data connection to Stony Man Farm and began sending the data Bolan had collected. Perceiving the data to be scanned fingerprints, an application had already begun the systematic search through the in-house databases, which were, in fact, downloaded copies of some of the most secure intelligence systems in the world. The Farm mainframes ripped through their stored data with immense speed. Later the computers would turn automatically to the remote systems of the world for up-to-the-second verification.

In this case, IDs were pulled out of the Stony Man Farm data dumps in minutes, while Bolan was still giving an account of his eventful evening.

Aaron "The Bear" Kurtzman swore softly when he saw the IDs flash on his display.

"I guess that means they were who they said they were," Bolan said.

"Yeah. The guy at the wheel really was the personal driver for General Edwin Juvenal, U.S. Army. The rest were special forces types culled for personal security. They had official duties for the books—like secretary—but they were bodyguards, assigned after the general survived assassination attempts in 2002 and last year."

"Why's Juvenal so unpopular?" Bolan asked.

"Unknown. I'll look into it. Have you had a chance to talk to our friend from the pen?"

"Not yet. I'm distancing myself from the scene at Fairchilde. Another twenty miles and we'll have a chance to talk."

"You think he will talk?" Kurtzman asked.

The phone was quiet for a moment, then Bolan said, "He will."

THEY TOOK the state highways, and Bolan found a lonely spot to make the transfer. He halted on the rocky shoulder and hoisted up al-Jabir, extracting him from the steel shaft that had once mounted the machine gun. The trussed-up fugitive was dumped into the passenger seat, an extra length of high-tensile wire used to secure the line from his neck to his wrists to the seat back. The man was helpless and distracted by the continuous effort needed to keep his head leaning back and his arms unnaturally stretched.

"I'm not saying a word," al-Jabir announced.

"I'll start the conversation," Bolan offered as he started to drive again. "Here's an interesting subject—the Seven Scorpions."

"I don't follow American pop music," the captive said, sneering.

"You won't see them on MTV. They're a U.S. special forces unit."

"The name makes them sound like a bunch of vapid teenagers."

"Just a name," Bolan said. "And just because you never heard the name doesn't mean you never heard of these men. They were a specialized Army Rangers team that was dedicated to covert assignments. This particular group vanished."

"Sorry to hear it." Al-Jabir had been undercover in the U.S. for years, and his American accent was nearly perfect. Now he was distracted by the struggle to reduce his discomfort and his speech became heavier, even if the colloquialisms were still baseball and apple pie.

"They disappeared in Iraq, specifically," Bolan said. "That was in 1991."

Al-Jabir tried to hide the glimmer of interest that showed in his face. Bolan caught it out of the corner of his eye as he steered the Excursion through the predawn darkness.

"Your turn to talk," Bolan said.

"If you remove all the bindings, I'll consider it."

"Not a chance."

"Then I'm not saying a word."

Bolan hit the brakes and the Excursion slowed quickly from 60 to 35 mph, and the effect on al-Jabir was dramatic. His entire body was pulled by inertia, and the wire tying him to his chair grew taut on the line connecting his wrist cuffs to his neck. The wire was strong and inflexible and didn't stretch. Al-Jabir's throat was garroted, and his arms were yanked even farther out of their sockets.

He gagged and choked as his body settled back into position. Bolan was already bringing the car back up to speed.

"Ready to talk yet?" Bolan asked.

Al-Jabir glared at him and started to talk—but the words were Arabic. Bolan had picked up enough Arabic over the years to catch the gist of what al-Jabir was saying. Something about the late Mrs. Bolan and her association with the neighborhood canines.

He allowed the invective to continue until he hit 70, then he hit the brakes and slowed to 20 mph. Al-Jabir gasped and thrashed, throat pulled shut, arms dragged back and up. His eyes began to protrude from his head, and his lips visibly swelled and smacked like a gasping fish, but the fugitive made no noise until a muffled pop came from him somewhere.

When Bolan finally accelerated, al-Jabir fell back against the seat and he gasped and shouted in pain at the same time. When he finally became coherent he said, "My arm, my arm!"

Bolan glanced at the man and saw that his shoulder was unnaturally shaped. "Dislocated shoulder," he announced like an emotionless doctor on the sidelines at a college football game.

"It hurts!" al-Jabir growled.

"Just wait." Bolan glanced at the speedometer. "Ready to talk yet?"

"Go to hell—"

Bolan was going 80 mph, but within twelve seconds he brought the SUV to a dead stop.

It was the longest twelve seconds in the life of the Iraqi terrorist Khalid al-Jabir. His lungs screamed for air, but it was nothing compared to the agony of his shoulder, where the bones flopped uselessly and the muscles and tendons stretched farther than they had ever been stretched, then began tearing one after another.

He was fighting off the darkness of unconsciousness at the moment he found himself breathing again in loud, pig-grunting heaves. Al-Jabir felt foolish and weak as he brought himself under control, but every thought was dominated now by the need to avoid more pain. He despised himself for the first time in his life when he said, "What do you want to know?"

"Three months ago you tried to strike a plea deal in federal court. You claimed to have information on a special ops outfit that was captured inside Iraq in 1991 and held prisoner."

"Yes."

"Tell me about it," Bolan commanded.

"The deal didn't go through. Nobody believed me. My own lawyer didn't even think my claim was credible."

"I have news for you—somebody thought you were credible enough to launch a full-scale cover-up," Bolan said. "Your plea deal wasn't shrugged off. It was squashed."

"Why?" Al-Jabir breathed heavily.

"Now you need to start giving me the information you would have provided in court if your deal had been accepted."

"Yeah, and what do I get for it?"

"You get my promise of an easy drive in the country."

4

The first glint of morning sun peaked through a gap in the hills of eastern Pennsylvania. Mack Bolan reached for the visor, then stopped.

He saw a speck.

It was as small as a gnat and hung in the air like a thumbtack in the sky. Bolan watched it grow a degree larger, and that gave him an idea of how big it really was—and how fast it was moving. And it told him the speck was coming directly at him.

They were tracking the SUV, of course, probably through a transmitter tied into a GPS. He should have dumped the vehicle an hour ago.

But he no longer needed it, and he no longer had any use for its cargo. He yanked the wheel and spun the massive Ford into a controlled skid that ended with the vehicle facing the opposite direction, shocking his passenger out of his fitful sleep with more screams and curses. The stench of burned rubber assaulted them, then was left behind in a burst of speed.

"What are you doing now?" the Iraqi whined once his pain became bearable.

"More VIPs interested in you, al-Jabir," Bolan said. "You're a popular guy."

The fugitive looked confused until he spotted the dot in the side mirror, where it had become more than a bug. The helicopter was closing in fast on the SUV at an airspeed that far exceeded the upper limits of the V-10 under the Excursion's hood.

Al-Jabir had to laugh. "I don't know who you are, American, but I know you're about to be taken out by your own countrymen. Even if I go too, it will be satisfying to see you die."

"Don't hold your breath." Bolan adjusted the cruise control and tapped the brakes suddenly, pulling the SUV around a gentle curve and aiming it down a long straight stretch of state highway as its speed decreased.

He grabbed a sturdy rifle case from the back seat, and al-Jabir tried to look at him.

"What are doing?"

"Leaving," Bolan stated.

"We had a deal!" al-Jabir pleaded. "I told you everything!"

"Which is why I didn't kill you," Bolan said, watching a small overhang of roadside trees come closer and holding the door latch.

"But they will!" al-Jabir cried.

"Then the world will be a better place," Bolan said, and opened the door just a foot. As he maneuvered his powerful frame through it, he touched the resume button on the cruise control and wedged the rifle case between the seat and the steering wheel.

"Wait!" al-Jabir exclaimed.

But Bolan was already gone.

THE EXECUTIONER hit the ground running as the trees masked the SUV from the approaching helicopter for a few short seconds. He'd been going fast and barely managed to stay on his feet as he ran out the inertia, then pulled himself under the cover of the trees and examined his handiwork.

The SUV was accelerating rapidly back to its cruise control setting of 60 mph, and the impromptu steering wedge kept it on the asphalt for almost a quarter of a mile. At about the same time the helicopter thundered directly overhead, Bolan watched the big Ford roll onto the shoulder and then into a fallow field. Those on the helicopter had to have thought their prey was trying to make an escape, and the chopper put on a fresh burst of speed.

For Bolan it was time to clear out, and he jogged swiftly alongside the road. He was exposed, in the open, and he didn't know how long the aircraft would be occupied with the fleeing SUV.

As he bolted over the empty highway onto an intersecting county road, he caught a glimpse of the fallow field where the SUV was skidding in the earth, front wheels cranked hard to the right. The prop had dislodged and the tires dug into the earth, stalling the vehicle. The helicopter put itself in a tight circular flight pattern, as if watching to see what the vehicle would do next, but it didn't do anything. It just sat there. Something arced out of the helicopter and plopped into the grass next to the driver's door. For a long, quiet moment the morning remained relatively peaceful in this lower corner of Pennsylvania, then the air was filled with a burst of fire and gray smoke. The air throbbed, and the sound reached Bolan a second later. The SUV's front end lifted off the ground. A big bite was missing from its front end and the driver's door was pushed in, but wasn't penetrated.

Bolan assumed that the occupants of the helicopter were actually the owners of the SUV. They knew precisely how heavily armored the thing was. They were simply making sure that whoever was inside would not have the constitution for a quick flight to freedom.

Something else came out of the helicopter, tumbled lazily through the air for thirty feet and came to a rest on the hood of the SUV. By then the helicopter was already in a quick ascent.

The timer was a generous ten seconds. Bolan wondered idly if al-Jabir still had enough of a hold on consciousness to be aware of it. Because he would know what the package contained.

Al-Jabir was a murderer, a man who targeted the innocent and the helpless. He specialized in civilian terror. He ruined the lives of people who mattered only as numbers in the eyes of global governments.

If there was anyone who deserved a little suffering it was Khalid al-Jabir.

But the moment was soon over, along with al-Jabir's life, when the device activated. Probably a low explosive charge to spread the phosphorous, Bolan decided, as the vehicle was engulfed in white-hot fire that ate through the metal, smashed the glass and digested the seven-thousand-pound vehicle like a coffin in a crematory furnace.

Bolan was pretty sure nobody was ever going to find any serial numbers inside whatever would be left of the SUV.

The helicopter dipped slightly, as if nodding to itself in satisfaction, then climbed steeply and disappeared into the east.

Mack Bolan, the Executioner, had his own reasons for feeling satisfied. What the men in the helicopter did not know was that he had already learned all he could from al-Jabir. He had also found and stripped a steel ID tag off the SUV, and it was now in his pocket.

He had even memorized the ID painted on the helicopter, and now he stopped long enough to extract his war book and record the alphanumeric string. If he was killed in action before he could get the data back to Stony Man Farm, and if his belongings somehow made it back there, then Aaron Kurtzman would have the wherewithal to track down those numbers.

Bolan started along the highway on foot, staying hidden from the road when emergency vehicles began speeding past fifteen minutes later in response to the burning vehicle.

Powerful strides eating up the miles, he chewed on every detail of the scanty intelligence he had so far. His satisfaction turned to aggravation as the pieces steadfastly refused to fit themselves together. In fact, the pieces looked like they came from different puzzles entirely.

IT WAS MIDMORNING when he hiked tiredly into a small Pennsylvania town. He had phoned the Farm as he walked and Kurtzman sent a driver. The pickup was in twenty minutes.

He smelled greasy food, and his stomach noisily reminded him that he had not eaten a meal in thirty-six hours. That was nothing new. Food was just fuel. It surprised him to realize that the decrepit wreck of a building adjoining the town gas station was not abandoned, as it appeared. It was a restaurant—an Eat Here, Get Gas–type diner that was open for business.

He strolled wearily inside and was stared down by an octogenarian waitress with a suspicious-of-strangers attitude. When he ordered not one but two dinners off the circa-1997 cardboard menu she let the corners of her mouth droop below her chin, silently but seriously disapproving of his gluttony. Bolan hoped she wasn't going to get hostile.

The way he felt, she just might be able to take him.

Kurtzman told him not to come to the Farm.

"The politics of the thing," Kurtzman explained apologetically. "Taking this thing on puts us on thin ice, no matter how low-profile the Farm is. If you happen to run into Hal, or he happens to find out you were here and asks me what you're up to—I just don't want to be forced to lie."

"You wouldn't lie," Bolan observed reasonably.

"Yeah. I'd tell all. Which makes Hal an accessory. This whole thing could get very ugly among the politicos, and if there's even a hint of his association it might have consequences on his career plans," Kurtzman stated grimly.

Bolan considered that silently as he lounged in the rear of the armored limousine. He felt the lethargy slip away, replaced by the expectancy that came with learning fresh intelligence.

After giving instructions to the Stony Man driver, Bolan raised the divider.

"Bear, time for a full report," Bolan replied into the speaker-phone mounted in the briefcase Kurtzman sent along with the driver. Inside, along with the telephone, was a laptop. Both the phone and computer communicated to the Farm, allowing them to be networked as needed. "Why don't you start from the beginning, in case I missed anything in last night's rush to the scene."

"Okay, I'll take it from the top." As he said these words, the image of Aaron Kurtzman appeared in a window on the computer's display. Bolan did not know the details of the communications link, but he understood that he was likely patched through to Stony Man Farm over numerous mobile phone lines to accommodate enough bandwidth for voice, data and video. The quality of the image in the small window was good enough for him to see the dark moons under Kurtzman's eyes.

"It starts in 1991, five days before the beginning of the end of Desert Storm. A Rangers outfit that called themselves Seven Scorpions made a deep insertion in Iraq under orders from an Army colonel named Edwin Juvenal. He's moved up a couple notches since to brigadier general rank. He sent them on a reconnaissance mission, ostensibly."

"You sound unconvinced."

"Something didn't sit right, so I ferreted out the original high-level reports. Even looking at low-res scans of the old paperwork I could tell they were doctored—altered after the fact. The orders to make the reconnaissance were not officially issued until Desert Storm was over and done with." A second window opened on the display next to the image of Kurtzman. It showed Bolan a slow slide show of black and white military report scans.

"Juvenal was covering his ass," Bolan observed. "Which means the insertion was not authorized by Desert Storm command."

"Yeah, and it means Juvenal got some of his pals with rank to sign off on falsified orders and reports," Kurtzman added. "Whatever their intent, the Seven Scorpions were inserted on what was planned to be a weeklong mission on a complete blackout."

"That's a long stint in hostile territory without support," Bolan said.

"Despite their comic-book name, the Seven Scorpions were the best. I've looked up records on all seven, and they were the cream of the crop. Skilled, intelligent, dedicated and extremely loyal. Juvenal handpicked each for his own personal special ops outfit."

"Picked them for one mission or several?" Bolan asked.

"Still working on that. Anyway, the official records list a

bunch of reconnaissance briefings that were supposed to have been provided by the Seven during the mission in question, but they're falsified. They were actually the work of another special ops mission and changed to add credibility to Juvenal's report. In actuality, only one communiqué came from the Seven. It was twelve hours after the U.S. offensive commenced and things were already going south for Iraq in a hurry. The radio message from the Seven was coded, but it was essentially a Mayday. They were vastly outnumbered and about to surrender. They were never heard from again."

"They were written off," Bolan said. "Juvenal sacrificed them to his own career."

"Yeah. My take on the thing is that Juvenal was out of the loop in Desert Storm. He didn't know and didn't think the final move against the Iraqis was coming so soon. It would have been a career killer to dampen the victory over Saddam with the announcement that seven unauthorized soldiers were at the mercy of Iraq. So he decided to forget they ever existed. Never mind that these were men with families. He probably figured the chaos of the second war with Iraq buried what was left of his tracks."

"Then our friend Khalid al-Jabir materializes," Kurtzman continued. "Tied to a Hamas-linked terror cell, arrested and charged." The second window now displayed mug shots of the late Khalid al-Jabir. "Since he was arrested as a preventative measure, there were only conspiracy charges against him, and he knew he could bargain. That's when he offered up information on a group U.S. special ops commandos being held somewhere in Iraq—prisoners of war for fifteen years. Juvenal got spooked, thinking the truth might come out after all these years."

"How'd you find out about al-Jabir's announcement, Bear?"

Bolan saw the grin grow on Kurtzman's weary face. "One of the new spiders Akira and I have been fiddling with over the past couple of months to watch terrorist activity worldwide. You wouldn't believe the how much good intelligence falls through the cracks. We're uncovering some good leads. We usually just pass them on anonymously to the agencies in charge. This thing with al-Jabir came through just like the others, but it caught my eye for some reason, even though I was sure it would turn out to be a bluff by al-Jabir. But I dug around and found the false reports and the man's credibility improved. At the same time I started watching his acquaintances closely. A couple of errant mobile phone calls told me about the prison break."

"And told Juvenal," Bolan added.

"Yeah." Kurtzman's face drooped. "I should have been keeping an eye on him, too, Striker. It never even occurred to me that he would make a move like this. Guess I screwed it up."

"Don't kick yourself, Bear. In the end it worked out for the best."

There was silence. Kurtzman stared from the display window as if the video feed had locked up. Finally he asked, "How so?"

"We've got a better lead on Juvenal," Bolan explained with a shrug. "We've got IDs on his enforcers, not to mention the SUV and the helicopter. We'll use it to build a case against him."

"Yes," Kurtzman said slowly. "I've traced them all, fingerprints and serial numbers. They're not convincing enough to prompt a court-martial against a general, I can tell that much. I'm still digging up dirt. But you haven't told me what al-Jabir had to say. How much did he really know?"

"Not much," Bolan said. "He oversold himself to the lawyers, but under duress he came clean."

"So? Are there or are there not POWs in Iraq?"

"There were, as recently as two months ago, Bear," Bolan said grimly. "And that was about all al-Jabir knew, when push came to shove."

"Not enough intelligence to purchase leniency," Kurtzman stated.

"No, it wasn't. But he gave me a name. Hamza al-Douri."

Kurtzman nodded and typed in the name, instantly initializing a search on the man. "Kuwaiti national. Government worker. Professional manager."

"And Iraqi spy."

"Oh."

"I'm going to see him."

"His residence is in Kuwait City."

"I'm getting a flight out now. I'll transfer planes in London and be in Kuwait in fifteen hours. I thought commercial was the way to go."

"Yeah," Kurtzman agreed. He could have arranged for Bolan to take passage on any military aircraft that might be heading for the Middle East, but Bolan knew it would be better for Kurtzman to keep a low profile. Calling in favors from the military was standard practice at the Farm, but Barbara Price might ask about it. Or Hal Brognola.

"What's eating you, Bear?" Bolan asked suddenly.

Kurtzman dragged his eyes away from the invisible horizon and looked at Bolan through the video window. "If Hamza al-Douri gives you the intelligence you need, you'll go after those POWs. You'll go into Iraq, Striker."

It wasn't a question so Bolan did not answer.

"If you put together a list of the world's unsafe places, you know what would come out as number one?" Kurtzman demanded.

This time it was a question, but Bolan still said nothing.

"I'm going to work on this on my end," Kurtzman said sharply, glaring at him. "If there's a way to tie this to Juvenal or even just prove that these men are really there, I'm going to find it. We can use that to force their hand—have them send in a rescue operation or something. I'll resort to a PR campaign if I have to."

"The politics around this are dangerous," Bolan observed.

"What do you call one man going in alone, without so much as official sanction? You're the best, Mack, but there are plenty of remnants from the old regime—they're fanatical. They're murderous. And there is nobody they hate more than Americans."

"I know all that."

"Don't go into Iraq. Not until I've done everything I can at this end. Not until we're both convinced there's no other way to bring those men out."

Bolan thought about that. He was not a man who took orders. Not anymore. He was the ultimate lone wolf, and there had been a time when the authority of Stony Man Farm had stifled his crusade, his War Everlasting, and he rebelled against it.

On the other hand, Aaron Kurtzman was about as good a friend as Mack Bolan had on Earth, and he was asking for a favor, not issuing commands.

Bolan nodded. "Okay, Bear. That makes sense."

Kurtzman looked relieved. "I'll have more to tell you in few hours."

BOLAN WATCHED the scenery as they headed south. Approaching Baltimore the development grew heavier, soon they had bypassed the city and were heading for Washington, D.C.

He was bone tired, but he would sleep on the plane. Right now his mind was spinning with a quiet rage against the military bureaucrats and power players who had done this deed. How could they rationalize abandoning loyal soldiers to a fate worse than death?

Bolan would deal with the bureaucrats later. First, if he could, he would save the prisoners. He would find them, wherever they were in the vastness of Iraq.

Intoxicated by exhaustion, his mind slipped from the sandy wastelands to the jungle. He thought back to the other men who had been left behind by the nation they fought for. Many of those men were unaccounted for to this day. Their fate became official with the slap of a rubber stamp on their military file: MIA.

How many of those men were not dead?

Bolan heard something crack, and it brought him back to full awareness. His hand, gripping the closed notebook, had been squeezing harder. And harder. The plastic shell was broken in the corner.

Minor damage.

But Bolan felt a sudden resolve. One way or another, dead or alive, the Seven Scorpions would be recovered.

Even if he had to do it alone, Bolan would bring them back.

6

Stony Man Farm, Virginia

Kurtzman started awake and grabbed the wheels of his chair when a gentle hand was placed on his shoulder.

"Sorry, Aaron," Barbara Price said.

"It's okay."

"Why not get some real sleep. Like in a bed."

Kurtzman nodded glumly. "Might as well."

Barbara Price, the honey-blond Stony Man mission controller, wanted to grill Kurtzman on whatever was keeping him busy virtually around the clock for the past thirty-six hours. She had a vague idea that he was protecting her—trying to avoid dragging her into troublesome territory.

Finally she asked simply, "Find what you were looking for?"

Kurtzman looked at the floor and began rolling away. All he said was, "No."

Kuwait

DAWLAT AL-KUWAYT, or the State of Kuwait, looked much like any other stretch of Middle Eastern desert. There were a few small patches of fertile ground and a major oasis, the al-Jahrah. But as with many Middle Eastern nations, its truly valuable resources were hidden underground.

Oil was discovered in Kuwait in the 1930s and, like many other Middle East nations, oil came to dominate the country's economy. In fact, despite its small size geographically, it was one of the largest producers of oil in the world.

But Kuwait became unique in the 1980s when the nation began to make more from its global oil money investments than it did from the oil itself. Kuwait was the kid on the block with the most toys, and Iraq was the bully next door who simply didn't have the self-control to hold his jealousy in check. Iraq stormed into Kuwait and confiscated all the toys it could find—and claimed the rich kid's house was actually on its property all along.

The invasion of Kuwait was motivated by petty jealousy disguised, in Iraq, by a propaganda campaign that even the Iraqis had trouble swallowing. Bolan had always viewed it as a brutal, foolhardy undertaking by a vicious, desperate despot. All these years after Desert Storm Iraq was still recovering from tyrannical leadership.

Kuwait, meanwhile, had used its vast riches to rebuild its single metropolis—home to almost all its people—and was again a shining jewel of the Middle East.

Mack Bolan wasn't rested, although the flight from Washington, D.C., and London had seemed endless, and he was pacing the cage long before the Saudi Air 747 settled ponderously on the runway in Kuwait City.

The updates from Aaron Kurtzman were not exactly comprehensive. There wasn't much intelligence available on the guilty parties in the U.S. military or on the Iraqi spies in Kuwait, but Bolan didn't allow this to discourage him. If the world's greatest cybernetic intelligence gatherer could not find the data, then the data probably did not exist.

It was Kurtzman who was truly disappointed, plagued by a growing concern about sending Bolan alone into Iraq. Kurtzman wanted evidence. He wanted to nail the U.S. military bureaucrats who were complicit in the deed and the cover-up.

In fact, Bolan wondered about the intensity of his friend's interest in the POWs. Kurtzman had experienced countless missions. Why take this one personally?

Bolan thought he knew the answer—part of the answer, anyway. It had to do with the changed mood at Stony Man Farm, which was like the altered perspective of someone recovering from the loss of a limb in a serious accident.

The full weight of the analogy settled like a black cloud on Mack Bolan as he strode through the airport terminal. He was thinking about the loss of a friend, a one-armed man. Then he was thinking about the loss of many friends.

And then he was thinking about the loss of loved ones.

His eyes scanned the airport like the alert watch of a hunting cheetah, assessing every human being for threat potential. His jungle warrior skills evaluated every movement, every affectation, looking for suspicious behavior.

But that was all below the surface. In his consciousness he was as alone as the sole survivor of nuclear holocaust.

April. Katz. He almost spoke the names aloud.

Sam Bolan, the father who went mad with shame and rage and resorted to murder.

He had long ago forgiven Sam Bolan.

He was standing in the afternoon sun of the Middle East. He didn't notice the glare, or the burning on his skin, or the searing desert heat. His thoughts were leading him into the darkest, coldest dungeon of his memory.

Cindy.

She was a child. The innocent with the heart of gold. She sold herself into prostitution to rescue her family, to save her father. That was the shame that drove Sam Bolan over the brink. She was slain by the father she would save.

It occurred to Mack Bolan that even if he did not understand what in particular struck a chord with Kurtzman about the POWs, he understood that fervor. That motivation. That drive.

To him, every battle in his War Everlasting was a personal undertaking. With every breath he took he fought to avenge his family, the victims who could never, ever be avenged.

With one hand, Mack Bolan shaded his eyes from the brilliant light of the sun.

THE ASSISTANT DIRECTOR'S 100-watt smile lost some of its brilliance when he saw the man his secretary ushered into the office. The American was tall, with a build somehow both agile and powerful. He had dark hair and chiseled, hawklike features. He was Caucasian but his skin was dark, like desert workers who spend a lifetime out in the sun.

Unlike the desert laborers, this man had eyes that were glacial blue, as sharp as the glinting blade of a freshly stropped steel razor. They saw all, those eyes, while commanding the assistant director's complete attention.

They commanded the attention of his secretary, too, apparently. The young man was usually annoyingly cool and in control, but now he practically stammered the introduction. "May I present Mr. Matthew Cooper. Mr. Cooper, this is Assistant Hamza al-Douri." The secretary blushed scarlet. "Assistant *Director* Hamza al-Douri."

"Mr. Cooper," al-Douri said, shaking the American's hand. A moment of contact told him it was a hand that had killed. Maybe frequently. Al-Douri waved at a chair.

Bolan sat, comfortably, not quite smiling, supremely confident.

"Tea, Mr. Cooper?" asked the secretary. It was a breach in etiquette. It robbed al-Douri of the opportunity to take the role of host.

"No, thank you."

Another breach in etiquette. In Kuwait, and globally, Americans were known as stumblers when it came to following local traditions. Kuwaitis didn't take offense—it wouldn't do to be irritated with the saviors of your nation. But for many Kuwaitis, who often attended university in the UK, tea was a tradition worth pushing for.

This Cooper was not a stumbler. Al-Douri did not push the tea. He glared his secretary out of the room and took his place behind the desk.

"Your visit has caught me unprepared, I am afraid, Mr. Cooper."

"I can imagine," Bolan replied.

Al-Douri tolerated the silence for a few seconds, but the American refused to explain further.

"As an assistant director, I serve as an adjutant for members of the National Assembly, so your discussions should probably begin with the actual members of the Majlis al-Umma, whatever the nature of your business may be…." He looked expectantly at Bolan, who didn't even blink.

"So! Please tell me how I can be of service."

"One moment," Bolan said. And he sat there.

Al-Douri became increasingly agitated over the next ten seconds. Something beeped, and Bolan extracted an unusually large mobile phone from his lightweight sports jacket, scanning the display.

"I've been waiting for this information," Bolan explained, nodding at whatever was on the display as he pulled out a slim notebook of battered black leather. He quickly and efficiently copied the information from his phone display onto paper. "You'll find it interesting, too."

Al-Douri's mystification grew. His dealings with assorted Americans and other Westerners hadn't prepared him for this oddball character. This Cooper would have been amusing if he didn't carry with him a sense of menace, as potent as the growl of a carnivorous big cat pitched almost too low to be heard. With a knock, al-Douri's dapper secretary poked his head in.

"Will you be needing anything else, sir?" He spoke English for the American's benefit but pointed at his watch. The workday was officially over, and young Kuwaiti professionals did *not* work overtime.

Al-Douri offered tea again, but when the American refused it the secretary was dismissed and his footsteps retreated down the hall until the door clicked shut. As if waiting for the sound of the latch, Bolan announced, reading from his notebook, "Ar-Rutbah. You were born there. November 18, 1953."

Al-Douri became a statue.

"You served in the Iraqi army, joined the Ba'ath Party, eventually made your way into Project 858, the communications monitoring sector of Iraqi intelligence know as al-Hadi. After Desert Storm you went undercover, eventually establishing yourself as a Kuwaiti citizen and worming your way into various ministry positions, usually handling foreign affairs and immigration issues."

Al-Douri's hands were on the desktop, but Bolan's attention was riveted to his notebook, so he moved one hand casually, slowly—and in an eye blink found himself staring down the barrel of a suppressed handgun.

The weapon had appeared like magic. Like when the cartoon mouse whips a huge mallet from behind his back, where he could not possible have hidden such a mallet. Again, almost amusing, al-Douri thought. This Cooper had not broadcast the move, which happened with the speed and noise of the shadow of a bird.

"Who are you?" al-Douri demanded. He was disgusted—it was clear he was up against a professional. Al-Douri's years of work establishing this cover would be for naught if this man exposed him, and the consequences would be unpleasant.

"You are the big mystery, Assistant Director," Bolan growled. "What's a nice Iraqi intelligence and communications expert doing in an office of the Kuwaiti government?"

"Why did you come here?" al-Douri demanded.

"To talk."

"About my childhood in Ar-Rutbah?" al-Douri said sarcastically.

"About seven U.S. prisoners of war, held in custody in Iraq since 1991."

Al-Douri was baffled. Then he became afraid. Whoever this man was and worked for, he was clearly an enemy. And any enemy who knew such secrets would kill him—or turn him over to those who would kill him.

"There are no U.S. prisoners in Iraq." He couldn't think of anything better to say.

"You're lying," Bolan replied.

The man with the ice-cold eyes made the smallest movement with the handgun. It was a Beretta 93-R, a monster of a pistol that could be set to fire 3-round bursts of 9 mm rounds. The aim was extremely difficult to control when fired in triburst mode, so the weapon was actually fitted with a secondary, foldable handle under the barrel. The handle was still in its folded position, but al-Douri did not doubt for a second that this man Cooper had the strength and skill to hit his target one-handed.

"What if I talk?" al-Douri demanded, licking dry lips. "Do I go free?"

"I'm not negotiating. I'm delivering an ultimatum. Start talking or start dying."

Instead, al-Douri panicked. He flopped to the floor behind the desk and jerked a mobile phone from his pocket, thumbing the button that sent out an emergency call signal.

Then he found himself rising to his feet again, suspended by his jacket collar, in the grip of the man with the icy eyes. Al-Douri's years of training came back to him. He twisted his torso and snapped one fist at the Beretta handgun in a single explosive movement. His perfect execution of the move pushed the aim of the handgun away from him while throwing his assailant's defenses wide-open—al-Douri exploited his window of opportunity by striking a lightning kick at the American's groin.

Bolan raised a shin to deflect the kick, and before al-Douri could make another move he saw the American's left hand come out of nowhere, with the fingers locked flat and driving under al-Douri's chin. The Iraqi who pretended to be a Kuwait bureaucrat gagged and crashed to the ground, choking up bile.

BOLAN HEARD POUNDING footsteps approaching. He knew that five or more Iraqi undercover agents worked in this building, and it sounded like all of them were responding to the emergency summons from al-Douri.

The soldier snatched the spy off the floor and walked him into the door, which crashed open. Several men were approaching in a controlled run, hands empty. At the moment they saw al-Douri and his assailant, the Iraqi agents simultaneously reached the same conclusion: their cover was blown. No reason not to put up a fight. They scattered for cover and produced weapons.

"Don't shoot!" al-Douri croaked in Arabic.

The nearest gunner lined up on Bolan with a small-profile handgun, but the Executioner beat him to the trigger pull, firing a 3-round burst from the powerful Beretta 93-R. The 9 mm shockers cut down the gunner and splattered the wall behind him. A second gunner cut loose, but a quick step aside pulled Bolan out of the line of fire and dragged al-Douri into it. The spy jerked when the small-caliber bullet slammed into his rib cage.

Bolan reached around his prisoner with the 93-R held sideways and triggered a triburst. The rise of the recoil carried his aim in a horizontal sweep of violence that slammed first into the gunner, then gut shot his nearest companion. Both of them fell to the floor.

Behind them two figures burst from the stairwell, then pulled back into the protection of the door. Bolan swore silently—the newcomers had folded-stock rifles or machines guns. This wasn't going well.

"Hand him over!" one called in English.

Bolan ignored him, walking al-Douri backward in the other direction to the stairs on the opposite end of the narrow government building. The soldier kicked open the door—and heard approaching footsteps.

Someone shouted a command in Arabic, and Bolan found himself facing gunmen in uniforms. He pointed the 93-R at the ceiling—he didn't shoot police.

"Help me!" al-Douri bawled and collapsed, allowing his body weight to drag him out of Bolan's grip and carry him down the stairs. At that moment a burst of automatic gunfire slammed into the swinging stair doors from the hall.

Bolan weighed his options, then dived into the hall as the burst halted. He landed flat, arms reaching above him, and triggered a triburst at the exposed gunner. The man went down, his Russian-made AK-74 clattering on the carpeting. Bolan bolted off the floor and down the hall. The last surviving gunner was taken off guard but got his finger curled around the trigger with amazing speed. The rounds spewed out of his weapon into the floor, ricocheting noisily around Bolan. The warrior squeezed out a triburst that sent the gunner to oblivion.

There was another command from behind him as the MPs, or whoever they were, took cover in the stairs.

Bolan ran in the other direction.

7

Police were on the scene for hours, trying to make sense of the gun battle that had been waged in the government building. In a fifth-floor hotel room not a hundred paces away, Mack Bolan stared through a pair of binoculars and thought dark thoughts.

The probe had not gone well.

Al-Douri was more efficient than most of his ilk. For a man who had been undercover for years he still kept his team prepared for instantaneous response, and it paid off. Bolan had been unable to gain control of the situation in the few seconds he was allotted prior to the arrival of the police.

He wasn't given to self-recrimination. That was counterproductive behavior. And he knew there was no way he could have anticipated the near-instant response from the Iraqis and almost-instant arrival of the police.

But the results spoke for themselves. He had no intelligence from al-Douri. He'd achieved nothing more than exterminating a few Iraqi moles.

Al-Douri would be questioned closely by whomever the Kuwaitis had investigating the shootings. Whatever story he told them, it would feature himself as an innocent bystander. Unless the Kuwaitis already suspected al-Douri, they'd let him go.

Then he'd come after Bolan.

It was time, the soldier decided, for a nice steak dinner.

THE HOTEL COULD HAVE BEEN anywhere. New York. London. Tokyo. The rich decor of the lobby didn't exhibit even a glimmer of originality, and the atmosphere was maintained at a consistent seventy-two degrees Fahrenheit. The machine-cooled air felt unnatural to the young doorman as he moved from his podium inside to the cobblestone drive under the veranda, where the stifling heat persisted long into the evening.

The doorman recognized the passenger emerging from the taxi. At their first meeting he told the doorman to call him simply Alb. He held the door for Alb and they stood at the doorman's podium, as casually as if Alb were asking for directions to a local restaurant.

The information wasn't so mundane, and the doorman's tip was better than the typical ten-dinar note. The doorman had to stifle a grin as he fanned the five hundred-dinar bills.

"Talk," Alb said.

"He came in here just a minute before the police started showing up down the street at the ministry offices," the doorman said eagerly. "As soon as I got the word from your guys, I knew I'd seen a guy that fit the description. Then I look up and here he comes out of the elevator and I stood here watching him eat his dinner."

The young doorman nodded at the section of the lobby where decorative fencing made a faux outdoor café. Circle-T Ranch Fine American-Style Steaks and Barbecue was the less formal of the hotel's two restaurants.

"He ate at the corner table. He asked for it special. I know because after he was done I went and asked the host," the doorman explained. "It's the best view out the front, and he watched the police the whole time he was eating. Then when he was done eating he kind of casually walked up to the doors and watched some more."

"What then?"

"Went back to his room," the doorman said with a shrug.

"Which room?"

Out of sight behind the podium the doorman fanned his bills.

"Room 509. His name is Mike McKay. Passport says he's a journalist."

When there were no more questions, the doorman looked up and found himself alone. Alb was heading across the lobby.

He wondered briefly who Alb really was and why he was so interested in Mike McKay, the journalist in room 509. Maybe he would arrest him. Maybe kill him.

Not that he cared. He was a Saudi, in Kuwait because that was where he could get a job that paid decent money, and he thought every Kuwaiti he came in contact with was arrogant and elitist. He couldn't care less what they did to one another or to visiting Americans.

In fact, the doorman hoped there was more trouble coming, because these occasional five hundred-dinar payoffs did wonders for his standard of living.

ALNAKEEB ALB requested suite 509. The young man at the desk was perfectly polite and utterly bored. He explained that room 509 was occupied, but there were several other suites available on that floor and would Mr. Alb like to see a diagram of the rooms? Alb glanced at it and requested suite 511. The desk clerk was pleased to inform Mr. Alb that suite 511 was indeed available and could he please provide a credit card? Did he have any bags that would require a porter?

Had the desk clerk possessed any genuine interest about Alnakeeb Alb, he might have met the man's gaze and seen an odd mixture of ruthlessness and manic self-control. They were the eyes of man for whom killing was a career choice.

But, the clerk might have thought, at least he enjoyed his work.

ALB DID LIKE HIS WORK. He enjoyed nothing *but* his work. There was the excitement of the hunt, the adrenaline rush of the kill, and every other waking minute was tedium.

He also had self-mastery. Without it he would have been a wild man, an indiscriminate killer, one of those freaks who was hunted ruthlessly, displayed in the media like a monstrosity when apprehended, then beheaded. At least, in Iran he would have been beheaded—he wasn't sure about the Kuwaitis. But Kuwait was where the money was, with a concentrated population of entrenched wealth. These were families who had become rich on oil, but who were not too far removed from the territorial battles of only a few generations ago. Some of them had enough fight left in them to make use of the services of a man like Alnakeeb Alb.

Alb was now as rich as some of the men who hired him, but to him the real measure of his success was continued steady employment.

This time he had to be careful. He knew what happened in the ministry building and was impressed by the reports he heard. The man was as professional as Alb himself.

Alb didn't know enough about the American perpetrator, though, to be sure of his affiliation. Was he some sort of agent? Not CIA, certainly. In fact, no sanctioned agent would set himself up in a hotel like this. Hamza al-Douri had offhandedly mentioned that the American's attack was unwarranted, but that was a lie. Hamza al-Douri was not what he said he was, either. Certainly an innocent Kuwaiti bureaucrat wouldn't have hired a contract killer to take care of this problem, or the other problems Alb had solved for al-Douri in recent years.

He was staring at the printed paper folder containing his two key cards as he stepped from the elevator and scanned the fifth-floor hallway, finding it deserted. There was a highly polished wooden table and a brass vase arrayed with fresh flowers, and the carpet was fancifully printed with beige, gold and umber geometric shapes on a burgundy background. The design was repeated a hundred times in each direction, unbroken by other furniture or human beings. No one was strolling this hall trying to look like a hotel guest while actually guarding room 509. Maybe the guy really was working independently.

Alb liked the idea of going against one of his peers head-to-head.

His ears strained to hear any sound behind the door of 509 when he strolled past. Nothing.

His suite was lavish and huge, with a parlor, bedroom, and dressing room that adjoined a bathroom. Alb pretended he was impressed with the place, but as he strolled through it he was searching for any sign that he was being watched by his neighbor. Satisfied that there were no hidden cameras or planted video monitoring devices, he searched the room for audio bugs. Nothing. Finally he examined the door that adjoined the two rooms. He saw the dead bolt firmly in place, and behind it was a second door, also dead bolted.

Maybe this was overkill. Maybe he was being too careful. But if half of what he heard about the ministry building battle was accurate…

He pulled out a stethoscope and listened to the wall, hearing CNN Europe playing on the television. After a few minutes the TV was turned off and Alb heard faint footsteps, then water. The shower. Alb was almost disappointed at how easy this was going to be.

He jammed face towels into the narrow space around the door to help muffle the sound as he picked the lock on the first door, listened again, then jimmied the dead bolt on the second door. The hotel's key-card system did not extend to the doors between adjoining rooms, but that made no difference to Alb and he had the all the locks neutralized in three minutes.

The shower was still running, but there was a chance that his target was not alone in the room, and before he barged in Alb took a peek. He had purchased the video device from a Mexican Web site for less money than he had just spent to rent the suite for a night.

The flexible wire was an eighth of an inch thick, and when he wiggled it under the door it fed an image to a three-inch LCD display that was low resolution but more than adequate for a security sweep. The suite was just one big room, and there was nobody in it.

Alb withdrew the M-85, an automatic handgun with a medium-size frame that meant it wasn't hard to conceal. It was his firearm of choice, but his intended lead weapon was an Israeli combat blade, stolen from one of his first victims. He removed the sheath from his sport coat and clipped it on the front of his pants.

He opened the door. The shower was still running.

Too easy.

BOLAN USED A DENTAL MIRROR to monitor his hotel suite from inside the bathroom.

He had made himself the bait. Dinner in the hotel steak house had been like wiggling the hook to attract the attention of the fish. Not much later a new guest had arrived to take the overpriced, oversize adjoining suite. Bolan observed through the peephole that the man had no luggage and no companions.

Despite the newcomer's skill, he couldn't pick the locks on the adjoining doors without making some small sound—Bolan had stood with his ear almost brushing the door's surface and heard it clearly. Then he had moved to the bathroom.

His dental mirror showed him the little metallic worm that poked under the bottom of the door, then retracted, and that was when Bolan changed positions again. He moved fast on bare feet, the carpet deadening the sound, and put himself behind the door in the spot the intruder had already observed as empty.

The door opened and the intruder's handgun came through first, then his shoulder. Finally his torso and head appeared.

Bolan lashed out with one foot, propelling the door with immense force into the gunman. The steel fire door and the steel doorjamb caught the intruder down the middle like spring-activated pinchers clamping down on an insect.

The gun thumped on the floor and the intruder's head lolled momentarily before Bolan grabbed his arm and jerked him into the room, dropping him face first and cuffing his wrists behind him. The gunner had not made a sound.

After a quick pat down Bolan flipped the gunner onto his back to find his mouth bubbling with blood. The carpet was puddled with it. The Executioner took the knife, found an extra knife and narrow-profile .22 tucked away on the man's shins, then pulled him into an upright sitting position. The blood cascaded down his chest. The killer looked at Bolan with a simpleton's gaze.

"How did you do it?" he asked in broken English. "How could you have been there when I opened the door?"

"You were sent by Hamza al-Douri," Bolan said. "Where can I find him?"

"I do not know," the killer man said offhandedly. "How you got the drop on me? There is no place you could have been hiding in this room."

"Why do you care?"

"So I can do better the next time," the killer said reasonably, blood trickling from his lips.

The man was in denial of his own impending death, despite the rapid blood loss from internal injuries. Bolan felt no pity for the death of a man who killed for profit, and he felt no compunction about taking advantage of his poor reasoning. "Okay, we'll trade information," Bolan said. "I'll tell you how I got the drop on you. You tell me where to find Hamza al-Douri. But you go first."

The killer considered this dumbly, the glimmer of life visibly dimming in his eyes with each faltering heartbeat, and Bolan had the urge to grab the man and try to shake this vital tidbit of information out of him—but it would have been wasted on a man who didn't even feel the pain of a shattered rib cage. Finally the man nodded briefly.

"I will have to trust you as a fellow professional," the killer slurred. "Hamza al-Douri is in the home of a powerful friend. A rich man named Jasim is giving him secret sanctuary. Jasim has a villa on President George Bush Boulevard." The killer grinned. "I have been there more than one time for assignments. I have seen its security system. I know that even expert men like us will not get in."

Bolan committed the information to memory. Kurtzman would know more about this man Jasim and about the villa.

"Now tell me how you did your little trick," the killer said. "Keep your promise."

"It wasn't one little trick but a simple bait-and-switch, which you swallowed like an amateur." Bolan stooped, looking the man in the eyes and began ticking off items on his fingers. "First I made myself obvious in the lobby because I knew somebody would be willing to talk about seeing me when the underground began a citywide survey of the hotels. I picked this room because it's between two expensive suites. Then you showed up—alone, no luggage—and rented the suite next door, even though the hotel is just half-booked. You couldn't have been more obvious if you were wearing your lapel pin from the *Killer for Hire Guild*. So I turned on the TV for a while, turned it off and started the shower, and you bought into the scenario without a second thought. Pretty soon I heard you picking the locks between the doors. At least as a lock pick you're not totally inept, but you still made more than enough noise for somebody who was listening for it."

The killer was bubbling with indignation but couldn't summon the energy to respond to any of the insults.

"Those are all the stupid moves you didn't know about. The one you did know about was trusting your video probe. Sure it could tell you if I was standing there about to ambush you in the middle of the room, but it couldn't see the high technology surveillance device that I was using to monitor the door from the bathroom."

Bolan reached into his back pocket and withdrew a slim dentist's mirror with a plastic handle.

The killer's mouth slackened, and he made a low stuttering noise as if to protest a violation of the rules. Bolan continued without letting him speak. "As soon as you withdrew your video worm, I knew I had a few seconds to get into position behind the door. You came through and got snapped in a trap like the rodent you are, smashed up and too stupid to know you're minutes away from being dead."

"Dying?" Even the one slurred word took great effort. The killer looked down at himself, and for the first time became aware that his clothes were drenched, and his blood-sodden cotton shirt clung to a chest that was oddly misshapen with a deep channel that couldn't have existed if any of the bones on the right side of his rib cage were intact.

The killer didn't have the energy to panic. His body flinched, and his eyes flitted wildly around the room. "Call for help."

"You're not worth it," Bolan replied.

Bolan picked up his mobile phone and dialed his dedicated number into Stony Man Farm in Virginia. The scrambler on the phone itself made the voice transmission indecipherable except by the receiver, and the protocol that dictated the decoding was itself dynamically altered at irregular intervals during each conversation. Still, the call was routed through a bewildering series of global cutouts, filters and untraceable rerouting. It took almost five seconds before Bolan heard the first ring, which never finished.

"Striker, how's it going?" Kurtzman asked.

"Could be better."

"The Kuwaiti media is buzzing about your handiwork at the Ministry of Bread and Circuses."

The killer tried to say something and choked on blood. He hefted himself to his knees momentarily, then collapsed with a grunt.

"What was that, Striker?"

"My informant."

"Send me his prints and I'll get you a background."

"I don't think there's a need for that. He's strictly local muscle. Hired help. But he gave me a lead. Hamza al-Douri is taking refuge in the home of a man named Jasim. Get this—he lives on President George Bush Boulevard."

Over the line Bolan heard the tapping of fingers, then Aaron Kurtzman said, "Huh."

"Got anything?" Bolan asked.

"Striker, I've got results on this joker streaming in from all over the place. CIA, FBI, M-16, the Russians, the Israelis, the Italians, the Japanese. Hey, get this—this guy has a police record in *Daytona Beach*."

"Give me the basics," Bolan suggested.

"Yeah, okay. Maysaloun Jasim. He's a Kuwaiti, born on the fringe of oil money. His father was a top oilman, but the family has been suspected of evil deeds since forever. Jasim parlayed his contacts into a thriving business of protection and facilitation."

"Kuwaiti Mafia?" Bolan asked.

"Not quite. The picture is fuzzy, but he's clearly in the good graces of the powers that be in Kuwait, so he has made a point of not stepping on toes. But he has a network of contacts and small-scale businesses outside the country. Arms. Prostitution. Drugs. And more business deals than I can count."

"But why is he hiding an Iraqi undercover agent?" Bolan asked.

"Here's why," Kurtzman announced. "Remember the Arab Summit in early 2002? The one that Israel wouldn't let Arafat attend? Iraq used the media attention for a little public-relations spit-and-polish. They formally declared their acceptance of Kuwaiti's status as an independent nation, renouncing the claim that Kuwait was a renegade province that Iraq had legal claim to. Nobody in his right mind would take that claim at face value, but it did create better conditions for Iraqi-Kuwaiti trade—the legal kind and not-so-legal kind. Guess who spends most of April 2002 in Baghdad setting up trade ties?"

"Jasim."

"Here's the interesting coincidence. Jasim's Grand Cayman accounts were fortified in May 2002—to the tune of twenty million U.S. dollars. And that's doubled in the interim. This is information the Farm has culled—I don't think the Company has a clue."

Bolan got the picture. Jasim was a man who played the system and kept his dealings legitimate—if not ethical—as long as they served his ambitions. When those opportunities dried up, he wasn't about to compromise his standard of living, so he gravitated toward less legitimate sources of income.

"Jasim's enough of a traitor to hide out an important Iraqi agent when the situation calls for it. Bear, I'll need to know anything and everything about the security at the house on President

George Bush Boulevard. It's supposed to be sophisticated. I'm on my way there now."

"Not sure if I'll have that kind of intelligence, Striker, but I'll do my best," Kurtzman said. "Can your informant give you any more details?"

Bolan crouched and put a pair of fingers against the throat of the figure sprawled on the carpet.

"No."

8

A man like Hamza al-Douri, backed up by the resources of millionaire Maysaloun Jasim, would have sent in an anonymous killer first. That would make for the cleanest kill with the least chance of comebacks. But just in case the hit man blew it, Bolan knew al-Douri would have a Plan B.

So did Bolan.

The Executioner had spotted his Plan B in the parking garage during a quick surveillance after his too obvious dinner in the lobby steak house. Plan B, a Suzuki GSX-R1000, was still parked there when Bolan came down. It was probably the property of the son of a wealthy Kuwaiti who had likely gone to college in the UK or the States and learned some Western ways. Chances were the kid who owned the Suzuki would never have reason to test its capabilities, but Bolan might.

The backup team would be watching the hotel doors and keeping tabs on Bolan's rental car, a plush Mercedes parked in a VIP spot on the bottom level of the parking garage. The soldier had paid the parking staff well to keep an eye on his high-priced toy.

He had the Suzuki hot-wired in minutes but kept the big 988 cc engine rumbling at idle as he wheeled it out of its parking place and allowed the spiral decline of the garage carry him in neutral down the levels, from five to two. He braked and tucked the motorcycle against a concrete support column while he crept to the bottom level on foot. His reconnoiter paid off when he spotted two conspicuously occupied cars on the lower level, parked well apart from each other but both in places where their occupants had a line of sight on Bolan's rental Mercedes.

The soldier disregarded a capture-and-interrogate scheme and decided to try for a clandestine exit. After all, if this bunch was still sitting here with their thumbs up their noses when Bolan entered the Jasim villa, it would be that many fewer hardmen to face down.

He moved catlike, his black clothing making it easy to merge with the shadows between the cars, and found his way alongside a black Saab sedan. This was the car closest to the exit but also the easiest to get to without moving into the open. There was just a driver inside, and Bolan assumed this was the transport for a foot patrol that was now canvassing in and around the hotel.

A quick inspection revealed specialty body panels and runflat tires, and he saw the tiny logo on the rear window glass that told him it was bullet-resistant. But whoever put a lot of cash into hardening the car forgot to invest in some commonsense classes for the driver, who was so overconfident he had the door opened to stretch his long legs.

Bolan carried a prepped booby trap. It took him only seconds to tie one end of the polymer monofilament to a reinforcing bolt under the Saab's rear bumper. The fragmentation grenade dangled from it, a few inches off the pavement. Another strand of monofilament was threaded through a small gap in the inside rim of a rear tire. Bolan pulled the pin on the grenade and tied the loose end of the second line around the bomb and the pin with a slipknot.

He tightened it to reduce the slack, and the trap was set. When the tires moved the line would be pulled tight and it would slip easily off the grenade. Unless the sedan's armor was better than it looked, it would be rendered undrivable.

Silently he crept away from the sedan. The man with the long legs was still lounging in his seat, watching the rental Mercedes. His range of vision was restricted by his kaffiyeh, the centuries-old traditional Arab headwear.

Bolan duck-walked silently alongside the sedan, the driver

unaware of his presence until the soldier suddenly stepped over his stretched legs, grabbed him by both ankles and twisted powerfully, sending the relaxed driver into a full-body corkscrew that landed with him facedown on his car seat. His shout of alarm was muffled by the seat. Bolan stayed low and hauled on the killer's ankles with all his weight, dragging the driver's body from the car. It hit the pavement hard.

The driver flopped like a fish, twisting onto his back and grabbing for the handgun holstered under his arm. Bolan snatched him by the belt and yanked the heavy bodyweight toward him while he lashed out with one foot at the driver's jaw.

The jaw was jelly and sagged open, full of blood, but the driver reached again for the gun. Bolan was unbalanced in an awkward crouch on one knee, and his next kick was a weak effort that he aimed at the hand, barely dislodging it from the holster before the driver got his grip. Then the Executioner rammed his knee into the driver's abdomen with all the force he could muster.

The explosion of breath was the loudest sound to emerge from the battle, and it created a geyser of blood. Bolan was surprised to see the driver still conscious, still weakly going for his handgun.

Bolan crabbed in close to the man and rained heel blows on the lolling head until he was certain there was no life left in it.

He dragged the kaffiyeh off the corpse and looked it over. It was a plain ivory color, but the blood spatters weren't large enough to be obvious from a distance. He took the garment and crept back up to the second level in a hurry, not knowing how long it would take for the driver to be missed. When he reached the Suzuki, Bolan dragged on the kaffiyeh and quickly tied the *agal,* the woven band of cords that held the cotton fabric in place. When it was lengthened slightly to fit his skull, the headwear felt natural.

He pulled it around his head and drove the bike at an unhurried pace down the ramp to the bottom level, where he found the scene unchanged. The driver's corpse lay undiscovered alongside the sedan, and his oblivious companions were smoking cigarettes in their sedan near the doors into the hotel.

Bolan felt their eyes on him, but he didn't turn to look. Even if they had his photograph they weren't going to see enough of his face to make him.

The hotel parking attendant at the entrance gave him a brief, uninterested nod.

Then Bolan was on the street. As he cruised leisurely alongside the parking garage, he saw a pair of headlights sweeping through the second level, followed by a chirp of brakes. The grisly remains of the driver had just been discovered.

It was time to make some distance.

THE YOUNG MAN working the late-evening shift in the parking garage didn't hear the footsteps. He was too worried about what he had just seen.

"Hey, Rumi."

It was just Ilah, who worked the front door some evenings. They had come from Saudi Arabia together on a work program designed to teach work skills to young Saudis from poor families. They were making better money than they could have hoped for in Saudi Arabia, but neither had learned what they would have called a skill.

"What is the matter with you?" Ilah asked.

"I think somebody just drove out of here on the Suzuki that belongs to that guy who does the accounting," Rumi said.

"You mean somebody *stole* it?"

The doorman never got his answer, because things started happening fast.

Someone was honking his horn, then there was a woman screaming. When the two hotel employees left the tiny glass booth, they saw a woman standing outside her car with both hands held to her head, looking at something on the pavement while she wailed.

Three men were already running to her aid—although they weren't very helpful. They took one look at whatever it was on the ground and ran back down the drive to a waiting car.

"He's dead!" one of them shouted. "Somebody kicked his head in!"

"Shit!" said the driver standing half out of the sedan. He now jumped back inside. "It was the dog on the motorcycle! Come on!"

They tore out of the parking garage, one of them shouting into a cell phone.

The woman figured out that the men in the sedan were not going to be of much help. She ran toward the glass booth, hysterical, at about the same time three more men emerged from the hotel in a hurry. They rushed past the woman and bumped her to the ground.

The doorman and the parking attendant were not sure what to do about all this. Especially when they saw the trio of newcomers kick the body out of the way and jump into the black Saab. The hotel employees helped the woman to her feet. The Saab moved about a foot before it exploded, and the three of them hit the ground again.

BOLAN WAS GOING the speed limit and driving defensively when he saw the police car stopped at the light. The lights on the police car blazed to life before Bolan was halfway through the intersection. So much for blending in with city traffic.

With a whoop of sirens the police muscled into cross traffic and tore after him. Bolan watched the car come up fast in the bike's mirrors. There was a blare of Arabic from the loudspeaker, probably telling him to pull over. They didn't sound friendly. Some sort of APB had to have gone out pretty fast to make Bolan a wanted man already.

He slowed the bike and steered for the side of the road. The cops stopped, and Bolan heard their doors open. One shouted an order. They probably wanted him to turn off his engine, and they just might have a revolver aimed at his back.

Bolan waited for his moment as a pair of cars approached shoulder to shoulder in both lanes of the street. When they were just close enough he twisted the accelerator handle and yanked the Suzuki onto the pavement and directly into the path of traffic, its uncontrolled fishtailing accompanied by discordant blaring horns and screaming brakes. There was a crunch of body panels behind him when a pair of the skidding cars made contact. Bolan brought the bike under his control, heading back the way he had come with the police nowhere in sight—yet.

He turned the Suzuki around the first corner and killed the lights, cutting into a cobblestone pedestrian walkway between buildings. It was less than an alley, too narrow for a car, and as the tip of the handlebars scraped the brick on the left or right he found himself steering by feel. It widened only for a narrow alcove holding a trio of plastic garbage cans.

At the end of the passage he rolled to a stop in darkness, looking out onto a district of boutiques with understated signage almost entirely in English. Bolan's realm of expertise did not include the fashion industry, but he knew he was looking at names that would inspire admiration in those who cared about such things. The inventory in these small shops would be worth millions. They were all dark now and the manicured grounds and walkways were empty, but Bolan didn't need a warrior's instinct to know the place wasn't as deserted as it looked. There would be regular patrols. Maybe the place had cops stationed here permanently.

He heard the sound of sirens from the street he just left, the sound distorted by the odd acoustics of the narrow passage, and a glance over his shoulder told him at least two emergency vehicles were on that side of the block. He wasn't going back that way.

Was he?

His mind was suddenly boiling with strategy that crystallized in seconds. He went over it again. Looking for a hole. Looking for danger. Not to himself, but to the local police who would be his pawns. Bolan didn't kill police. Even getting them wounded to further his own ends didn't fit the Executioner's strict ethical code.

But perpetrating a little mind game on the Kuwaiti cops? About that he had no qualms whatsoever.

THEY WERE JUST sitting there, listening to the action on the radio and straining to catch a glimpse of the other squad cars a block away—and heading in the opposite direction.

Neither of them said a word. Both of them were wishing they could be in on the chase. Both of them were regretting their frivolous conversation about their supervisor—which happened to be overheard and happened to be reported to the supervisor and happened to be the reason they were stuck with glorified security guard duty for the next three weeks. They were bored silly while every other National Police Force officer in Kuwait City was enjoying chasing a madman on a stolen motorcycle.

Like a pair of puppets on the same string they sat up straighter in the seats of the squad car. There it was! A motorcycle on the cobblestone pedestrian walkway, lights off, moving from the shadow of one awning to the darkness of a small boutique entrance alcove.

The action, against all odds, had come to them.

"Call it in." Sa'doun, a four-year National Police Force veteran commanded.

"Are we going after him?"

Sa'doun would have glared at the man in the passenger seat if he dared take his eyes off the spectral motorcycle. His partner was worse than a rookie—he was a stupid rookie. He had no future in the police force. His stupid comments—which Sa'doun had unfortunately laughed at—had landed them with one of the worst assignments inside the city.

"We're going to get all the backup we can muster in a hurry and trap him inside the mall by closing every exit. If we try to go after him alone, he'll slip right by us on that thing."

Stupid Rookie got on the radio. Minutes later, from all around the desert metropolis, the Kuwaiti National Police Force converged on one of the richest shopping districts in the world.

SA'DOUN FELT his heart pounding.

If he was instrumental in nabbing this foreigner—and that was about all he knew about the man, that he was a foreigner run amok—it might restore some of the luster to his dulled professional reputation.

When the motorcycle reached the end of the mall and paused in the shadows, Sa'doun almost took the risk of leaving the car to follow on foot. He would not risk starting his car—that motorcycle would be long gone before he could shift the Fiat into Drive.

Even following on foot was a long shot.

But he didn't have to. The biker peered up and down the cross street and apparently disliked his chances in the occasional traffic. He turned and drifted back, moving from shadow to shadow, in search of another escape route.

"What is he up to?"

Sa'doun didn't bother to glare at his partner. "Looking a for a way out."

"Why?"

What kind of an idiotic question was that?

"I mean," the rookie continued, "why does he think he's safe here? It doesn't make sense."

"Why not?" Sa'doun demanded, without really caring.

Before the rookie could respond there was a call from the radio. Squad cars were staged, ready to move into position at both ends of the boulevard and converging side streets.

"Hold off," Sa'doun responded. "He is heading back the way he came."

"Alert me when he is dead center—we will get him when he's farthest from any escape route," radioed the patrol commander. "Just in case."

Yeah. Just in case. This one was as slippery as a fish, Sa'doun thought, and they were going to set the hook deep.

Sa'doun waited. Finally he reported, "He is in position."

"Move in, all units! I want this street locked down now!"

9

Bolan heard the distant chirp of tires in two directions and saw lights converging on the far end of the blocks. Then the squad car that had been tucked in the shadows across the mall came to life. Bolan spotted them during his initial reconnoiter and guessed what they would do about him. He cranked his head at the squad car, gave them an openmouthed look of pure shock, then hit the gas and sent the Suzuki roaring down the street of boutiques.

At one end of the street a squad car turned in and headed directly for him, another Fiat patrol car coming up behind it with a ten-yard gap between them.

Bolan waited for the first squad car to drive over the spot where he dropped the device, then hit the button on the detonator. An orange ball of fire swelled and expanded fast on the heels of the first cop car, not quite able to catch up to it. Car two skidded wildly with the driver standing on the brakes, the tires screaming on the cobblestone surface. It veered onto the walkway and into a storefront. The finely etched name of an Italian fashion designer was obliterated in a fantastic explosion of plate glass and an inhuman-looking mannequin wavered then toppled, its head plunging through the shattered windshield of the patrol car.

More patrol cars were close behind. The next slalomed head-on into a concrete planter. Its headlights went dark, and the interior filled with white air bags that engulfed the occupants.

That left one squad car still in motion, and when its driver managed to get it under his control he headed straight for Bolan. The Executioner waited until there was just twenty feet separating the cop and the next explosive package, then hit the red button.

It was inside a stone-decorated trash receptacle. The garbage can flew apart in a belch of flame and litter. Bolan had been careful to make the charge small enough to be nonlethal, but the cop didn't know that. He swung the wheel and escaped in the only direction open to him. The Fiat flattened a hedge and smashed through the gilded front double doors of a tiny shop that sold women's shoes priced like top-grade gemstones. Display after display of colorful pumps were mowed down before the car came to a halt against the rear wall.

At the opposite end of the block more squad cars were screeching their tires and staging an impromptu roadblock, unwilling to get any closer to the madman who was apparently tossing incendiaries.

Bolan sped behind a concrete pillar molded like a Roman column and watched the scurrying officers of the Kuwaiti National Police Force.

A man with a bullhorn started shouting something in Arabic, but Bolan pressed a button.

The first charge went up a hundred feet from the roadblock, neutralizing the patterns of flashing headlights and emergency lights in a single sphere of brilliance. The gunners with their rifles and the bullhorn man scrambled behind their vehicles.

Sa'doun spotted the hand appearing from around the column yet again holding a remote-control device.

"Down!"

He and the rookie ducked behind the dashboard, and this time the blast was more distant. Sa'doun risked a look and spotted the smoking hole in the pavement from the next blast, not ten paces from the roadblock. The officers were fleeing on foot.

Sa'doun watched them go and knew there was no one left to stop the madman except himself. And the stupid rookie. Sa'doun slid from his car and bolted for cover behind a concrete bench.

The night was now oddly quiet except for the puttering of the motorcycle engine.

"Surrender or I will shoot!" Sa'doun called out in English. The madman likely spoke English. He tried it again in Arabic. There was no response.

Time to strike fear into the man, Sa'doun decided. He rose up, leveled the combat shotgun on top of the concrete bench and found the madman standing in the middle of the street waiting for him. The big handgun bucked in the man's grip, and the powerful rounds took big bites out of the top of the bench. The first was five feet away. Then four feet away. The shot that was two feet away came just after Sa'doun hit the deck.

Hearing the motorcycle rev up, Sa'doun peered under the bench, seeing the lower half of the vehicle speed up the street, then slow and turn into the buildings.

There was a pedestrian entrance between the buildings, big enough for the motorcycle. The son of a dog was going to get out of the block without ever putting himself in range for the backup teams waiting it out at either end of the boutique street. *He was going to get away.*

Sa'doun launched himself to his feet and raced headlong down the middle of the pavement, stopping to fire a single wild shot at the bike as it was swallowed up by the buildings.

Officers on foot were coming from the squad cars that had crashed into the planter and the storefronts.

"He went through there!" Sa'doun shouted angrily as he ran for the narrow slot. "Did you block this exit?"

Before anyone answered the gap between the buildings was filled with fire, which reached out for Sa'doun like a hot, burning hand and swatted him to the ground like a man swatted a bug.

BOLAN HEARD the officer shouting as he ran toward the passage between the buildings. The soldier had dropped another explosive there to block his escape, but if he didn't detonate now he'd risk killing the cop. On the other hand, Bolan might be the one killed if he used it too soon.

He pressed the button and yanked hard on the accelerator si-

multaneously, and the charge burst into life, creating a fireball
that became a moving wall of flame that rushed up behind him
like a living thing—a burning behemoth of incredible speed.
Bolan felt a tidal wave of heat crash into him, and his mind struggled to ignore it while he concentrated on maneuvering the motorcycle. At near-highway speeds, every time the handlebar tips
scraped the wall on either side the motorcycle threatened to rip
out of his hands. At that speed, one solid scrape against the wall
would twist the handlebars, jackknife the bike and result in a
crash the likes of which Bolan could only imagine—the relentless inertia of the disintegrating steel mass contained in this narrow passage would chew through him like the blades of a meat
grinder.

Then the world rushed at him and the confining walls of his
makeshift oven fell away. Bolan found himself rocketing across
four lanes of a city street. He heard the screech of brakes and the
honk of a horn.

A vehicle veered around him, then did a punishing 360 that
had white smoke coming off its tires. It was the sedan he had
last seen in the parking garage below his hotel. Well, you start
tossing around explosives, Bolan told himself, and you're bound
to attract some attention. His friends from the parking garage had
to have heard about the commotion on the police scanner and
come looking for him.

Bolan got the motorcycle moving again. So far the 144-horse-
power, 988 cc power plant had served him well. The bike had
impressive specifications: zero to 100 mph in less than six seconds. Top speed was better than 170. Every indication was that
the wealthy Kuwaiti kid who owned the bike took good care of
it, so its performance was as good as new.

Let's see if that's good enough, Bolan thought as he watched
the car come at him.

Bolan upped his speed as the front end of a man emerged from
the passenger-side window. Bolan aimed the motorcycle at the
front end of the car and for a microsecond made eye contact with
the driver. The man at the wheel saw death in the eyes of the Executioner. He thought the big bike was being used as a suicide

weapon. He slammed on the brakes, spun the wheel and sent the car into a wild swerve, while Bolan maneuvered the Suzuki easily in the other direction, stopping just in time to see the car screeching to a halt.

The man protruding from the window had dropped his gun to cling like a stuntman, but the sudden stop was too much and he ejected onto the street, rolling to the curb.

Bolan hit the gas and came at them, his free hand jutting over the Suzuki's low windshield with the big Desert Eagle extended like a tank cannon. The car's right rear passenger door flew open and a man with an assault rifle emerged in low profile, making himself a small target.

But Bolan was an exceptional shot. He triggered the Israeli-made handgun, filling the hot night air with the retort of the .44 Magnum round. The round slammed into the gunner's shoulder, bursting it apart. An AK-74 clattered on the concrete and the gunner collapsed alongside it, his usable arm moving rapidly but uncontrolled until he came into contact with the barrel of the gun. Bolan fired the Desert Eagle again, and this time the target was an easy one. The gunner went limp.

The sedan jumped into motion before Bolan closed in and the rear door slammed shut. The soldier accelerated after it, and just as he was getting a bead on the driver the rear window rose like a shield. Bolan fired into the narrowing gap, but the car veered and the round that would have splattered the brains of the driver zinged off the metal trim and flew harmlessly into the night.

Bolan fired into the rear windshield, proving it was bullet-resistant, then backed off enough to plant a round in the right rear tire. The rear quarter sank suddenly as the run-flat tire made the steering mushy.

Bolan increased his speed and pulled around the driver's side of the car. The windows were firmly closed.

The Executioner smiled and waved. It was just the right thing to do. The infuriated driver swerved at the motorcycle, and Bolan used that moment to blast the front tire and fall back fast.

The handling of the car changed dramatically and the driver found himself wrestling with the steering wheel, unable to control the swerve. Bad tires on two opposing corners were more than the all-wheel drive was designed to handle and the car wavered sluggishly, hit a curb and slammed into a light post.

Bolan heard sirens. They were now a few blocks from the chaos of the explosions, but the gunplay was bringing the police to them.

Suddenly the car was in motion but gave Bolan a wide berth. Then the warrior saw their purpose. They were going to get the man they left behind. The gunner ejected from the window was now on his feet, shambling to meet the car.

Bolan pocketed the Desert Eagle to give himself two hands to control the bike. He gave the accelerator a vicious twist that sent the bike careening down the street as if rocket propelled. The power plant purred noisily, but the motorcycle flowed around the wobbling car like river water around a mossy rock.

The gunner froze—to him the motorcycle had seemed to emerge from nowhere. Maybe he thought Bolan was long gone. He had retrieved his weapon and faced the warrior with a sawed-off combat shotgun that was no match in range for the deadly Desert Eagle that had emerged and was again thrust over the Suzuki's windshield.

The shotgunner looked wildly around. There was no place to hide. Bolan triggered the big handgun but at that moment the shotgunner, running for a dark storefront with amazing speed, jumped a brick planter and avoided the second round by a hairsbreadth. Bolan tracked his prey, but the man seemed to sense the shot and fell to his hands and knees as a third round burned the air where his chest might have been.

The gunner rolled to the side, putting a low concrete island between himself and Bolan, then jumped to his feet in a crouch behind a steel merchandise display.

Now Bolan understood what the gunner was up to.

Although it was designed with the elegance of a jewelry store, the tiny building was actually a gas station. The concrete-based humps out front enclosed pumps. Bolan saw himself barreling into another conflagration.

He triggered the Desert Eagle at the low shadow that scampered for the protection of the station. The shadow vanished. Then it was there again. The gunner's face was a mask of glimmering scarlet in the security lights. Bolan made that blood mask his target and squeezed out a round. The mask of blood became something else without any resemblance to a human face, and the gunner stood there momentarily, dead on his feet.

He toppled, and the trauma of sudden death discharged an electrical tempest. Dead muscles convulsed. Dead fingers clenched the trigger of the combat shotgun. The gas pumps were just ten feet away, and the broad spread of the round meant the dead man wasn't going to miss.

Fuel hoses parted with a spray of liquid and sparks from buckshot ignited the gas. Bolan felt as if he were wrestling a python in slow motion, but in reality it took him just seconds to slow the motorcycle enough to twist it through a sharp turn.

The orange flames snaked around the gas pump and crawled across the narrow drive to the storefront, almost licking the motorcycle's tires. The emergency fire system responded with a laughably tiny snowstorm of foam. A few puddles of flame blinked out, then the snow was gone.

The gas pump burst apart and covered everything with raindrops of flame, including a distinctive plumbing connection, where a breath of fumes seemed to burrow belowground like a flaming mole. Something moaned underground, the pressure building fast.

Bolan raced away as an abrupt release of pressure sent burning gasoline spewing from the piping. He felt the spray of liquid, then felt it burning. He smacked out flames on his legs and arms, then ignored the fire while he brought out the Desert Eagle. There was the sedan, still plodding along after him.

He saw his own orange aura on the pavement. He was still burning. No time for the car. He left it behind before the occupants could figure out what to do about him.

Bolan turned off the street and rode hard, getting away from approaching sirens and pounding at his upper arm and shoulder until the flames were gone—but the burning continued. He could feel it.

He took the Suzuki over a curb and into the wrought-iron fence around the small outdoor café area of a darkened restaurant. The gate popped open, and Bolan found himself plowing through spindly rattan chairs stacked on flimsy tables. He dropped the motorcycle and looked for a water source.

His eyes fell on the ubiquitous restaurant fountain, there to help create a temperate ambiance even on a scorching hot day in the desert city. But the inside of this shallow vessel was just a dry crust of mineral deposits. Bolan stooped, yanked at the shutoff valve and tepid water spurted from the nozzle, set in the stamens of a concrete bloom. He thrust his burning arm into the water as the escalation of agony told him the smoldering embers had eaten through his jacket, burned his shirt and were consuming his flesh.

His teeth clenched at the hiss of superheated steam, then the fountain spray belched and turned to a stronger stream of cool water that engulfed the heat and extinguished the fire completely.

Bolan gave himself the luxury of thirty seconds under the fountain, breathing deeply, knowing the moment he withdrew his arm from the flow of water the pain of the burn would escalate again. In the darkness he tried to see the damage, but couldn't tell what was charred linen sport coat, what was scorched cotton shirt, and what was cooked human skin.

The worst possibility was that the pain would be intense enough to distract him. Bolan could not afford anything less than one hundred percent of his mental capacity. He was just becoming fully aware of his situation: this restaurant had to have closed down. The dry fountain and a few pieces of litter told him the place had gone unused for weeks.

As the countdown in his head ended, Bolan withdrew the arm from the water, and when the pain hit him it was as bad as he had expected. That was bad enough. His teeth flashed like the fangs of a starving cat and he tore a chunk of charred linen from his arm like a bloody hunk of fresh meat, his jaws grinding into it, his forehead bathed in a fresh layer of perspiration, while his brain strove to think clearly.

It was almost impossible—the injury was bad. His body was

trying to shut down. It wanted to collapse into recuperative hibernation, and Bolan knew fighting it would be folly.

His eyes fell on the open gate, and he half stumbled across the courtyard through the scattered chairs and tables, grabbing on to the rails of the gate for support, feeling a wellspring of anger come to life. *He would not surrender to pain.*

With a force of will he mentally blocked the agony, stomping it into a vault inside his brain. The vault contained it—barely.

The street was empty, but the whooping of emergency vehicles was drawing closer.

Bolan examined the lock, then swung the gate closed.

Mack Bolan began to put the scattered tables and chairs back the way he had found them.

10

The first dark blue Fiat with the National Police Force logo cruised the street three minutes later, piercing the interior of the cafe courtyard with the white blade of a searchlight.

That was just seconds after Bolan had completed his cleanup job: restacking the chairs, shutting off the fountain and wheeling the Suzuki into a dark alcove. The pain was still under control, but his body was laboring with every movement, intoxicated with exhaustion.

The searchlight blinked out. The squad car moved on.

The courtyard's roof was heavy foliage on a lattice, but he wouldn't trust it to hide him from the helicopters that would be making their own search, probably soon.

He heard the thrum of rotors.

Bolan went to the heavy steel doors with his tools. It was like watching someone else's shaking fingers at work. The stranger's hands became dappled with moisture, as if in a light sprinkle of rain, the hot drops of his own sweat.

The door opened, and Bolan wheeled the motorcycle inside the dark restaurant. He bolted the door at the same instant the courtyard became awash in brilliance from the spotlight on the belly of the police chopper just overhead.

Bolan did not care to contemplate the number of times he had been pushed to his own limits, forced to endure what he had never thought endurable. His life had left him with a highly accurate sense of his own strengths and capabilities. Right now he knew he had limited resources. Every movement had to be efficient.

The closed-up restaurant was a stroke of luck—but only if the Kuwaitis didn't check it out carefully. Any close examination of the front gate would show the lock was broken, and then the place would be swarming with police.

And Bolan would be here waiting for them, because he knew he didn't have the energy to go farther—not with any stealth.

How bad was the burn, exactly?

Such speculation agitated the demon in the vault.

In the kitchen, alongside a walk-in cooler that was open, warm and stinking, was a rickety steel rack of dry goods and cleaning supplies. He nudged it away from the wall a few inches, until there was enough space behind it for a man to lie on his side, at least partially obscured by the shelf contents. This would be his hospital.

As he crawled into the niche behind the dry goods, scattering a nest of beetles, he wondered if he would awaken in a Kuwaiti prison. He ripped off more of the sleeve and dressed the burn with what first-aid supplies he had. The last thing he did was pull out painkillers—narcotizing codeine pills—and swallowed several.

Bolan had done all he could for himself, and his energy was depleted. His only option now was to allow his body to rest and heal. As the first distasteful surge of the narcotic slowed his thoughts, Bolan closed his eyes and felt the demon in the vault weaken, its screams dying to mere howls of fiery agony.

HAMZA AL-DOURI SWIGGED more vodka from the bottle.

"You really think that will dull your senses less than a pill?" Maysaloun Jasim asked his question—for the eighth time—with the ball-cheeked smirk he always wore. Jasim had a baby face and supreme overconfidence that went far beyond everyman arrogance.

"It's a known entity. I don't trust those pills because I don't know what they'll do to me," al-Douri replied, seething.

Jasim shrugged, still grinning. Except for the narrow beard on his chin, Jasim's face was shiny smooth, like the flesh on the face of a prepubescent boy. His face was heavy and fleshy, and his perpetual smirk made his cheeks into polished apples. He looked ridiculous, like a merry old man from a fairy tale, and that was just one more reason to despise him.

At the moment al-Douri despised everybody. The pain of the gunshot was throbbing, and he constantly fought to keep his temper in control.

Shot by his own man! The idiot was dead now, and he deserved it. The round was small caliber, but it had slashed an ugly flesh wound across his ribs. The doctors had stitched him up under anesthetic, but it left al-Douri dopey and loose tongued. He'd still been muddled when the police tried to question him, and he knew he shouldn't allow himself to be interrogated, but even feigned sickness didn't put them off.

Al-Douri was surprised when he was allowed to leave the scene of the attack. His doped-up answers had to have been good enough to raise no overt suspicions, but who knew how long he'd be in the clear.

He went right to Jasim's, a designated safe house, part of Jasim's contract with Baghdad. Jasim's wealth and influence made his home virtually untouchable by the police.

Jasim efficiently handled the rapid citywide quest that tracked down the ministry attacker in just hours, then al-Douri hired a hit man to solve that problem. Two teams of mercenaries—Jasim's personal security staff—were sent in to take care of any loose ends.

Now they were waiting, and al-Douri turned to booze as the doctor's pills wore off. He had to have something to take the edge off the fire in his gut. Jasim encouraged him to sleep, but al-Douri insisted on sitting up to monitor news from the field.

The wall-mounted television screen was set to low volume, but the murmuring voice of the male news anchor repeated what little was known of the attack at the government offices that afternoon. Aside from the screen the room was outfitted like a sheikh's parlor, not the office and command center it was supposed to be.

Al-Douri was about to ask yet again what was taking so long when a phone tittered electronically somewhere, and Jasim reached into a lurid decorative pile of wooden furniture, extracting a phone.

"Yes?" Jasim's face transformed into an ugly frown and a large amount of flesh curled off his forehead over his eyes. All at once Jasim looked every one of his fifty-one years. Al-Douri was momentarily amused to see the man lose the facade—then he wondered what made it happen.

Jasim hissed orders and slammed down the phone. "He escaped," Jasim declared as he picked up the phone again and jabbed at the buttons. "He killed one of my men and got past—"

Al-Douri thought about this as Jasim turned his attention to the phone, speaking in a hushed, angry voice. Then Jasim blurted, "What? Get in here!"

Seconds later a man appeared with a portable radio set, which he placed on the garish desk and twisted the volume.

It was the Kuwaiti police. The man was monitoring the emergency frequencies. There were frantic calls for fire and emergency medical teams, and they caught in passing the name of the hotel.

"There was an explosion. Car bomb," the radio operator reported. "It was in the garage, and three men were reported getting into the vehicle just before it blew. Now Mehdi's car does not respond."

"How long have you been trying to raise them?" Jasim demanded.

"A few minutes—since I sent you the call from the other car."

"Keep at it."

"Yes, Jasim."

The news got worse as the night wore on. It didn't take long for a runner sent by Jasim to confirm that the destroyed car was indeed his. Four of his security staff were dead.

They listened in amazement to the police confusion as the hell-raising biker was trapped, only to be lost in a series of explosions. There was a moment of elation as Jasim's patrolling enforcers reported stumbling across the man on the bike. Even Jasim's smirk had returned.

But not for long. The last confused radio reports from the enforcers told them two of their men were dead already. There was chaos out there. Jasim was insisting there had to be more attackers—one man couldn't have pulled it off.

About the time Jasim's mercenary team stopped transmitting, the emergency scanners came to life again. Another explosion not far away. Bodies in the street. A tiny gasoline storefront guttering out the last of its fuel tank and a burned corpse visible in the inferno—but unreachable.

How could it be? Jasim wore a face that reflected his internal confusion. He'd been defeated. The Jasim family was never outsmarted, outmuscled, overcome. Maysaloun Jasim was in unfamiliar territory.

The Jasim family was rich. Oil rich now, but even before the 1930s the dynasty had old money. The legend was they became wealthy trading slaves, two hundred years ago, harvesting Africans from the continent and penning them in their own secret harbor on the west coast of what was now Gabon. They were middlemen—a sort of slave convenience store for European and American shippers who did not have the manpower to do their own reaping. Just as often they were patronized by slavers who had done their own gathering only to find their cargo withering from disease. The bad cargo was jettisoned, and the slaver would be forced to buy from the Jasim outpost—an expensive proposition, but Jasim's quarantined slave pens were more likely free of disease.

Once slavers recognized how the Jasim preconditioning made their cargo more robust, and more likely to survive the despicable conditions of the voyage to the auction block, the cost per head was easier to swallow. The Gabon outpost became one of the largest slave distribution centers. Only British and American harassment could have driven the Jasim family out of the business—but finally a small fleet of slave patrol warships converged on the outpost and dismantled it. The Jasims were forewarned by Americans and Europeans who were firmly in their pocket, and the family members and staff were on their way home twelve hours before the warships anchored.

The slave business was no more, but the dynasty found continued success, generation after generation, and their ethical code, such as it was, had only deteriorated from their days as traders in human beings. Now the Jasim dynasty patriarch sold out entire nations.

But he did it for the money, and that galled Hamza al-Douri.

Al-Douri was born poor, grew up poorer and scraped his way into a position with the Iraqi government. It wasn't until his skills were noticed and he was conscripted into the intelligence bureaucracy that he began living well, but times had changed and he was back to struggling for every meager comfort.

Jasim had never worked for anything, never struggled. But Jasim had been instrumental in getting al-Douri established in the Kuwaiti government. Tonight he was giving the spy sanctuary— probably because he did not understand the risk, al-Douri decided.

"He'll come here," al-Douri declared.

"We'll turn him away at the gate." When he saw al-Douri's sour look, Jasim shrugged with his eyebrows and added, "He won't get inside."

"You think your security system will keep him out?"

"I do."

"I do not. I've met the man, looked into his eyes. I knew at that moment if he was as good as he seemed I was in big trouble. He has proved that he is that good."

That was when they got word of the police investigation of a body, found in the hotel where the killings occurred. The man was a known criminal, the news said, and gave the name of the deceased. Al-Douri's hit man.

"He's beat us," al-Douri declared through the throbbing of his wound. "He's outsmarted us every step of the way. You still think your security system is going to keep him out?"

Jasim glared at him. If he was angry enough to wear his emotion on his face, then maybe al-Douri had actually reached the man. "The security system will keep him out if he ever comes here, and he won't," Jasim declared flatly. "You forget that he does not know where you are or who I am."

"Alnakeeb Alb did though."

The statement shocked Jasim.

"He'll be here," al-Douri said simply.

"He will not get in!"

"How many times in one night will you let this American show you for a fool?" al-Douri asked.

Jasim gave him a hateful, withering glare and said nothing.

"Once more, anyway," al-Douri said with a liquid chuckle as pain filled his mouth with saliva, and he sucked on more of the vodka.

Stony Man Farm, Virginia, U.S.

AARON KURTZMAN STARED at the reports on his screen, his mouth as dry as desert sand. The latest articles filed with the news agencies and correspondents in Kuwait City were confusing and conflicting. Nobody had a clue.

It appeared no one knew who was responsible for the attacks against a minister in the Kuwaiti government. He had been ambushed right in his own office by a single gunman who was, witnesses claimed, an American. At least an English speaker with a North American accent. He was clearly a terrorist or a murderer with an unknown agenda, gunning down several government employees in cold blood. Curiously, however, these employees had come prepared for the battle, armed with high-powered weapons. The midlevel government official who had been the subject of the attack was not known to be dead or alive, having vanished after being questioned by police.

Questions about the curiously armed ministry officials were being rebuffed by Kuwaiti investigators. None of the National Police Force officers who served as building security had been harmed.

Kurtzman was one of the few people who knew who was responsible for these attacks, and why, but then came a whole new series of events that left Kurtzman guessing too.

A string of violent events shook an upscale street in the city. More deaths—in the parking garage and a room in the same hotel. All the victims had questionable backgrounds.

There were eyewitness accounts of a madman on a motorcycle stolen from the hotel. All that could be agreed on was that he had been spotted in one of the overpriced shopping districts and hemmed in by the police. A series of explosions followed. The subject escaped. The police couldn't quite explain how he escaped, although they stated with conviction that there had to have been accomplices. Only one of the reports effectively drew together the facts and implied that the explosions were carefully used to provide an escape for someone who was beyond the law but did not want to hurt anyone in law enforcement.

Then, less than two miles away, another strange altercation minutes later. No witnesses this time, but there was a dead man in the streets and another smoldering in the ruins of a burned-out gas station.

The dead men could not be identified. The gunshot victim was described as "probably" Kuwaiti, which implied a complexion darker than that of Mack Bolan's. But what of the man in the fire? The reports said dental records would be needed to identify the man—if his dental records existed anywhere.

Bolan failed to check in on schedule. He wasn't in jail. Kuwait was one of the few Middle Eastern countries with computerized law enforcement and immigration record keeping, designed to keep tabs on the huge percentage of foreigners who worked in the country at any given time. Arrests were electronically recorded with the speed and efficiency of a supermarket checkout.

So if not under arrest, *where* was Striker?

Kurtzman couldn't stop thinking about it: Were the charred gas station remains all that was left of Mack Bolan?

"Aaron."

Barbara Price was standing right next to him. He hadn't even heard her. When her hand rested on his shoulder, he reached for it, taking it in his own.

"Phoenix's ETA is sixty-five minutes," she said, but it sounded like she wanted to say something else.

Kurtzman's mind made the instant leap to the other situation, which had materialized out of nowhere the day before. He and Price had been sitting on the front porch of the old farmhouse sipping coffee, enjoying the quiet time, when Carmen Delahunt had come out to summon them to the latest crisis, so fresh it was still playing out for the global news media.

What a difference a few hours could make. This morning Mack Bolan had been alive and well and doing what he did best. Phoenix Force and Able Team, the two commando units that were the official field units of Stony Man Farm, had been on stand-down.

Then, simultaneously, fire erupted on one oil tanker after another. The tankers were thousands of miles apart and originated at various Middle Eastern ports, but a common element became apparent to the Farm cybernetics team: all the tankers were U.S. bound. Kurtzman and his staff traced communications between parties who seemed too interested and too handy to the fires, then tracked those communications to what might turn out to be another series of attacks on shipping vessels.

Kurtzman hoped it would be a false alarm—every other U.S. agency involved shrugged off Kurtzman's clues pointing to possible attacks on shipping vessels in the equatorial Pacific.

Kurtzman, morosely, knew he was right, and knew people would die soon because the U.S. failed to react strongly enough to the threat.

When Phoenix Force was on the scene in the Pacific they would need one hundred percent of Kurtzman's time. The cybernetics team would have to follow the sporadic communications signals step by step, even anticipating their movements, if they wanted to get Phoenix Force on-site when and where the perpetrators made their move.

Bolan would be on his own. There would be little Kurtzman could do to help him out at that point.

"What's all this got to do with Kuwait?" Price asked finally, noticing one of the windows on his screen with a Kuwait City map.

"Nothing," Kurtzman said.

"Is Mack there?"

"Yes."

"Is he in trouble?"

Kurtzman glared at the yellow map image, cubed by a grid, and said, "I think so."

11

Kuwait City

Mack Bolan's eyes came open and read the time before he quite
realized he was conscious. Five minutes past 4:00 a.m. Motionless, he examined the physical sensations his mind was getting,
like a pilot taking readings during preflight engine start. Pain was
there, but tamed. Bearable.

He got to his feet, brushing away beetles. The real test was
how his body acted when he moved, and in a heightened state
of self-awareness he cleaned and dressed the burn on his arm,
stretched out his body like a master in a dojo, then moved
through the dark restaurant to the motorcycle.

Other than lingering lethargy from the pain pills he felt fit
enough. Not quite reinvigorated, and certainly not healthy. His
body had been shocked by the wound. It was still demanding recuperation time, but Bolan couldn't afford that luxury. He had
appointments to keep.

He walked the Suzuki outside, stood in the dark alcove and
listened to the night. Six long hours ago this part of the city had
been swarming with law-enforcement vehicles and aircraft, but
now there was silence. Bolan walked to the gate and watched the
stillness until he found the anomaly.

It was a movement so slight he couldn't tell if it was real, but
that made it all the more suspicious. He found his field glasses

in his pack and probed the shadowy place. There was a concrete office building with just enough stylized trimmings to differentiate it subtly from office buildings anywhere else in the world, and rich fabric banners hung around the entire roof line gave it a softened look, like window draperies. The sign in the front was in Arabic and English, telling Bolan it was an art gallery. He was still in the neighborhood of high-priced retailers—or he had left one and entered another during the chaotic flight from the street of boutiques where he ran into the Kuwaiti police.

The circular drive from the street to the front of the gallery was lined on each side with palm trees in heavy pots, turned so the trees curved inward and their leafy foliage came together eight feet above the drive, forming a leafy carport, a shady place for shoppers to enter and exit their vehicles when they came to their gallery appointments.

Bolan was sure that the car he now made out in the moon shadow amid the palm trees was not a gallery customer. It was a dark Toyota with a tinted windshield. No Toyota driver would be able to afford the merchandise—not to mention the fact that it was seven more hours until the gallery would open for its first appointment.

There was another movement when the invisible occupant of the Toyota shifted in his seat. Bolan imagined a detective or cop inside, fidgeting to keep from nodding off.

So the Kuwaitis had suspected he might still be in the vicinity. Maybe they were too understaffed to go door-to-door. More likely they knew better than to risk the fallout that was inevitable if several dozen retail managers were called out of bed when the cops started opening up every building on the street. These people had pull with the wealthiest and most powerful residents of Kuwait. Better to just stake out the neighborhood and watch for the fugitive to show himself.

Bolan allowed himself the time to move carefully, thinking through the problem as he ate a ration bar and drank water from the fountain nozzle. He was feeling better every minute. The lethargy was receding until the only discomfort or stiffness came from the burning around his arm. One compromised limb he could work around.

He moved a table to the brick wall that surrounded most of the patio and crouched on top, then raised himself until he was peering over the top. The stakeout car looked abandoned in the darkness.

Bolan pulled back to put a section of lattice between himself and the car, judging it would be sufficient to hide the flash of the Beretta, and rested the suppressed barrel across one arm. He aimed, unsure of his drop compensation on such a long shot, and pulled the trigger.

The harsh cough was the loudest sound the street had heard in hours. The round was high—Bolan knew it before his glasses found the puff of dust coming off the side of the gallery where the descending 9 mm round impacted. The stakeout car was motionless. The sound didn't carry that far. The bullet strike fifteen feet overhead had not been noticed.

Bolan adjusted his aim very slightly, unwilling to risk sending a bullet into the stakeout car, and triggered another shot. He experienced a moment of satisfaction when a window on the gallery's second story shattered. The tinkling of glass was like music.

Bolan was off the table and heading for the gate with the Suzuki by the time the stakeout car swung in a tight circle to face the building, headlights blazing. A pair of officers stationed themselves in the open doors of the unmarked car and shouted at the gallery. Bolan, in darkness, emerged from the front gate and walked the motorcycle around the restaurant before quickening his pace. The last he heard of them were their fading shouts—apparently they were attempting to place the art gallery under arrest.

He had no illusions of safety. It would take them only a few minutes to figure out the ruse, then the hunt would be on again. He started the Suzuki when he was a mile away, finding himself in a low-rent apartment district where the buildings were tall and utilitarian. Keeping to the unlighted alleys and walkways was easy enough now, but the motorcycle was too obvious. He parked it next to a Ford that had been manufactured in a European factory in the distant past. Bolan was inside and driving away in under sixty seconds.

Corroding body panels rattled continuously during the drive, but the old car managed to hold on long enough to get him across town. Bolan parked the junker a half mile from his destination and hiked to President George Bush Boulevard.

The Jasim estate was one of the largest homes in Kuwait City and could be better protected than the Bayan Palace. But Bolan had friends in special places. Aaron Kurtzman had already identified Jasim's Achilles' heel, and knew just how to fire an arrow into it.

Bolan pulled out his mobile phone.

Stony Man Farm, Virginia

"AFFIRMATIVE, PHOENIX FIVE," Barbara Price said into her headset. "Aaron's isolating the message."

Kurtzman was working fast, using radio monitoring equipment in the field with the commandos, as well as that aboard a U.S. Navy escort aircraft, to triangulate the source of a low-power radio transmission being sent out over the waters of the equatorial Pacific in Micronesian waters. His efforts were wasted. There was nothing he could learn from that brief tidbit of a voice transmission. It could have come from anywhere.

On the other hand...

"I did what I could with the message," he reported on the line.

"Get anything from it?" asked a man with a distinctly British accent. It was David McCarter, leader of the commando team known as Phoenix Force, all five of whom were right now bobbing on the surface of the Pacific on personal watercraft and wishing they weren't.

"Not a thing and I don't think it matters," Kurtzman responded. "I suspect the message was transmitted from the closest of the nearby islands. If so, we have a destination."

"Bear!"

Kurtzman and Price were both distracted by the too-loud exclamation. There was a young Japanese man coming at Kurtzman with rapid strides, buzzing stereo headphones pulled down around his neck.

"I'm sending you the coordinates," Barbara Price radioed distractedly as Kurtzman and Akira Tokaido held a conference in urgent whispers.

"Got them," came the radio reply that didn't sound British at all. It sounded slightly cowboy.

Kurtzman was grinning. Relieved about something, obviously. He looked at Price and the grin faded a little.

"Striker's okay?" she demanded.

They were closer in many ways than a lot of married couples, so Kurtzman wasn't too surprised that she had figured out that he was worried about Mack Bolan's safety.

"Yeah, and he needs an assist. Can you spare me for three minutes?"

"Phoenix won't be on approach to the island for another fifteen," she said with a sharp nod. "But there's a price to pay."

"Huh?"

"You can take five if you agree to bring me in on this thing with Mack as soon as there's time for a briefing."

The grin was gone. "That's not a good idea, Barb."

"Why?" she demanded.

"Striker and I are stirring up trouble. Political trouble. *Pentagon* political trouble."

Price's eyebrows went up. She was intrigued, and at the moment she was on less than good terms with the powers that be that had a hand in the operation of Stony Man Farm. She said darkly, "Sounds like fun."

Kurtzman shrugged. "Then welcome aboard. But I don't know about fun."

With Price in the loop he didn't need the privacy of the computer lab. He snapped the keys of his workstation and opened the channel on his headset.

"Striker!"

"Morning, Bear."

Kurtzman felt his joy dwindle. He could count on one hand the times he had heard Mack Bolan sound dog tired.

"What's going on?" Kurtzman demanded.

"Rough night," Bolan said.

That's about as much of an explanation as you could expect from Bolan when he was describing his own condition in the field. "Rough night" could mean he'd hit an annoying number of stoplights en route to the hotel, or it could mean he'd lost a leg to a grenade.

Before Kurtzman could probe further Bolan said, "I'm at the Jasim residence. Want to ring the doorbell for me?"

"Glad to," Kurtzman said. "Sure you're up for this?"

"I'm up for it," Bolan growled.

End of discussion, Kurtzman thought. The Stony Man cybernetics maestro dialed into the proper network with a few keystrokes, shrugged off the security system with the activation of a single preprogrammed macro and sent the signal he needed to send.

"It should be going down now," he announced.

"It's going down in a big way, Bear. Thanks."

Then Bolan was gone.

TENSIONS HAD MOUNTED as the night stretched interminably, and Hamza al-Douri's temper was stoked by his throbbing pain until it came to a boiling point. Maysaloun Jasim's practiced composure crumbled as his fear mounted.

Yet when al-Douri tried again to convince the Kuwaiti millionaire that relocation was the best answer, Jasim wouldn't be budged. He was a stubborn man. He would not be convinced that his fortress could be penetrated.

Al-Douri was in no condition to strike out on his own, and the dangers didn't end with this man. He was by now a wanted man in Kuwait. He could not let himself fall into the hands of the government. That would mean prison, and that meant death for al-Douri.

Jasim could protect him. Jasim could move about without being searched. Only with Jasim was al-Douri safe from the Kuwaitis.

In another hour, when the sun rose, they would go to the boat with an escort of Jasim's remaining security staff and a few hired cars. A police bomb squad was already aboard the yacht, responding to Jasim's claim that he'd received a phoned-in threat.

"We move when it is light. We'll be safe when the sun is up," Jasim declared. "Until then, we stay here where we're protected."

Then the lights died.

"You fool," al-Douri said. "Now I think you will see how wrong you are."

Jasim knew it, but he could never let the wretch al-Douri see it. As the emergency lights blazed to life, he got to his feet and grabbed the radio from his pocket.

"What is happening?" he demanded.

"The security system went down," his security chief shot back.

"That cannot happen!"

"It just did—somebody got in from the outside."

"That cannot happen!" Jasim sounded foolish even to himself, then he heard the distorted response from the security man. Something about "police override."

"What about the police?" al-Douri demanded.

"They hacked into the security system through an override reserved for the police," Jasim said in a stunned monotone. "It is supposed to be accessible to the antiterrorist units of the National Police Force and nobody else. Just in case I am held hostage in my home."

"Now it is being used against you."

"What is our security status?" Jasim radioed.

This time the security team did not reply.

Behind him, choking on the agony of every step, al-Douri chuckled.

BOLAN JOGGED to the grounds of the Jasim mansion as it seemed to suddenly wither and die, the system of lights that illuminated every square yard of the grounds powering down. A moment later banks of harsh emergency lights streaked the grounds behind the twelve-foot iron fence.

So far so good. Kurtzman had made him a promise: he would disable the security system on the grounds of the Jasim family home, sneaking in through a security override system supposedly accessible only to the Kuwaiti antiterrorist units. Then he would cut the power to the grounds. And that was about all he could do. If he was able—if he wasn't actively needed in the current field operations of the other Stony Man Farm teams—he would monitor the Jasim situation and lend an assist if and when he could.

Bolan wasn't counting on it.

He crossed the dry, open ground around the outside of the gate in a steady trot, unnoticed by the video surveillance systems, and unceremoniously jammed a finger of putty into the massive steel box of a lock on the gate. He added a tiny detonator and jogged away, taking a position behind one of the mortared stone columns that anchored the gate every five yards. He heard shouting from across the grounds and waited it out.

Bolan's Arabic language skills, picked up piecemeal during more Middle Eastern missions than he could count, wasn't up to the task of deciphering the rapid-fire exchange between the pair of security men and their unseen radio contact, but the tone of their voices indicated they had not spotted him. They were mildly alarmed by the power loss, and they were on the alert for signs of an intrusion that had to be imminent.

It was time to meet their expectations.

Bolan scuffed the hard-packed earth with his foot as he stepped away from the column. The guards turned toward him, trying to sight him through the bars, but he put the column between them again. Their voices told him precisely when they reached the gate, and he pressed the detonator.

The gate burst open, making a metallic clang, and with the hum of vibrating metal still hanging in the air Bolan raced for the opening. The gate swung wide, the lock box reduced to singed strands of steel.

One of the flattened guards staggered to his feet. He was deafened by the blast and one eye was destroyed, charred along with half his face. He screamed, and blinked frantically to clear the blood from the good eye while spraying the air with 5.45 mm rounds. Bolan triggered the Desert Eagle into his chest.

The one-eyed guard collapsed, but the second fallen guard rolled onto all fours—never making it to his feet before Bolan's second .44 Magnum round crashed like a sledgehammer into the top of his head and liquefied the skull contents. The electrical activity in his brain shut down so fast the man received none of the benefits of his brief flash of postmortem consciousness. For him there was only blackness.

Bolan snatched at a fallen radio, then bolted across the lawn as fast as he could move, heading for the sprawling Jasim mansion.

The building was built on high ground, a hill engineered by the Jasim family to create a majestic view over the other ocean-front homes and the huge bay that was an extension of the Persian Gulf. The backside windows were infrequent—it was the front windows of the stepped building that were designed to offer the magnificent views, but Bolan kept his eyes on the fragments of light coming from them. He reached the wall and found the utility alcove, where the underground electric and other utility maintenance equipment was housed. A decorative gate—no lock here—hid the unsightly equipment. Bolan grimaced as the gate clicked shut behind him at the moment the generator in front of him rumbled to life.

The emergency CPU and operating system for the building was here somewhere. Kurtzman had learned the generator was on a two-minute delay. Kuwait had a reliable utility infrastructure, and power outages were infrequent and usually momentary, so there was little need for the generator to kick in every time the power went out. Still, Jasim should have thought through his need for emergency power.

Bolan explored the equipment and wiring, then planted a series of tiny charges. Each one was a receiver with a tiny detonator for a thin finger of plasticized RDX. The little packages were the size and shape of cigarettes, and white paper coverings and a bit of tobacco packed in the end completed the disguise—not that they would survive a close examination.

This was off-the-shelf military componentry, but Cowboy Kissinger, Stony Man's armorer, was proud of them. "Smoking kills," Kissinger joked about his little explosive creations. He placed them using waterproof strips that stuck them in place like vicious little bandages. Each unit would do devastating damage in a controlled area.

These weren't single-button blowups. Each was armed with a three-digit signal from the remote control, or a single detonate button would blow all the currently armed devices.

Conversation came over the radio Bolan had acquired from the guards. He understood enough to know they had discovered the corpses at the entrance. Somebody asked something about a radio. Bolan knew they would quickly figure out their intruder was listening in. Sure enough, the radio went dead.

He had better things to do than hunt for another frequency. Like pulling the plug on the generator. He found a red rubber switch recessed in the cabinet where the rain wouldn't get at it, and he jabbed it.

"THIS IS Team South reporting."

"Where is Adnan?" Jasim's voice exploded into the radio.

"We heard shots. We're on our way to the front gate."

Jasim stared at the radio in his hand as if he couldn't believe the device had dared say what it just said. Al-Douri chortled.

Jasim glared at the Iraqi. "Can you see them yet?" he demanded into the radio.

"I see bodies—"

"Whose bodies?"

"Not close enough yet. The gate is wide-open. All teams be aware—intruders are on the premises."

The generator kicked in. The lights came on weak and yellow, then rapidly brightened to full strength.

The Team South security man was silent for a moment while Jasim glared menacingly at the wall, refusing to meet the eyes of the Iraqi. Somehow he still sensed that al-Douri was grinning bitterly.

"Two bodies. It is the gate team," the man squawked over the radio.

"Is Adnan dead?" Jasim demanded. He didn't know or care who his security leader's partner was.

The radio transmitted a gagging noise. "He is dead."

"Are you absolutely sure?"

"His head is blasted open. I just stepped in some of his brains."

"That sounds very dead to me," al-Douri commented mockingly.

"We do not see Adnan's radio," the guard reported urgently. "They are eavesdropping. All personnel, switch to the backup scramble."

"Wait!" Jasim shouted, but it was too late. Just as their protocol dictated, the guard had instantly clicked off. He would now be calling in to Jasim on the new frequency, and the system would automatically alter the scrambling software. The other guards would initiate this week's numerical code on the radio, giving them access to the new frequency and decoding protocol.

Just one problem. Maysaloun Jasim stared miserably at the electronic device.

"You were not paying attention at this week's security meeting, were you?" Al-Douri's drunken voice was full of scorn.

Jasim's eyes seemed to have retreated into his skull in the last few minutes. He had never seen the need to change the code every damned week. He couldn't remember the last time he had actually bothered to commit the backup code to memory.

Al-Douri's chiding became hot anger. "Even I would not have believed it! Your stupidity and arrogance goes beyond my wildest imaginations!"

Jasim's body trembled with rage and he crossed the room in two great strides, snatched al-Douri by his sweat-dank shirt and wrenched him half off the couch.

"I have had enough of you!" Jasim barked. "No one may insult me—no one! I will kill you!"

"You have already killed us both," al-Douri replied with a drunken smirk. "Do me a favor and put me out of my misery now."

Jasim flung the man back into the couch.

"Coward!" al-Douri said with fresh laughter.

The lights went out again, and they were in darkness. Jasim cursed his decision to put the emergency system on a two-minute delay.

"If you had any mettle whatsoever, you would not be standing here waiting for death to come." Al-Douri shrugged.

Through his bafflement the Kuwaiti millionaire heard the words, and then he knew the truth. He couldn't think straight, but al-Douri was not panicking. As intoxicated as he was, al-Douri was lucid. If he was going to survive, Jasim had to put his trust in the repugnant little worm.

"How do we escape?" Jasim blurted. "Tell we what to do—I will follow your directions, whatever they are."

Al-Douri nodded. "It is about time. Help me up."

BOLAN ARMED THE FIRST of the explosives as he went hunting around the vast building, and heard footsteps coming his way. A pair of armed guards headed for the gate. They came to Bolan like willing victims and jogged within a yard of the decorative palm tree that half hid him. The second man had to have noticed something strange in the shadows and paused to investigate, turning back. He saw the glint of light and knew what it was. He tried to make a sound but could not, for the glint of steel had vanished into his throat.

Bolan extracted the combat knife as his victim fell, mute and dying, then broke into a run that brought him up on the second guard. The guard noticed something wrong and glanced over his shoulder just as a leg came out of nowhere and hooked his foot. The guard plopped down hard but reacted fast, turning onto his back instantly, but his attacker was already coming down on him. The same foot that tripped him landed on his throat, shattering the jawbone and crushing the airways. Bolan slashed open the aorta, and the dying man's lifeblood rushed out.

He had another radio, already set to the new security frequency. The squawking was tremendous. Chaotic. Something was going wrong. They wouldn't have noticed the sudden silence from this pair already.

Were they saying Jasim was out of contact?

Was that a good thing or a bad thing?

Bolan continued around the building, heading for the motor pool. The lengthy garage was hidden under a decorative garden.

Three of the eight car bays were open and empty in the emergency light glare.

He heard voices. Thumbing the stolen radio volume to silence, Bolan stepped over the retaining wall, landing with a tiny scrape on the drive, and crept inside the carport. He moved into a crouch behind the imposing front end of a restored Packard Town Car that dated from the late 1930s.

A trio of gunners hurried into the garage and piled into a military-style jeep without even considering the possibility of danger creeping up behind them in the darkness. Bolan unclipped a high explosive round and when the last man was in his seat the warrior leaped up, passing so close to them they could have grabbed him by his belt loops.

They were too off guard to do anything before the black figure fled into the night, and only the man in the back seat sensed the grenade that bounced on the seat beside him. He shouted, grabbed for the grenade, only to feel it jolt past his hands to the floor, where it was invisible in the darkness.

The man left the jeep with a mighty leap that carried him to the low roof of the next car, a disco-vintage Lamborghini Countach, before tumbling to the ground. The pair in the front seat had too much information to process, but their fleeing comrade's shouts of "grenade" registered. They were halfway out of their seats when the HE blew.

The topless jeep filled with orange fire like a bathtub overflowing with lava. The effect was witnessed only by the backseat man, flashing across his vision just before the wall of fire expanded to fill the garage, incinerating the top half of his head. It had been a mistake to look back.

But nothing he could have done would have saved him, because the intense heat of the high explosive was augmented an instant later by the detonation of the jeep's fuel tank, then the entire carport burst apart with a series of fuel-tank explosions that swelled the conflagration.

BOLAN WATCHED the fire just long enough to be sure none of the jeep's occupants had the catlike reflexes necessary to survive the blasts and come after him. It was soon obvious that nothing would emerge alive from the curiously contained blaze, which looked like a bonfire in a pit, surrounded by darkness.

JASIM STOPPED RUNNING and stared out the window. Now, when he should be running for his life, he stopped to admire the view.

"Come on, you fool!" Al-Douri spit each word as if it were its own insult.

"All my cars were in there!" The Kuwaiti millionaire spoke as if he could not believe what he was seeing. His terror was turning to numbness, and that was dangerous. Al-Douri knew he wasn't getting out of here without Jasim's help.

"Not all your cars—the most important one is waiting for us out front. It is the one we are getting away in, remember?"

Jasim nodded and plodded after him, shell-shocked.

"WHO IS LEFT?" al-Douri demanded as he staggered from the building toward the vehicle that had been sitting out front all night long, just in case.

"I am not getting any responses!" the driver replied. "None of them!"

"What about the remote security force?"

"They are on their way."

"Get him in there!" al-Douri snapped at the gunners, nodding at their employer. One of them stepped from the exposed rear deck of the gun-mounted Hummer and jogged to Jasim, who was moving like the walking dead. The gunner propelled his boss unceremoniously into the open rear door of the Hummer, lifted the man's legs inside and slammed the door. The Iraqi had collapsed onto the floor of the front seat. The gunner repeated the process on al-Douri, pushing his legs inside and slamming the door, ignoring the Iraqi's yelps of pain.

The gunner was a hired Syrian. He liked to think he was a mercenary, but the plain truth was he was just an opportunistic murderer, wanted for slayings in Syria and Egypt. He thought his problems were solved when he took a position with the Kuwaiti millionaire Jasim. His mind flashed back to a night he had spent on the run in Damascus after he was caught red-handed with the corpse of an old woman. Half the neighborhood had been incensed by his depravity and became a mob. He was like a caterpillar in a sand pile trying to escape an army of ants. He'd been lucky, somehow avoiding the mob and the authorities, but it had been the worst night of his life.

The Syrian clambered back into place on the rear deck of the custom-made Hummer, which had a truck bed built behind the passenger compartment with enough room to mount a pair of .50-caliber machine guns. When he was back behind his gun, feeling the big powerhouse of the Hummer rumble to life, the Syrian's fear became determination. Fuck them, whoever they were. He didn't care if it was a neighborhood mob or the whole Kuwaiti National Police Force. Whoever got in the way of this Hummer was going to get mowed down by him personally. His companion was watching the rear, and he'd mop up whatever was left.

The Hummer jerked and the Syrian held on to the machine gun for support, scanning the landscape illuminated by the vehicle's floodlights. They steered for the nearest entrance to the grounds, which the Syrian guessed was on the opposite side of the enemies' entranceway, judging from the pattern of events. But that did not mean there wouldn't be a reception party waiting outside.

The gate was closed. The Hummer jerked to a halt. The driver shouted out his window at the Syrian.

"Get the gate!"

The power was out. The Syrian vaulted to the ground, jogged to the gates, and scanned outside frantically while unlocking the gates manually. The broad streets were quiet. The nearest rich man's house was in darkness behind its own set of steel gates.

The Syrian's back muscles knotted against the gates. They were not meant to be operated manually and were heavy. Then he climbed into the rear of the Hummer, swinging his torso inside just as the big vehicle careened out the narrow opening.

His own people were going to get him killed, but he grinned

when he got to his feet and into his position of power behind the machine gun. The path was clear, in front and behind. They were no longer the hunted.

All they had to do was get to the boat.

12

Bolan heard the frantic radio exchange and came to an unpleasant conclusion: he wasn't going to get to Jasim and al-Douri before they made it to an escape vehicle parked on the other side of the building. But the rats had been flushed out, and he knew where they would scamper.

He bolted for the gate ruins that had been his entrance and jogged to the Ford junker. As he brought the car to life, he mentally scanned the Kuwait City map in his head. He guessed that Jasim's driver would take the most direct route to the docks. Jasim would have called for police help, and he might very well have an escort all the way down to the docks.

Bolan went by the side streets, pushing the tiny car to rattling speeds and taking bone-jarring off-road shortcuts, always keeping the descending slope of the land in front of him. Twice he slammed the undercarriage of the Ford into obstructions and thought the vehicle would simply die on him, but it kept going, complaining every foot of the way. When he reached the docks, he scanned for the slip that held Jasim's boat.

It was easy enough to find. The 102-foot, white-hulled pleasure cruiser was ablaze with light, and a police vehicle was parked near the entrance to the wide wharf, engine running and headlights on.

Bolan saw at a glance that he had won the race, then spotted the vehicle carrying Jasim and al-Douri. It was a military Hummer, piercing the night with a collection of floodlights. Beyond the glare Bolan made out a pair of mounted, belt-fed machine guns.

His shortcuts had put him in the lead, but not by much. They had a half mile of travel left before reaching the wharf. Getting between the vehicle and the cops wasn't an option. The machine guns would cut him down and endanger the police. He'd have to stick to Plan A, if possible.

With the lights cut on the Ford he revved it up from the top of the last stretch of the long, narrow access road that was taking him down to the bay. He pushed the car until its engine whined and was incapable of further revolutions, and the tires slithered uncertainly on the gravel. Then Bolan cut the engine.

He was a bullet, barely controlling the rattling Ford as it careened out of the curve and barreled down the last stretch of incline. If it were daytime, he'd be fully exposed to the police and Jasim. He reached level ground and shot across open space to another dock, the plank surface, rattling under his wheels. Would the cops hear that?

The end was in sight. The whitewashed wharf ended in blackness. Bolan slalomed the Ford to slow it without resorting to brakes, then snatched his pack and leaped out. He was suddenly churning his legs at a sprinter's pace to avoid a high-speed tumble.

As he slowed to a jog, the receding lump of the Ford reached the end of the dock and dived off with a mighty splash.

Bolan ducked behind a thirty-eight-foot cruiser, breathing steadily to bring his body aches under control. Ache, hell, he was in pain. And he didn't have time for pain. He didn't have time for any distraction.

The cops were out of their car, but they were watching the approaching Hummer. Neither vehicle showed alarmed behavior. Bolan was far enough away that he had gone unheard, unnoticed.

So far. Bolan crammed every piece of hardware on his body into his pack, a water-resistant SEAL stow that Kurtzman had appropriated for him with a few bureaucratic maneuvers from the local U.S. military. Bolan kicked off his shoes and went in after the Ford.

The water was cool enough to soothe his abrasions and burning arm and gave him a fresh burst of energy, which he needed to make the powerful strokes that carried him across the open water to Jasim's big pleasure cruiser. Pausing to watch, he saw the vehicle disgorge its occupants at the end of the dock. Apparently they didn't trust the planks to support the Hummer. Bolan saw al-Douri being supported between the cops. A man in an expensive suit and headwear had to be Jasim himself, but he was being propelled down to the boat by one of his men as if he were without a will of his own. Two gunners guarded the rear, armed with portable assault rifles.

Bolan made for the aft end of the yacht and dragged himself onto the folded diving platform. He clung there, riding out a wave of exhaustion, feeling like the prototypical drowned rat.

When he heard the boarding party and crew activity, Bolan extracted the Heckler & Koch MP-5 SD-3. He aimed it over his head, ready to fire into the first face that poked over the aft end.

No one came. The engine thrum intensified, and the cruiser pushed away from the dock on lateral maneuvering thrusters, then made a tight turn. Bolan found himself looking at the shore. The police were pulling away unhurriedly.

Jasim's pleasure cruiser was heading out to sea at a leisurely pace herself. The danger was behind them.

But not nearly as far behind them as they imagined.

The Executioner's workday was just beginning.

THE SYRIAN PACED the deck nervously, watching the receding lights of Kuwait City.

Good riddance.

But he couldn't shake the feeling of being hunted. He would never have admitted it, but he had been afraid—was still afraid.

He forced himself to breathe deeply. The air was almost cool in the near-dawn. In an hour it would be hot again, but right now it was comfortable. He tried to feel at ease.

They were safe now. Unless their attackers came after them with speedboats. Could that happen? Well, why not? Whomever they were, Jasim's enemies had shown remarkable resources and skill. Why stop now? If they knew how to get into the mansion grounds, then they had to know about the cruiser.

The Syrian squinted across Kuwait Bay. There was a light on the water, maybe two klicks back, and he made out the faint lines of a boat in the graying dawn. Was it pursuing them?

He quickly strode to the rear and glared at the light. Maybe it was just a fishing boat.

Then he heard a sound, a human sound, and it was so close it seemed impossible. The Syrian's head jerked. He had one endless heartbeat to realize that his instincts had been correct. He *was* still being hunted, but the hunters—make that *hunter*—was not on the fishing boat.

He was one soaked and battered human being, hanging on to the back of the ship like a lemming on a cliff face, but with an intensity in his eyes that bordered on mania.

This man seemed beyond caring about his own life, driven by an obsession. The Syrian didn't know what the obsession was and didn't have time to think it over, because before he could shout or aim his weapon he found himself airborne.

He was in a watery hell. He thrashed to the surface and saw the big white cruiser was already being swallowed by the gray light of morning.

The Syrian couldn't swim. He tried to scream at the boat, but instead he heaved up salt water and he went under heaving again, so that the spasm channeled another quart of water into his lungs.

He watched the gray surface recede.

BOLAN CROSSED the long rear deck to the boathouse and found a small utility door leading into the mechanical area of the cruiser. He descended the tight steel stairs quickly. There was a single man below, and he had just finished some maintenance chore when he found himself face-to-face with the Executioner.

Bolan spun him and put the crewman down on the steel stairs, face first. The man grunted and when he tried to turn his face the barrel of the Beretta 93-R nudged his forehead into a steel stair edge again.

"Speak English?" Bolan demanded as he patted the crewman

down with one hand, finding him unarmed other than a deep pants pocket full of screwdrivers.

"Some English."

"Who are you?"

"I am Jasim's boat engineer man. I was told to come get boat ready for a trip. Now they brought me with them, and my wife does not know where I am."

Bolan made a quick visual check of the compact, spotless engine room. No weapons. His instincts said the man was telling the truth.

"How many other crew?"

"No crew," the man said.

"There were at least two people aboard before Jasim arrived."

"Yes, yes, two of Jasim's men, and me, and then Jasim came."

"Did the first two men have weapons?"

"Yes, yes. Big guns tonight, too, not just little pistols."

Bolan used plastic disposable cuffs on the engineer's hands and ankles, looping the leg ties around a generator mounting bolt. That would keep him out of the way.

The man was dumb with terror. Bolan relieved the engineer of his belt and tightened it around his head, splitting his mouth in a sturdy gag.

"Don't worry, friend," Bolan said. "I'll try to have you home to your wife in time for lunch."

The engineer nodded, and maybe the fright in his eyes faded a little. Bolan hoped the man did not take it as a promise.

There was no certainty in the War Everlasting. Every battle could be the final fight. Bolan intended that he and the engineer would survive to leave the big pleasure cruiser—but there were no guarantees. Maybe everybody on this ship was doomed, Bolan included.

Then so be it.

BOLAN CREPT OUT onto the open deck once more, scaling a narrow set of stairs to the topside sundeck. He went flat when the fore guard strolled into view, carelessly letting his AK-74 assault rifle dangle by the stock from one fist.

The guard stood along the front rail and tucked the rifle between his legs, then fumbled in his pockets. Bolan crept up on him, his bare feet as silent as a stalking lion. But the water was still dripping from his clothing, and maybe it was the tiny drops that alerted the guard. He spun as Bolan closed the last two paces, and in surprise he allowed the cigarette to tumble from his lips. He flung the orange plastic lighter at Bolan's face, but the warrior ignored it and struck hard at the only unprotected flesh he could find. The combat knife slashed across the guard's throat. The man grabbed his neck and didn't put up a fight when Bolan launched him into the ocean with a quick shove. He snatched up the Kalashnikov and disposed of it over the side as well, then moved back into a less exposed position on the upper sundeck.

Two down. Two more gunmen, plus the Hummer driver, plus Jasim and al-Douri. He was going to have to get inside unless they decided to cooperate by coming outside themselves.

He heard the door slide open almost directly under his feet. One man walked casually to the middle of the front deck and, after the sound of the door sliding closed, another man emerged. They were in the white uniforms of a hired yacht crew, but this pair toted AK-74s, aimed at the deck but clearly at the ready. They were conversing in unhurried murmurs for just a moment before one of them interrupted the other with a question. They had noticed the missing guard. A moment later one of them strode to the rail and peered at a dark spot on the deck beneath his feet.

The man cursed in Arabic and both of them were instantly in full alert mode, but they were too late. Bolan found his moment and squeezed the trigger on the HK MP-5 SD-3 submachine gun. The morning breeze was disturbed by the coughing sound of the gunshots from the factory-installed sound suppressor.

A 9 mm burst brought down the first gunner. His companion made a mad dash toward the cover of the deckhouse, but Bolan cut him down from above with a burst to the chest.

No more enemy gunners were likely to present themselves now. He heard the shouts inside, beneath his feet, and he raced toward the rear, slipping down the stairs and moving under the overhang alongside the rear deck entrance to the interior.

The door burst open with a kick and the man inside spun out of it like a whirlwind, sweeping the deck with his assault rifle. He was extremely fast, and Bolan had a muzzle in his gut before he could dodge it, but it took a microsecond for the Hummer driver to realize he had the enemy right where he wanted him. The driver squeezed the trigger but Bolan twisted and swept the gun barrel aside, then delivered a powerful jab with the barrel of the MP-5 that almost penetrated the driver's skin. The driver had removed his body armor if he had ever worn any. The gun barrel crushed some internal organ.

The driver staggered and tried to run, but Bolan targeted him with a quick burst that left him sprawled lifeless on the deck.

SUPPRESSED MACHINE-GUN fire came from just above their heads, and Maysaloun Jasim watched his two best men, both with military special forces training, collapse in bloody piles.

Al-Douri was propped on a nearby chair, barely holding himself upright, but he managed to curse violently. The driver grabbed his Kalashnikov and went out the rear.

Jasim snapped out of it. The horror of those sudden, violent deaths sent a fresh supply of adrenaline into his veins. He strode across the room and opened up a hand-carved wall shelf. It was designed to serve as an elegant buffet when he hosted large dinner parties on the yacht and turned this parlor into a dining room. He reached up into the wall and withdrew a 12-gauge, sawed-off shotgun, then a box of shells. He cracked the shotgun open and inserted shells in both barrels, then pocketed the box.

"Anything else useful stashed up there?" al-Douri asked.

"Here." Jasim handed him an AK-74. Al-Douri made quick work of checking the magazine, and he smacked it back into place with his palm as another burst of machine-gun fire came from the rear. It was definitely suppressed, definitely not the retort of the driver's Kalashnikov.

Al-Douri was shaking his head dourly. "It's him."

Jasim knew who he meant. Al-Douri had been insisting all

along that they were under attack from just one man—the same American who attacked him in the ministry building just twelve hours before.

"I will believe it when I see him," Jasim retorted confidently, feeling self-assurance welling up in him. He'd been in a stupor of what? Fear? Whatever. He was himself again. Supremely confident. Al-Douri called him arrogant. Well, he was a Jasim. Anyone who was a Jasim had the right to be arrogant. No American cowboy was going to take down a patriarch of one of the premier families of Kuwait.

They silently watched the door at the rear of the parlor, where the driver had disappeared. They heard nothing now except the thrum of the engines, carrying them at a leisurely eight knots into the Persian Gulf.

Then the engines stopped. Someone had to be on the bridge, above them at the rear of the sundeck. Where would he come down? Jasim wondered. Fore or aft? He backed away to the far side of the parlor, eyes flitting between the two entrances.

The rush of the water traveling under the hull silenced as the big pleasure cruiser came to a halt and rode the waves gently. The door at the back of the room creaked on its hinges, opening slowly. The bottom of the door was obscured by a chair. Had the door latched when the driver went through it?

Al-Douri was shaking his head—he had a clearer view of the rear door. No one was there.

Jasim turned his attention to the fore end. The sun-reflecting drapes over the huge picture windows were closed, but through the glass door he could see enough of the deck. Nobody was coming in without his knowing about it.

He liked the heavy feel of his father's old sawed-off. It was the kind of weapon nobody would mess around with. In any sort of a confined space it was a no-miss weapon.

Then the boat bobbed and Jasim saw movement. He triggered the shotgun at the door, shattering the glass and shredding the curtains. The big picture windows had only begun to disintegrate when he triggered again, and the windows smashed onto the deck with a crashing noise that went on and on. The morning sun was peaking over the horizon and came through the tattered drapes to create bright jagged shapes on the walls of the parlor.

Then he saw the same movement again and realized he was seeing the limp lolling head of his dead guard. The bobbing of the boat was moving his skull. The face rolled over and looked directly at Jasim with mocking dead eyes.

"Fool!" Al-Douri was covered in glass and was trying to wipe the blood out of his vision, but there were so many splinters imbedded in his flesh that he created only more blood.

Then Jasim saw more movement, behind him this time. A dark shape was coming through the open door at the rear. The tall figure swept down on al-Douri, snatched the Kalashnikov from his hands, then backed away covering both of them with a suppressed submachine gun.

It *was* al-Douri's attacker, the one-man American army.

"Damn you!" Jasim blurted.

"Don't move."

"Go to hell!" Jasim cracked open the shotgun and fumbled in his pockets for more shells.

Bolan raised his weapon and sent a 3-round burst into the ceiling tiles. Flakes of them sprinkled onto the Kuwaiti millionaire. Jasim froze, finally understanding the danger, and when Bolan gestured at the floor he dropped the shells, then the shotgun.

"No, shoot him!" al-Douri screamed, trying to smear the blood out of his vision.

Bolan snatched the Iraqi spy by the wrist and quickly bound his hands in front of him. Then he ordered Jasim to the carpet on his face, trussing him up like some elaborate roast about to go in the oven. He searched them both, removing three blades and a small handgun from al-Douri, along with a bottle of pills.

"Kill me," Jasim pleaded.

"That would be way too easy," Bolan said. "You're going to get all the publicity you deserve, Jasim. I'm going to see to it. By sundown you're going to be famous worldwide as the Kuwaiti millionaire who sold out his country to the hated Iraqis."

"I'll be ruined."

"You'll be more than ruined, you'll be shamed," Bolan

replied. "Your family will become pariahs, and your money will be taken away from you. The name Jasim will be used like the word 'shit.'"

Jasim was sobbing. He rolled onto his side, struggling to get to his feet. Bolan knew he wanted to throw himself over the rail, but he wasn't going anywhere with his wrists bound to his feet.

"What about me?" al-Douri demanded.

"You're the whole reason I'm here," Bolan said, backing into an antique chair in the corner of the room, where he could keep an eye on his prisoners. "You would have saved us both a lot of trouble if you'd simply answered my questions yesterday."

"And if I don't talk? What will you do? Kill me? You've already done that. I'll be dead soon enough."

"I don't think so," Bolan said. "You'll pull through if you get some medical attention. The Kuwaiti prisons have good medical facilities, I'm told."

"I'd rather be dead than tell you what you want to know."

"I think you'll feel differently in about an hour," Bolan said. "You've taken two of the pills in that bottle. Your breath stinks like bad booze, so I assume you're deadening the pain with alcohol. Whatever is keeping the pain at bay, it will be wearing off soon enough."

"So what?"

"So then we negotiate." Bolan glanced at his watch. It was just after six in the morning.

"Never."

By 7:30 a.m., al-Douri was pleading for the pills and telling Bolan everything he wanted to know.

13

The young Ranger emerged into the bay of the Chinook CH-47D helicopter. When he was close enough he spoke loudly to be heard over the steady thrum of the twin rotors.

"Sir!"

Bolan opened his eyes. He'd used their flying time for a quick nap. He was tired. He couldn't afford the slowed reflexes that came from sleep deprivation. On the other hand, there was every chance the someone in Iraq would soon learn about the secrets al-Douri had spilled and make haste to change the facts of those secrets. There had been no time for real rest.

"ETA ten minutes, sir," the young man said, not quite sure how to address this maybe-civilian.

"Thanks."

"Sure you want to do this?"

"I'm sure."

The Ranger looked like he wanted to say more, but what the hell did you say to some guy who had the wherewithal to get himself air-dropped into the middle of nowhere in Iraq by the freaking U.S. military?

Besides, this guy looked like he knew what he was doing. He even looked like he might have the ability to pull it off—whatever *it* was. The young Ranger had seen some very scary dudes during his half-dozen years in the military, but this guy looked lethal in his *sleep*. The Ranger was glad the guy was on the American side.

"What can I do to help you out?" the young Ranger said finally. "I'm fully prepped."

The Ranger nodded. "Good luck, then, sir. Stay frosty."

It sounded stupid, saying it to a guy like this, but the dark figure grimaced in what had to have been a smile of appreciation. "Thanks. I will."

THE CARGO RAMP OPENED on the bleak vastness of a remote section of Iraqi desert. Kurtzman had found recent Homeland Security intelligence reports hinting at the recent failure of the Iraqi air-traffic monitoring radar over the area. Defense technology failures inside Iraq were an everyday occurrence, and the U.S. military was correcting them when it could. This particular event was just a blip on the screen at the DOD, without much urgency, but Kurtzman saw the opportunity it offered—and the danger. When he suggested it to Bolan, the warrior had not hesitated.

"Sounds ideal, Bear, so long as it is safe enough for the insertion crew."

"They can fly in low to avoid commercial air-traffic radar, so they'll be unseen, unless the Iraqis get their equipment repaired within the next eight hours."

"Not likely," Bolan said. Technology parts and expertise were rare commodities in Iraq. "But what if?"

"They'll scramble up an air defense. I'll know about it. So will the entire air command in the Middle East. You'll have to turn tail and get an ASAF escort back home."

Bolan grunted. "Hal won't like it."

Kurtzman laughed. "Striker, Hal's not going to like any of this."

Bolan considered that. "Sorry to put your ass in a sling, Bear."

"But it's worth it."

"Yeah."

"Besides, this is my pet project, remember?" Kurtzman added. "I'm the one who called you in. You're just my subcontractor."

Bolan really did grin at that.

IF HE HAD BEEN SMILING now, the climate would have scoured it right off his face the moment the doors opened to the blast of gritty wind coming off the surface of the desert. The Chinook wasn't fully settled on the baked, cracked earth, the pilot reluctant even to put her full weight down on this stretch of dangerous ground. Bolan understood his caution. Resistance fighters could be holed up anywhere. He waved to the Ranger as the ramp touched the earth, and he rolled the old Lada SUV out onto the craggy flats of what had once been the bottom of a thriving inland sea.

The Chinook was ascending again so soon the ramp almost snagged the rear fender, and by the time Bolan had steered out of the billowing dust clouds of the downdraft, the Chinook was heading for home.

They had every reason to move fast, and so did Bolan. He pushed the SUV hard, picking his way over the cracked and rutted surface of the salt desert like a stunt driver on an extended obstacle course. He wanted to put as many miles between himself and the landing spot as he could, and do it as fast as possible.

Then he saw the flatbed truck emerge from a small outcropping in a rocky ridge. Barely slowing the SUV he snapped up his field glasses and examined the truck. It was miles away, and with proper time for reconnaissance the Chinook crew would have spotted him and landed elsewhere. By chance, this section in no-man's land was not deserted at all. In the widest corner of the teardrop-shaped desert, where the land was mostly flat, the helicopter insertion could have been witnessed clearly.

Who knew who was in the flatbed? Probably Iraqis searching for scrap metal. The big rusty tank for liquid that was lashed on the flatbed suggested they might be poppy farmers with a verdant swath of arable land hidden in a desert ravine.

Bolan had one option, and that was to get the hell out fast. The flatbed truck may or may not be radio equipped. The occupants may or may not be inclined to report what they had just witnessed. He grabbed his radio as he edged the Lada's speed up to and above what he had previously judged his safe speed. He raised the Chinook, quickly explaining what he had seen.

"Understood," the Chinook pilot replied. "We're haulin' ass already but we'll haul faster. Good luck."

The pilot signed off. The Chinook would be okay. Within minutes she would be back on her regular flight path, and no one would take special notice of her. Bolan was the one who was at real risk. The pilot had said as much in his sign-off. As far as the Chinook crew was concerned, Bolan was as good as dead.

The Executioner had been as good as dead on numerous occasions.

He had always beat the odds. He couldn't remember how many times he had cheated fate, but he was going to do it again. This was about saving lives. This was about rescuing the forgotten prisoners of a long-ago war. Failing now meant failing those men.

The Lada's special suspension and hardened power train carried her over the mogul-like ridges with teeth-rattling vibration when his speed exceeded 80 mph, and in a quarter hour he had crossed the vast flatness to a long, low ridge of rock that blistered the desert like scar tissue. He was out of sight of the flatbed truck, and there was nobody else within his line of sight. He used another three precious minutes clambering to the top of the rock and scanning in every direction to be sure he was alone and unseen.

Convinced, he leaped and skidded back down to the Lada and started her transformation. He found one of the tiny steel tabs tucked under the rim of the headlight and gave it a careful, firm pull, which lifted up a film of plastic clinging to the Lada's body. Pulling steadily toward the rear, he stripped off a two-foot-wide section of the plastic sheeting that ended at the driver's door. The front quarter panel of the SUV had been transformed from a dirty white, designed to camouflage it in the salt desert, to an aged, sun-faded brown, which would be far less conspicuous on the streets of Iraq. Bolan had intended to wait to perform this process until he was farther away from the insertion point, but if the Iraqis had somebody coming to investigate suspicious activity, he needed every advantage.

Ten major sections of the plastic coating came off easily enough—a small miracle in the heat, which made the plastic soft and gluey and easily torn. Only the hood section ripped down the middle, and Bolan wasted a few extra seconds clawing off the scraps. When finished, he was left with a mass of sticky film the size of a basketball. He lobbed it up into the rocks, where it disappeared into a crook.

The vehicle he was left with was not a pretty sight, but she was tough. So Bolan had been told.

It was a Lada Niva Model 21214 to all appearances. Aside from the frame, there wasn't much left of the vehicle that had rolled off the factory floor. All the body panels had been stripped off for insertion of armor plating, or simply replaced entirely with armored body panels. One hundred percent of the glass was replaced with the bullet-stopping variety. The 1.7-liter GM power plant had been unceremoniously removed and replaced with a 2.5-liter 6-cylinder block. It was an acceptable set of wheels as long as it proved to be reliable.

He watched the skies as he raced the brown Lada, coming into difficult terrain when he emerged from the salt desert. Even with his windows open he barely heard the thrum of an aircraft approaching, and he veered the SUV into the nearest cliff side and parked it. He wasn't kidding himself into thinking he was hidden. The aircraft was going to fly almost directly over him. It wouldn't spot the Lada on the first pass, maybe, but one backward glance by the crew and he'd be found.

The plane was a twin-prop aircraft with the Iraqi flag on the small tail. It looked like a personal aircraft, maybe a four-seater, converted for low-flying reconnaissance missions. Just the right tool for finding a one-man invasion force. If he'd still been in the open flatland, he would never have eluded the little prop plane.

It vanished over the next ridge.

Bolan waited, watching, but mostly listening. He knew when the aircraft changed its heading by change in the pitch of the twin propellers.

He thought fast and bought himself time by trying the same trick over again. He yanked the Lada into gear and pulling it into a tight U-turn to bring it up against the wall on the opposite side of the shallow chasm of rock, then examined his surroundings and came up with a plan.

The plane was skimming the ridge tops when it passed over again, but once again it failed to spot the SUV. It was just a matter of time—they knew he was down there somewhere, and the junkyard of scattered rock piles wasn't all that large. But once they saw him and broadcast news of their find, the place would be swarming with Iraqis.

He had to take down the recon plane, and he had to do it with such speed they wouldn't send out a Mayday first.

Bolan drove down the narrow chasm and veered around the end of the rocky ridge, then shot straight out into the desert. He found what he wanted—a soft spot where the baked salt surface was weakened by sand from an ancient beach. He'd spun his wheels through several of these desert pockmarks in the past half hour.

He came to a halt with all four wheels in the sandbox and slammed his foot on the accelerator, spinning the wheels up through three gears. The sand spewed and salt dust billowed up and around the Lada like a desert demon released from his bottle and swelling with the rapture of freedom.

It was better than he could have hoped for. Bolan donned desert goggles and grabbed a face mask from the medical kit, snapping it over his nose and mouth as he heard the small prop plane turn again in his direction. They would spot the dust cloud any second. They would want to see its cause before they reported it to their superiors.

The props slowed and the plane sounded like it was coming in even lower. Bolan repeated his trick with the Lada, spinning her wheels in the loose sand and creating a white cloud that obliterated the sun like the densest San Francisco coastal fog. He jumped out of the SUV and felt his way around to the front end, satisfied that the vehicle would be invisible underneath it.

Hidden in plain sight, the Executioner waited.

"DID THEY BLOW themselves up?" the copilot wondered out loud.

"That's dust, not smoke," the pilot replied, his voice a mixture of scorn and elation. "The fools have got themselves stuck in a sand trap!"

"You would think they would have a car that could make it out of a patch of sand," the copilot said doubtfully as they steered at the white billowing mass that hugged the desert floor, sluggish in the stagnant desert air.

"Let's take off the mask and see for ourselves!"

The copilot was about to protest, then thought better of it. The pilot was his immediate superior officer and disliked being second-guessed. The pilot kept the airplane going just above stall speed and brought them over the last ridge, then descended to just forty feet. He headed directly at the dust cloud, buzzing the top of it, the prop draft whirling the cloud away in a sudden maelstrom.

The copilot craned his neck to see below and gasped.

"Pull up! Pull up!"

"What? Why?"

BOLAN'S M-16 A-2/M-203 combo led the twin-engine prop plane and he clearly saw the momentary look of horror on the face in the window. He triggered the M-203 grenade launcher a fraction of a second later, and watched the 40 mm HE round crack into the body of the aircraft with instant catastrophic results. The fiery detonation chewed a hole in the fuselage and filled the interior with flame. Every window, door and rivet opened to allow fire to stream out. A moment later came the fuel-tank explosion, which jettisoned the burning contents of the interior through the empty windshields. The pilot and the copilot were the largest chunks of burning waste.

The aluminum frame of the aircraft somehow managed to hold the wings together for another five seconds, carrying the burning hulk out over the desert, her flight amazingly level. Then the heat became too intense. The aluminum cross braces parted, and the wings folded. The aircraft dropped to the desert floor and began to burn in earnest.

Bolan watched it happen in his rearview mirror as he put the scene behind him. Fast.

14

Lada automobiles started as a product of the Soviet Union, which meant they were unimpressive by any measure. During the Communist era it was typical for a new Lada to come off the factory floor with so many mechanical problems it could not be driven.

After communism was shed like a moldy raccoon coat, Lada found itself competing with automobile companies that designed cars to roll down the street when the driver wanted it to. Significant changes and privatization of its supply chain helped Lada improve quality. Bolan, however, wouldn't have made the car his first choice.

But he didn't have a choice. There was precious little available in the Kuwaiti car pool of hardened vehicles. Kurtzman had a difficult enough time allocating this one, on top of the long list of other equipment he wanted for Bolan, without setting off alarms throughout the Department Of Defense.

"Trust me, this is ideal," said the Army captain who handed him the keys. The man had high-level security clearance and was charged with equipping various special ops details, but even he had been told only the basic facts about Bolan's mission: a one-man penetration into rebel territory in Iraq.

"Why is it ideal?" Bolan asked suspiciously.

"Check it out," the captain said, blowing his nose on a red grease rag and tucking it into his back pocket. "It changes color like a chameleon." He went on to show Bolan how the thermally applied plastic film could be removed within minutes to remove the light desert camouflage. "Underneath that it's brown and ugly, just like every other piece-of-crap La-dee-da you're gonna see driving around in the place where you're going. You're not going to stand out."

"Are the improvements strictly cosmetic?" Bolan asked.

"No way," the captain protested. "The block is bigger and better, and most of the components have been replaced with milspec desert-grade parts. The transmission is upgraded, too. Everything is greased up so that somebody looking under the hood won't see anything that's out of line—not unless they know their mechanics really good, know what I mean?"

"Suspension? Brakes? Tires?"

"All upgraded. Good tough parts," the captain said defensively. "Not so's you could tell by looking."

"Mileage?" Bolan asked.

"I dunno, why don't you check the sticker on the window?" the captain blurted sarcastically, wiping his hands rapidly on his soiled coveralls. He had done much of the work on the Lada himself and didn't like the big guy's attitude.

Then he noticed the big guy wasn't talking. He was just staring.

The captain saw something in those eyes that he recognized from some of the SEALs, the Rangers, even the fields grunts. The ones who went into the field again and again, who saw horrors that no one should witness, who survived battles where the odds for survival were minimal. And they went back every time their CO asked, without question, because they were America's warriors.

And along comes this guy, who's going into the worst possible field and going alone, and some smart-ass grease monkey Army captain is giving him shit. Well, when you looked at it that way... The captain's attitude altered abruptly.

"Sorry, sir," the captain said. "Didn't mean to get cocky on you."

"Mileage?" Bolan repeated.

"You'll get five to seven hundred miles with the reserve tanks we've got tucked up in the body panels, but a lot less if you do some stop-and-go desert driving."

"Captain, I think you know you probably won't get this vehicle back," Bolan said.

"Yeah, but that's out of my hands."

"You wouldn't try to get rid of one of your problem vehicles, would you? The one everybody around here knows about? The one that probably wouldn't make it round trip to the off-base convenience store?"

"No, sir! We don't even keep them around here—we transfer the troublemakers over to the regular car pool for local use."

"Good. Anything more I should know?"

"Well, we did install a bank of 20 mm heat-seeking missiles that launch from under the headlights." The captain chuckled briefly.

The joke hung in the air like a heavy, wet blanket, but then Bolan grimaced.

"Q you ain't, Captain," Bolan said.

The captain smiled, relieved, thinking, And you're not James Bond, either, buddy, 'cause *nobody* would want to watch a movie with a grim bastard like you running around for two hours.

THE LADA SUV took him swiftly into one of the remote villages, then on the road to Balad, where he lost himself in the heavy auto and pedestrian traffic by noon. He struggled through the city to the Tigris highway, which ran alongside the river on its northwest to southeast path from the three-corners intersection of Iraq, Turkey and Syria, into Baghdad, then continued all the way to the Persian Gulf. Bolan stayed on the main road despite the possibility of roadblocks. He was counting on the confusion of the Iraqis over the meaning of the intruder to delay a measure that drastic.

Soon the Iraqis would know their missing recon plane was shot down. But who was trespassing and why?

The sun was blazing and the interior of the SUV became like an oven. By late afternoon he was muscling through the dense throngs that crowded the streets of Baghdad.

Bolan wasn't formally educated in ancient history, but he knew enough to feel a sort of reverence for this place. Baghdad, the great city that dominated the Fertile Crescent, had been one of the birthplaces of civilization. In this place, where the beneficence of the two great rivers, the Tigris and the Euphrates, made agriculture highly productive, human beings for the first time found themselves freed from the struggle for survival long enough to expand their interests into art, science and written language. Tiny slivers of advancing knowledge were diffused by merchants into that other infant civilization in the Nile Valley. Bolan knew that scholars argued over which of the two was really the first true civilization, but that was just intellectual minutia.

What was important was the soul of this city. Baghdad was one of the ancient hearts of the world, now reduced by decades of despotism and the devastation of war to nothing more than a sprawling slum. The struggle for democratic rule still faced pockets of resistance.

Someday maybe Baghdad, standing on her ancient but rock-solid foundation, could become a great center of civilization again.

Bolan shook off such thoughts as he found the safe house Kurtzman had located for him—stressing that there was nothing "safe" about it. Just a hole in the wall set up by an Iraqi spy who was more or less on the CIA payroll and thought to be more or less dependable. Bolan drove by the alley entrance to the dank-looking bottom-level flat three times before deciding there was no one watching it from the street.

Then he went to find the CIA agent.

NATEQ HATIM HAD WATCHED as his grandmother was beaten to death by high-ranking Republican Guardsmen when they caught her stealing fruit from a street cart. Hatim was already a rising star in Saddam Hussein's Ba'ath Party when he brought official charges against the Guardsmen—only to realize too late that embarrassing the upper-echelon Guard was an insult to the prime minister himself.

With the help of a family contact the bureaucracy gave Hatim what amounted to a free pass: the complaint was essentially wiped off the record books. It had never officially happened.

The men who made up the Ba'ath Party remembered the event, and questions about Hatim's naiveté slowed his advancement up the party ranks for a few years, but his otherwise stellar record made him a favorite once again. There were talks of him eventually moving out of the vast middle-management pool and into the select, top-level Party elite.

But Hatim was not what he seemed. He had changed his allegiance. The beating death had opened his eyes and made him realize that a regime that ignored brutality against its own people could not be good for the people. Hatim realized he had operated on a principle of self-empowerment. The Ba'ath Party was guided without a philosophy of its own and served only as a pool of men who also sought to empower themselves. Neither the party, nor the government, operated under a higher ideal, despite the slew of slogans that the government drilled into the people.

When this chilling, brutal truth became evident, Hatim understood other truths. Iraq was an aggressor that proclaimed itself a victim. Iraq slaughtered her own people and proclaimed it a necessity in the name of national stability. Iraq was ruled by a tyrant who called himself a freedom fighter.

Then the war changed everything.

New leadership was the only way Iraq could hope to escape the ways of the tyrant—and the succeeding tyrant who would inevitably emerge from the Ba'ath breeding pool if no external force prevented it. That external force was America, which Hatim had been educated to hate from the day he was born. It was difficult now to know who to trust.

The man who emerged from the crowds outside the café didn't even attract Hatim's notice until he had entered, passing a bill to the proprietor to be permitted entrance, and strode to the table adjoining Hatim's.

It was him. The man was walking around Iraq like he owned the place, but he gave the name Cooper in a low mutter, and repeated a series of numbers that were the total of an equation that was the agreed-upon password.

The man ordered lunch in Arabic, putting a Syrian-border accent on the words to hide his lack of fluency. When the proprietor left them the man called Cooper said, "I came in from Balad and your people know it."

"Have you been spotted yet in Baghdad?" Hatim asked as he sipped tea.

"I don't think so. They're looking for a white car and mine's not white anymore."

Hatim glared at a man on the street, who brought the stench of his clothes far too close to the café. The man understood the message and gave the café a wide berth. The café was for the social elite—as defined by their cash roll.

"Is the safe house secure?"

"I can't make guarantees. As far as I know, it is undiscovered. I pay a local boy to keep out squatters."

The American seemed satisfied with that, and he launched into his lunch hungrily. After a moment he said, just before taking a mouthful, "Former Republican Guard General Saleh Jawdat."

Hatim stiffened and forced himself not to react visibly. "What of him?"

"Who is he and where is he?"

"Who he is," Hatim replied evenly, "is very bad news. If he's part of your plans, then it's time to change them, my friend."

"Tell me why."

Hatim felt nervous. Suddenly this meeting was too unsecured, too exposed. "He is one of the worst. He makes people disappear. Many people. Sometimes important people. He is a sadist, a torturer."

"That's Iraqi standard practice."

"Yes, to some extent. But I say again, he is one of the *worst*. He crosses all the boundaries. He does the dirtiest work. When answers are needed from a strong-willed man, and all other persuasions fail, then General Jawdat is the last resort. He always extracts the answers no one else could."

"What's his command?"

Hatim grinned painfully. "That's difficult to pin down. He has several former Republican Guard groups of various sizes under his command, but I could not guess at the actual number of them. It is impossible to know how many people secretly support the old regime."

Hatim put down his teacup and casually adjusted his steel watchband, twisting the clasp to display a small white tablet adhered inside the hollow of the clasp.

"Cyanide. Your people provided it as a part of my agreement to do their work. If I fear capture by General Jawdat, I hope to have time to take this first."

Bolan nodded. "That's who he is. Now I need to know where he is."

"So you will know best how to avoid him, you mean?" Hatim said, chuckling in his throat. "No, I guess not."

"Do you know where?" the American asked evenly, but Hatim knew he was growing impatient.

"At this moment, no. But in four hours, yes. There is a party tonight at the building site of the World Trade Exposition Hall. Jawdat will be there, along with promoters from throughout the Arab and Asian worlds. There is a dream to transform Baghdad into the hub of commerce for all of Europe, Asia and Africa. So they are building a trade center that doesn't have any trade. The party tonight is part of the effort to make it happen. Dinner will be alfresco at the construction site, then everyone will retire to the World Trade Hotel."

"I think I'd like to attend the late-night entertainment portion of the evening," Bolan said.

Hatim nodded, a move too slight to be seen. "There will be many beautiful, cunning women."

"There's only one woman I'm interested in—the woman Jawdat is interested in. Does he usually take the same one?"

"It is never a woman. It is a young girl. A waif. Look for the starving street urchin with fear in her eyes, and you will have found Jawdat's partner for the night."

"I'll be there," Bolan said.

"This other matter you asked about in the communiqué that preceded you, regarding American prisoners. This I know nothing about. I think if there were prisoners the rumors would be rife in the streets."

"Not if they're Jawdat's prisoners. Not if it's a secret only Jawdat knows about."

"If they exist, the prisoners would be powerful leverage if their existence is made public at the optimal moment."

"You'll be at the party?" Bolan asked.

"Certainly."

"I'll need Jawdat's room number."

Hatim blanched. "I will try. How will I communicate this to you?"

Bolan thought about it, asking a few pointed questions of Hatim, and came up with a strategy.

"That might work," Hatim concluded.

"Do you object to bedding one of the women yourself?" Bolan asked. "You'll need to keep her with you all night."

"I will suffer through it," Hatim said with a smirk.

Bolan rose. "See you at the party," he growled, and strode out.

Nateq Hatim lingered over his tea for another ten minutes, thinking about Bolan's parting words. Surely, he thought, the man would not attempt to show himself at the World Trade Hotel.

That would be suicide.

15

"Come with me, please," he said to the lovely woman with the lustrous skin that contrasted beautifully with the tight, Asian-inspired dress.

She smiled demurely. "So polite, sir." She took his arm.

He grinned drunkenly. "You seem like a well-bred young woman, so you should be treated with respect."

By using me for sex? she thought, but still smiled as they entered the elevator. He continued to grin idiotically as he aimed a finger at the buttons and stabbed one, frowning at it. Then he shrugged, sloshing some of his drink on the elevator carpet. On the eighth floor—the highest floor of the twelve-story building in which construction was completed—he marched purposefully down the hall.

Ahead, the woman spotted the general. She felt a spasm of revulsion, remembering her nights with him. He had a partner, a young newcomer. This had to be her first time with the general. It was going to be a night the young woman would never forget. Maybe she wouldn't even live through it. In the old days, more than one of Jawdat's partners had escaped his bed and flung themselves from a palace window.

The drunken man, to her horror, seemed to be trying to catch up with Jawdat. Was the drunk one of Jawdat's friends? Staying in Jawdat's suite? Suddenly she wanted to scream and flee.

Then the drunk stopped short. He watched Jawdat and the girl enter the room and frowned at them, then nodded.

"Wrong floor!" he whispered. "I'm on seven!"

His consort almost fainted with relief.

She noticed his drink getting the better of him on the way down. He had insisted on taking the stairs. He didn't want to wait for the elevator to return, but he began reeling on the way down. There was a moment when she thought he was going to fall over and tumble down the carpeted steps. When he fumbled with the key and got the room door open he barged in, forgetting the manners he had used earlier, and spent five minutes in the washroom making retching sounds.

When he emerged, he was smiling weakly. "Let me help you to bed," she said with nursemaid kindness. She had been in this situation before—with luck, she would soothe him to sleep before he felt well enough to get aroused, then she would have a night off—she could stay here and relax. Maybe watch some satellite television.

But her companion seemed to have expelled his sickness and soon had her performing her function. Two things she couldn't help notice were the mildness of the alcohol taste on his breath and his need for loud music from the bedside radio. It was a French rock station, and it drowned out any other hotel sounds she might have heard.

BOLAN GOT THE CALL, sent ostensibly to a local office but bounced around the world to Stony Man Farm, where Aaron Kurtzman stripped out the audio performance by CIA agent Hatim, pretending to have accidentally dialed his office as he vomited into the hotel toilet, then drunkenly pressed the keys to get the portable phone to turn off.

The fumbling was an act, too. The three digits provided Mack Bolan with the room number of the ex-Republican Guard General Saleh Jawdat.

Bolan had memorized the layout of the World Trade Hotel and guessed the general would be provided one of the rooms on the southeast side of the building, where the best suites were situated to offer a river view.

Bolan guessed right, and when the numbers came in he left

the Lada, entered an older hotel and found his way up to the roof. In his decrepit uniform he gave the hotel employees just the right impression: an underpaid, surly, midlevel police officer with enough seniority to cause problems. Not that they would get in the way of an officer sent to keep an eye on the streets below during the expensive soiree occurring across the street.

The elevator had an operator. This was an old-fashioned touch but was actually required because the elevator had bare wires where the control panel had once been. The operator used canvas gloves to flip circuit breakers amid the exposed electrical wiring to make the elevator move and stop. The lift probably wouldn't have earned the required inspection pass certificate that most European and American elevators displayed. When the elevator descended, and the hall was empty, Bolan continued to the roof on foot.

He set up on the roof edge, keeping his feet on the patches of gravel so they wouldn't stick to the tar, which was still hot and gluey from the heat of the day. Finding some scraps of flimsy wallboard he arranged a kneeler for himself.

Getting to the roof had taken some time, but when he put his field glasses to his eyes Bolan found he had time to kill. Jawdat was freshening a drink in his room unhurriedly.

Bolan assembled his hardware. The heavy-duty Ruger sniper rifle had come with the heavy load of supplies provided by Kurtzman's contacts. Bolan's vehicle was loaded with enough hardware to outfit a small army. If he had come into Iraq on foot he would never have been able to justify the weight of a limited-use weapon like a sniper rifle.

He was glad he had it. The target was approximately 320 yards from his position, and he was aiming through the dismal Baghdad smog, through a window that canted slightly away from his position. He needed every advantage the Ruger offered.

Jawdat loomed large in the Leupold scope. The darkening of the night and the brilliant lights in the suite made it look as if he were pouring powder into the drink he was mixing. Concentrating on the magnified image, Bolan did indeed see a small envelope being emptied into the glass. Jawdat stirred the drink with his bony finger.

He looked like a gnarled dead tree in a suit, with scrawny wrists protruding from the ill-fitting sleeves of the shirt and jacket. His neck, distended and scrawny, looked even longer protruding from the too-low, too-large collar. He made a lipless, hard smile that demonstrated genuine pleasure. He was enjoying himself, whatever he was up to.

Bolan adjusted the Leupold scope minutely, scanning the suite from side to side, seeing no one, despite a range of vision that extended the depth of the room. Then a door opened to what may have been a washroom. The waif that emerged was smiling drunkenly, her head moving with the unfocused vision of the very intoxicated. She wore what might have been an expensive designer dress that draped her thin limbs without fitting them. Put her and the general on the same scale and they would weigh as much as a normal human being, Bolan thought.

Hatim had mentioned that Jawdat's rumored excesses were said to involve the use of various drugs, designed to make his women utterly compliant. But this wasn't a woman. Even in the up-close view of the scope she didn't have the spread of hips or the swell of breasts. What was he going to do to this child? Why did it require drugging her in addition to all the booze she had already consumed?

Whatever it was, Bolan wasn't going to let it happen. But that was secondary to his true reason for being here.

Time to make a phone call.

THE PHONE BUZZED. Jawdat cursed and put the drink on the bedside table. This had better be an emergency.

"Jawdat," he announced into the receiver.

"I have a gun aimed at you, General," said a no-nonsense voice in American-accented English. "I can get off at least three shots before you reach the door."

Jawdat stared into nothingness as he considered the threat, then slowly turned to face the windows, where the drapes and blinds were wide-open. The room lights made them a mirror, but he could see the faint black outline of a building across the street.

"You are looking right at me, Jawdat."

"Who are you?"

"Bounty hunter. A very good one."

"Hired to assassinate me?"

"Hired to free the American prisoners of war that have been in your clutches since Desert Storm."

Jawdat cursed audibly, despite himself. It was impossible that the man could know about the prisoners.

"I don't know about any American prisoners," Jawdat retorted. Bolan hadn't actually expected him to cave in so easily. Time to start showing the general that the Executioner meant business. Bolan aimed the weapon and squeezed the trigger.

The Ruger crashed against his shoulder. The .458 Winchester Magnum cartridge went through the hotel-room window, leaving a hole the size of a dinner plate and spraying glass around the interior. He saw the general cowering behind his arm and turning away. When the Iraqi looked up again, he was still holding the phone to his ear, forgotten.

"Get the message?" Bolan said.

"You stinking swine!" Jawdat roared. "You will die when we find you! You will die!" The petty threat was all his limited English could come up with at the moment.

"You are the one with a gun aimed at his head. Tell me where to find the prisoners."

"Never."

"Think again, Jawdat. Would you like another demonstration?"

Before Jawdat could respond the glass exploded in on him a second time. The round was closer, crunching into the wall above the desk and tearing into the brushed mauve wallboard. Jawdat made a wordless sound, and even he could hear the fear in it. It was a huge mistake to let the enemy see your fear. But he did not know what to do.

Then it occurred to him that he was more in control of the situation than he had at first thought. This man was threatening to gun him down to get the information he wanted—but it was information that only Jawdat had. The American needed him alive.

Jawdat smiled.

"You'll never kill me."

"Don't count on that," replied the man on the phone with confidence that made Jawdat second-guess his deduction.

He plowed ahead anyway. "You need me. You kill me and you have nothing."

"I'll have the satisfaction of destroying you. I haven't been simply watching you for the last ten minutes, General. I've been taking a little news footage, and it's already sitting on a computer in the state of Florida in the U.S.A. What will happen if I put it on the news tonight? Think the Iraqi people will appreciate one of their rebuilders getting shown up for all the world to see as a sadistic molester of children?"

Jawdat's face and hands became cold. The threat was worse than death. But was it true?

If it was, he was good as dead. He would have to kill himself or be killed.

But if it was a bluff, what did he have to lose by calling it?

"I am going to walk out of this room, American," Jawdat stated with a carefully controlled voice. "You will not kill me."

"You got me, Jawdat. I won't kill you. But let me give you something to remember me by."

There was another explosion of glass and the heavy-duty window disintegrated entirely. Jawdat screeched as the phone bounced on the carpet. He snatched at his elbow, where he found a mass of soggy flesh.

Jawdat staggered from the dropped phone to the young girl, slumped on her face on the bed—he had not even noticed that she had passed out. He used his good arm to grab the collar of her dress and hoist her to her feet. She was a sack of bones and skin, and Jawdat was a powerful man. She dangled as if from a noose in front of his body. Would the American risk shooting again with the girl in the way? He was an American. He would refrain.

Jawdat felt his body weakening, and he could only maintain

his shield for a minute or two, then he saw the clouds of darkness creeping into his vision and the encroaching numbness of shock settling on him. He tried to walk with the dangling prostitute puppet, but his strength was gone. He dropped her in a heap on the carpet, where she moaned. Jawdat careened to the door, expecting another shattering sniper round to tear into him at any second. If he heard the sound of more glass, it would already be too late.

But the sound never came. Jawdat fumbled with the doorknob, somehow opened it and fell into the hall. He heard a scream from someone, then he was in blackness.

16

Bolan knew with Jawdat unconscious it wouldn't take the others long to understand what had happened and where the shots came from. It was time to get out.

He descended unseen and exited a rear door of the second-rate hotel, the Ruger now disassembled in an old canvas sack held over one shoulder as he strolled through the unlit streets to the garaged Lada. The man whom Hatim had arranged to rent the space showed up, demanding an additional stipend to the already exorbitant fees paid by Hatim. The garage owner grew enraged when Bolan ignored his demands, putting himself between Bolan and the SUV.

Bolan didn't have to understand the rapid-fire language to know he was being shaken down. So he nodded and reached under his loose-fitting shirt. The garage owner's reaction showed that he had been expecting cash to be removed from Bolan's shirt, not the big Beretta 93-R.

The hands went up and the angry diatribe died on the lips that were the target of the suppressed handgun.

Bolan checked the Lada's contents without allowing the garage owner to slip from his sights. The specialty locks and hardened door mechanicals had foiled a break-in attempt that was evidenced by the scratches around the various locks. The garage owner saw Bolan notice the scratches, and the man looked like he would melt from fear. He began stammering. Bolan gestured for him to take off, and the man slithered out of the garage without turning his back or lowering his hands.

Bolan left the place and sought new cover.

It was time to hurry up and wait.

THE PLACE WHERE he waited was a shadowy alcove in the rubble of structure that had collapsed amid all the fighting over the years. The odd angles of the tight space inside the rubble somehow managed to accommodate the Lada, although there was paint from the SUV left on a skewed support pillar. Bolan had scoped the spot earlier. Inside he was invisible in the blackness but had a clear view of the VIP parking area. He observed General Jawdat's vehicle with impunity.

Jawdat would come. The wound was bad but not life-threatening. He would never allow himself to be taken to hospital, not knowing he was being hunted. He would trust only his own personal security. If there was one thing a corrupt bureaucracy fostered, it was a sense of healthy paranoia.

As expected, the guard posted at the car had abandoned it during the crisis at the World Trade Hotel to assist in the search for the culprit. As expected, Jawdat and his entire retinue came back to the squat, armored steel box that looked tough enough to withstand the crush of an avalanche, and powerful enough to drive out from under the mountain of snow afterward.

But it wouldn't stand up to the gift Bolan left under the front end. The engine grumbled to life, and Bolan keyed the remote that snapped a relay inside the device, causing its erect, flexible metal probes to discharge a flash of static electricity. The engine died without a sputter, and the car disgorged a trio of cursing bodyguards who made for the front and popped the hood. The rear doors were wide open, revealing the general sprawled on the rear-most bench seat.

It was time to strike. Bolan sighted the Ruger sniper rifle on the upper body of the Iraqi who was bent under the hood of the transport vehicle. When he pulled the trigger, the Ruger sent the round burrowing in through the side of his rib cage and tearing his upper body organs to pieces.

The other Iraqis saw their companion lay himself on the big engine block. Only a moment later, when the sound of the sniper rifle reached them, did they see and understand the sudden fountain of blood drenching the greasy engine. They spun, each in a different direction, covering front and rear with AK-74 assault rifles. They were shouting questions to each other when Bolan fired the second round out the window of his shadow-hidden car. The Iraqi facing him saw the flash, but a fraction of a second later felt the terrible shutdown of his body and sensed awful cold from the caved-in place below his collarbone. He stumbled back two steps, crashed into his companion and died on his feet.

The last man turned the momentum of his unbalanced stumble into a dodge, spinning himself to the ground as Bolan's third shot streaked from the barrel of the Ruger. The warrior calmly watched the figure slip along the far side of the vehicle and wrench at the door, only to find it locked. He shouted angrily at the general, who was moving sluggishly inside.

Bolan was out of the Lada and following a planned route along the back of the collapsed building, peering out from behind a corner of masonry into the space behind the armored car. He could see the dim outline of the fidgeting bodyguard, who was watching the place Bolan had been. He did not sense the warrior's presence elsewhere. The Executioner raised the Ruger, aimed it and triggered a round that took a big bite out of the darkened storefront beyond the guard. The Iraqi panicked and bolted around the front and sped to the open rear door of the vehicle, eyes sparking. But inside the car the general had been spurred to life. His arm snaked out of the car and grabbed at the door. His last bodyguard protested loudly. Bolan fired the Ruger sniper rifle at the crook of the door and the car, and the Magnum round crashed through the guard at hip level and sprawled his front end into the car just in time to serve as a doorstop.

Jawdat barked orders at the corpse and struggled to shove the body out of the rear door. Wounded and feeble, he didn't have the strength to do it. He collapsed in his seat, panting, wild-eyed, and then he saw Bolan.

The Executioner now slung the sniper rifle over his shoulder. The big, Israeli-made .44 Magnum Desert Eagle handgun was more than enough firepower to handle Jawdat.

"You need me alive," Jawdat spluttered.

"I need to know where to find the American special forces soldiers that you've held prisoner for more than a decade."

"Then we can make a deal." Jawdat was talking too fast, his eyes slitting from the accusing, wide dead eyes of the guard to the merciless grim gaze of the gunman who held his life in his hands.

"Who are you?" His voice was shrill.

"I'm an American."

"I know that," he spit.

"Where are the prisoners?"

"You think I'm going to tell you? As soon as I do I am a dead man."

"You've got it exactly wrong. The only way you might live to see the end of this week is if you tell me—right now—where they are." Bolan spoke the words with disgust. There was nothing worse than being forced to bargain for justice. He saw no alternative.

Jawdat sneered. "Next you will try to sell me the Brooklyn Bridge."

"Not all men wallow in cesspools of lies and deception—hard to believe, I know, but the entire world doesn't operate like the government of Iraq."

"Yes, yes, yes. If you're going to kill me, then get about doing it."

Bolan heard a blast of an air horn. Reinforcements were a few streets away. "I'm not going to kill you, you miserable son of a bitch," Bolan growled fiercely. "But I'm going to make you wish I had."

Jawdat was slipping into semiconsciousness, but he showed puzzlement on his craggy, pitted face. When he dragged his eyes up again, the American was gone.

Bolan trotted across the empty street and slipped into the wreckage of the collapsed building, backing the Lada out of its tight niche and speeding away in the opposite direction of the approaching lights and horns. In minutes he was tucked in his new safe house.

IT WAS an unused military staging garage, probably forgotten, unneeded by a military that no longer existed. Hatim said it was once one of the hiding places for equipment, which Saddam Hussein dispersed as widely as possible to avoid the frustratingly effective U.S. strikes. The equipment was probably nothing more than scrap now, rusting in some forgotten corner of the desert, but the official designation on the door kept this building free from squatters.

It amused Bolan to find haven here, although he wouldn't exactly be letting his guard down. No place in Baghdad could remotely be considered safe.

His senses were alert as he checked his new home, finding nothing but years of accumulated litter. He ate a military Meals Ready to Eat, and for a moment allowed himself the luxury of stray thoughts—his old friend Gadgets had been complaining about MREs a few months ago, going on and on about them in the way that only Gadgets could.

Hermann "Gadgets" Schwarz was a commando with Stony Man Farm's Able Team and his nickname suited him. He could tinker with just about any piece of electronics or mechanics you put in front of him and usually improved it. But what he really wanted to improve upon were the MREs he was forced to eat in the field.

He had been complaining to Cowboy Kissinger when Bolan found them. "You gotta help me out here, Cowboy," Gadgets pleaded.

Kissinger was the Stony Man Farm armorer. There wasn't a weapon he couldn't build or customize, from throwing knife to small arms to the sophisticated homing and computer-targeted missile defense systems deployed around the Farm. He gave Gadgets a look of disbelief. "Let me get this straight—you want me to drop what I'm doing to tinker with your ham steak?"

Bolan, sitting in the lonely blackness of the trash-strewed concrete box, felt a grin on his face. He realized he had just eaten a ham steak MRE himself. He'd stopped paying attention to his field rations years ago.

He wondered where Gadgets and the others in Able Team were now. Kurtzman had hinted that Able Team and Phoenix Force were both in the field but hadn't said where. He wished them safely home again.

They were all the family he had. Able. Phoenix. Stony. The men and women who devoted their lives to toiling in the shadows for a nation that was ignorant of their existence. Those who did know—the very few in the federal government—weren't always appreciative of their efforts. Or their sacrifices.

Stony Man Farm had lost some of its own. Yakov Katzenelenbogen, Stony Man's tactical adviser and onetime commander of Phoenix Force, was the most recent loss. He had been a warrior, with a list of impressive credentials and unmatched field experience. He was a friend. There had been others before him...

Bolan got to his feet in a single fluid movement, cutting off that distracting chain of thought. Right now he couldn't afford to wallow in the past. There was the present to deal with. But, before he could force his reminiscences back into their mental box, the memory of a face flashed in his brain, beautiful, young, smiling at him. He almost heard himself say the name "April."

17

Bolan increased his speed and veered around the turn in the barrier gate. He was using information and a list of targets provided by Kurtzman and Hatim. In the predawn darkness he spotted the lonely outpost of the outer-ring security guard. The pair of guards wasted no time when they saw the speeding, unlit vehicle coming straight at them. One of them raced for the tiny guard shack while the other took his stance and aimed his automatic rifle into Bolan's windshield.

The soldier flipped on the headlights and added the spotlights, mounted in the headlights but several times more brilliant than conventional high beams. The blinding light was like a physical blow, making the gunner shield his eyes with his arm and drop the weapon to his side. The man in the guard booth flung away the radio.

Bolan stood on the brakes at the last possible moment. The tires screamed and the Lada fishtailed at the guard booth. The blinded gunner ran for the safety of the entrance gate, plowing into it at crotch-level and flying heels over head and thumping on the pavement.

The radioman found the spotlights weren't on him and snatched at his rifle, but Bolan was way ahead of him. The Heckler & Koch submachine gun perforated the radioman with 9 mm shockers. Bolan jumped out and took out the second guard before the man got to his feet. Then there was silence.

Not for long. This was just the outer ring of a security system with many layers, and in the middle was the heavily secured compound of what remained of the old guard. It was here that attacks on coalition forces were organized. Here that resistance to democracy lived. It was disguised as a social club for what remained of Iraq's elite class. It was a transparent ploy. Still, the trickery and wrangling of the ruling class every step of the way had kept U.S. forces out far more than it had allowed them in.

Now the entire area would be on high alert in minutes.

Bolan jogged to the security booth and tucked his visiting gift up under the small shelf that held the communications equipment. It was out of sight. It needed to stay unnoticed for just ten minutes.

The soldier drove away.

FAEIZ FOUND twenty guards on the scene when he arrived. There was a general dispersal of the knotted groups when they saw it was the security chief in charge of the night command arriving.

"What happened?" he demanded. The head of the outer perimeter guard duty stood over a body. The dead guard was on his back, chest bloodied, rifle still gripped tight in his right hand.

"Somebody gunned down both of them." The captain nodded at the figure slumped inside the cramped guard shack. "He managed to get out a radio call."

"Did the attackers get inside?"

"My men saw an SUV pulling away. I have already started a full-scale search of the area, inside and outside the first perimeter. We will know if they are here but I think we would have spotted an intruder already."

Faeiz frowned and grabbed the radio from his belt, calling for another status report. No one had any trouble to report.

"Keep the status reports coming. Once each minute until I say otherwise."

He looked out over the buffer zone between this outermost guard station and the next, more formidable fence. The security lights were all on. It looked like noon. The grounds were barren and devoid of life.

"I do not understand this," Faeiz muttered. "Why execute these men? What purpose did it serve?"

"As a distraction?" the captain suggested. "Maybe they think we will lower our guard at some other entrance point if we focus on this gate."

Faeiz shook his head slowly, walking to the booth to stare down at the remains of the guard inside. "They would have to be head-in-the-sand fools to think that. But I have no better explanation." He said into the radio, "Have the city patrols gone out?"

"Yes, of course, as soon as the alarm was sounded," replied the mobile squads chief. "We're looking for an SUV or four-wheel-drive vehicle of some kind. We would find a better description useful."

"I'll let you know." Faeiz said. He bent at the waist, leaning inside the booth, and looked at the odd lump under the radio shelf brackets. He leaned in so far his head was on the dead guard's lap.

"What is this?" he called out, sounding like he had his head in a barrel, reaching for it.

Ten minutes were up. The odd lump detonated.

18

It was a house of prostitutes. Hatim had claimed he knew of at least thirty of them working the place, and probably more he had never seen. The place was funded by Ba'ath Party directors, who made certain that midlevel Ba'ath up-and-comers knew all about it. Nothing spurred success like sex.

"You know you are somebody when you get pleasure house privileges," Hatim had said with a taut grimace.

"You've been there?" Bolan had asked.

"Of course. I am a 'somebody,' aren't I?"

"Tell me about it."

Hatim told him everything he knew, which included some of the layout and most of the security measures, which were limited to armed guards and some well-hidden video surveillance pickups.

"Audio too?"

"Sure. The audio's most important. The resistance wants to know who's spilling secrets."

"What are the women like?"

Hatim began telling him and Bolan interrupted, restating the question.

"Oh. Which of them are dangerous, do you mean? I would say any of them who are over the age of fifteen or sixteen. If they are there that long, then somebody thinks their will is broken and they will stay loyal enough. Any woman older than that was surely an employee of the palace. The palace was where the very fetching girls went, and many came back to the pleasure house to run the place and of course continue entertaining the men of the Party."

Bolan thought about that, thought about a fifteen-year-old girl who had been in the place long enough to have her will broken. He said finally, "Hatim, how old are they when they first go in there?"

"If they're recruited or purchased, maybe eight, maybe ten. Some are there from birth—the daughters of palace women."

Bolan had never given voice to the next question: How old were they when they began to be used? He knew that it was at once.

That was rape, pure and simple. Even when marriages were arranged at birth, cultures did not allow for their prepubescent children to consummate it. Even fifteen seemed young to Bolan—Bolan, who had been horrified by the desperate choice his seventeen-year-old sister had once been forced to make.

This was not his reason for being in Iraq, but the Executioner was glad it had presented itself as a target.

HE WENT IN THE BACK of the pleasure house, scaling the concrete walls and snipping the nonelectrified barbed-wire mounted on top. He lowered himself inside the grounds, where meager attempts at beautification included a few gaunt, thirsty trees and some benches made from cast-off concrete block. Bolan had seen penitentiary recreation yards that were beautiful compared to this stark garden.

He stalked the armed guard stationed in the back, creeping through blackness unrelieved by lights.

The guard was there to keep the women in and to keep the would be rescuers of unwilling recruits out. He didn't come across as a skilled soldier. His flashlight was his way of finding his path, but he had to have walked it a thousand times and only used it when he reached the gate of steel bars. He tested the lock by giving it a hard rattle, and when he turned he found himself face-to-face with his killer.

The Iraqi knew the look. Battle cosmetics to darken the light complexion. A vest or straps on which were clipped the instruments of killing. All the signs of a western commando—probably American, maybe a Brit. Definitely the enemy.

The Iraqi reacted with a flash of movement, spearing the enemy hard in the gut with the bayonet on his AK-74. The only problem was his enemy moved faster.

Mack Bolan sidestepped the bayonet and yanked the weapon out of the guard's hands, then slammed the time-worn wooden stock of the AK into the Iraqi's chin, shattering the complex weave of skeletal components that had fused together to form his jawbone. The Iraqi gagged on a choking deluge of blood and felt the world explode when the same sort of blow broke his skull case to pieces.

Bolan left the body and entered the unlocked rear door. He found himself in a low, cramped room that stretched into the blackness as far as he could see. There had to be fifty narrow cots crammed together along the two walls and on every cot there was a sleeping form.

Not all sleeping. Three beds away there was a stirring under the thin sheet and the bed's occupant rose on her elbows. Her face was dappled with perspiration from the heat and stagnant air. She looked at Bolan, then lay down again. She had to have assumed he was just another of the guards.

How could she know better? She was a child. Hatim was wrong—that girl was younger than eight. Yet she was resigned to her life. He had witnessed it in the dullness of her eyes.

Mack Bolan was not a man who knew much about children, but nothing was so offensive to his sense of right and wrong as the destruction of a child's soul. How much humiliation and suffering it had to have taken to tarnish the sparkle of natural buoyancy was inestimable, and yet he had just witnessed it in the flesh.

Someone had to pay for the lack of luster in the eyes of that little girl. With grim purpose, the Executioner left the barracks and went searching for the warden.

SOMEBODY SPOKE in the long, shadow-filled hallway and came to catch up, talking urgently. It was another of the guards, whose rapid flow of words caught in his throat when he came alongside Bolan.

The warrior struck fast then, burying the stiletto in the surprised guard, withdrawing it, burying it again, then steering the dying man through a set of doors that turned out to be a kitchen. The filthy stench almost gagged Bolan. He heaved the guard into a bin filled with soggy vegetables and the man collapsed, hands dangling limply over the sides.

There was excitement at the end of the corridor, where a man slipped through a curtained divider and into a well-lit security office without noticing the warrior clinging to the wall. Bolan knew the cause of the apprehensive conversation: news of the attack on the compound was spreading among the city's security infrastructure. A higher alert state was being ordered citywide. Two voices in the office, two guards already out of commission, that left four or more guards patrolling the complex, according to Hatim's intelligence.

One of the four showed himself. He had to have noticed something out of place in the shadows, because he pulled back through the drapery divider before Bolan got off a shot. The newcomer shouted and fired through the divider, pockmarking the wall with a trail of holes that homed in on Bolan with lightning speed. Bolan dropped into a crouch, targeted the unseen source of the rounds by their trajectory, and triggered a long burst from his submachine gun. He heard a grunt and the fall of a body.

Bolan bolted for the office and faced the pair coming to join the gun battle. He triggered a quick burst into the nearest gunner, whose companion leaped for cover and squeezed out a long burst from behind a utilitarian room divider of steel.

Bolan answered by rolling a fragmentation grenade across the room. It arced behind the divider and the panicking gunner jumped into the open, firing wildly but desperate to escape the grenade blast. Bolan cut him across the middle and the gunner slammed down.

His eyes were open long enough to see Bolan retrieve the grenade and reattach it to his combat webbing.

Bolan had not bothered to pull the pin. He had to conserve when possible.

The outsmarted Iraqi's last words were probably not polite, but Bolan couldn't understand them anyway.

Back in the hall the scrape of feet on the other side of the draped archway alerted him to approaching danger. A hissed whisper, a grunt of agreement, then two of them barreled through the opening aiming high and low. They should have concentrated on left and right. Bolan's foot tripped one from the side, propelling him into his companion, and they both spent the last seconds of their lives struggling to regain their balance. A 9 mm burst chopped into the pair and they were still.

The guards were neutralized, if Hatim's estimate was correct. But Hatim hadn't been confident.

Bolan stayed where he was, instinct or intuition holding him there. Maybe he saw or heard something that was too faint to identify but nevertheless activated his warning sense. He was too good a soldier to ignore the impulse.

A moment later there was a an electric crackle from the floor. One of the corpses had a radio and was being asked to check in.

The request became more insistent and Bolan heard the voice in stereo—the caller was talking outside the draped door, maybe ten paces off and coming fast. Bolan listened to the near-silent slap of bare feet and determined it was just one man.

An automatic rifle prodded through the drapes tentatively. Bolan let a head wriggle through the opening, too, then the warrior's hand snaked through the darkness and latched on to the newcomer's collar, hauling him through the drapes, sweeping him in a fast circle, and propelling him bodily into the wall. The Kalashnikov was picked out of the man's hands, and before he could get his wits about him he found himself on the floor, trussed liked a goat about to be bled.

Bolan yanked off the drapes, tearing off a wide strip and twisting it into an improvised rope that he threaded through the series of slots constructed into the concrete bricks above the door to allow air circulation between the rooms. He hauled on the rope and winched the guard off the ground. The shell-shocked guard became agitated.

"Speak English or shut up," Bolan said.

"Who are you?" The guard was so surprised he'd stopped sounding angry.

"Just the hired help," Bolan said. "This place is all screwed up. Lots of unfit men running things in Baghdad. I'm here to send a message to those dogs."

"What are you talking about? You Americans have already taken over ruling Iraq."

"I'm not here for the U.S., dog, I'm here for my friend. My friend is a powerful man here, but he is not being appreciated."

"You are a mercenary?" the guard asked incredulously. "Hired by an Iraqi?"

"Now you've got it."

"Who? Tell me who hired you!"

"Not quite yet, dog."

The insult was just enough to goad the guard, who thrashed impotently, which pulled his plastic handcuffs painfully tight on his wrists and ankles and he swung into the doorjamb. Bolan watched the performance while waiting for the woman behind him to make her play. He had glimpsed her in the chaos, ready to come in with her snub-nosed handgun. He just didn't know whose side she was on.

"Keep moving and you'll cut the circulation to your hands," Bolan told the guard, giving the woman the opportunity to close in under the cover of his voice. She came to within a foot of his back.

"Drop your wea—"

Bolan spun and lifted the weapon from her hands so fast she didn't believe her eyes.

"Give me that!" she blurted foolishly.

"I don't think so."

She lashed out at his shin with a downward step, but telegraphed the move with a long lifting of her leg. The blow never landed. Bolan snap-kicked her other foot from under her, and suddenly the young woman found herself doing the splits. She sprawled to the ground.

"Are you the bitch that sired this whelp?" Bolan asked as he tied up the woman with strips of drapery—he had used up the last of the plastic handcuffs on the dangling man.

The woman tried to spit on him, which was impossible while helpless and facedown on the floor. She followed it up with a venomous string of invective.

"Whatever. You're old and ugly enough."

She screeched and tried to twist on her back, gnashing at him with her teeth. Bolan actually thought she had a pretty face, and she couldn't be more than twenty. But he wanted her mad. In fact, he wanted them both seething and humiliated. His goal was to offend them so severely they wouldn't even think about keeping it to themselves. This probe was a waste of time if it was covered up.

"You will be a dead man very soon!" she shouted.

"Listen to her if you know what is good for you, American!"

"Keep barking like that and you'll wake the neighborhood," Bolan said, as he stuffed wads of drapery into their mouths and lashed the gags in place with more strips of material. Finally he lashed their bits together with a short length of more rolled fabric. The woman's struggles jerked the suspended guard and slammed him into the doorjamb. He jerked back and wrenched her head off the floor on a backward-bent neck.

Bolan liked what he saw. These two wouldn't get free without help and would spend the night fighting each other. By morning they would be in severe pain and as mad as hell.

He went back the way he had come, finding the barracks crowded with worried-looking young women and girls.

He wanted to tell them to leave. To go home. But they had no homes to return to. Their fate was sealed. They huddled in a large frightened mass, eyes wide with fear.

Bolan knew what he had to do. He had to protect them from even the implication of blame in the humiliation he was perpetrating inside. He pulled the gate shut that locked them out of the rest of the residence. They were prisoners in their barracks. There was nothing these girls could do to help those inside.

He peered into the crowd, looking for the standouts—the older women, like the one he had just tied up in the next room. Shouldn't there be more experienced whores supervising the younger ones? The mothers of the girls who had been born and raised in this place?

Then it occurred to him that they were attending the party at the World Trade Hotel. Just the one house mother with the bad attitude had remained here tonight.

It didn't matter. The message he left was clear enough.

But there were many messages to send this night.

19

When Nateq Hatim drew up a quick list of possible targets, Bolan and Kurtzman had been able to choose the best targets. Best, in this case, meant high profile.

Bolan had a few predawn hours in which to work, and every probe had to be a slap in the face to the Ba'ath Party and to the still-powerful underground rulers. The slavers of Baghdad were going to be eating unforgivable insults for breakfast.

Which didn't mean they couldn't be effective antiterrorist countermeasures at the same time.

"You are a dead man," said the research doctor charged with monitoring the laboratory on the midnight-to-noon shift. "You will be killed!"

"You said that." Bolan yanked the rolled sleeves of the doctor's cleanroom coat into a hard knot. The doctor's arms were still inside them.

"What are you doing?" the doctor demanded, raising his voice. He said even louder, "You are not supposed to be here!"

Bolan had the submachine gun in his hands and when the pair of Iraqi soldiers rushed into the work area he squeezed the trigger, cutting them down in a harsh blur of 9 mm rounds. They were dead before the door had swung itself shut behind them.

The doctor's blustering was gone for the moment, and he began to whimper like a worried mutt when Bolan came at him with the submachine gun.

Bolan did not aim at the doctor but at the wall next to the man.

When the MP-5 SD-3 spewed 9 mm rounds into the electronic panels, it chopped up the controls and eviscerated the stand-alone cryogenics monitoring computer. The cryogenics CPU sensed multiple simultaneous failures throughout its systems and issued several alarm protocols, all within the few hundredths of a second before the redundant power and alarm systems were themselves transformed to scrap and the microchips themselves shattered. There was nothing left to control the cold box.

The doctor was silent in the aftermath, numbed by the tiny pocket of damage and its vast implications.

Bolan walked to the mess, found the last-resort emergency override circuit breakers and yanked out their electrical cables.

"You are very thorough."

Bolan's mouth was a hard line. "I'm not done yet."

"I know what you think this is," the doctor said in broken but rapid English. "You are wrong. It is just research. That is all we have ever done here is research!"

Bolan nodded. "Of course."

"Now what are you doing?"

Bolan did not bother to explain. He knew the doctor knew exactly what he was doing. He inserted his wire cutters handle into the steel latches on the wall-mounted containers and popped them off, one after another. The containers were as tall and wide as shoe boxes. Cold vapor breathed out of them when he flipped off the lids in quick succession.

Inside were brushed aluminum canisters, about the size of coffee cans. Bolan knew that if he placed his hand inside one of them it would have instantly frozen his flesh to crystal and preserved it just as perfectly as the tissue samples frozen inside. Each of the canisters was labeled with a name printed out laboriously in Roman and Arabic and each label had the word *Belinga* or *Booue*. At the bottom of each was the legend *EHF*.

It took him a moment to come up with the meaning of the words, but when he did he understood the entire enterprise. He glared at the doctor and said, "Just who is interested in researching a vaccine for Ebola hemorrhagic fever?"

The doctor stammered but couldn't come up with a reply.

"If I didn't want to risk infecting every person in this city, I'd make you eat one of your tissue samples and you could get a real firsthand understanding of what EHF does to you. I've been there. It's not pretty. It's inhuman to contemplate unleashing that on anybody, anywhere, for any reason."

The doctor was torn between denial and debate and didn't manage to say much of anything.

Bolan found printed stationery from the Centre International de Recherches Médicales de Franceville inside one box. "This is where you got the tissue samples. Let me guess—you paid some poor Gabonese to break into the medical research center and carve hunks of flesh out of EHF victims before the Ministry of Health could have the cadavers cremated. Am I right?"

Bolan could see that he was. "Did you even think twice about the fate of your burglar? If he was in there hacking out flesh in a big hurry, he wouldn't have avoided contact with infected blood. How many people did he infect? How many innocent men, women and children died of EHF so you could get these samples?"

The doctor spluttered, "We fight your oppression using whatever means necessary!"

"Nobody buys it, Doctor. Even you know that's a load of crap. Every tyrant who rules a wasting economy tries to cast the blame somewhere else. Kuwait or the U.S. or wherever. But a dictatorship is just a dictatorship, nothing more—a bunch of power-hungry wheeler-dealers without much ethical backbone. In this case, no ethics at all."

The highly insulative properties of the canisters made them extremely resilient in case of unexpected temperature alternations. Even if their outer refrigerated chamber failed catastrophically and reached room temperature, the canisters should keep their contents sustained at minus one hundred degrees Celsius for almost six hours. In fact, the only thing they could not stand up to was fire, which was why they were in a concrete-and-steel fireproof lab.

Bolan took a collapsible plastic canteen out of his backpack. The contents were not water. He flipped up the nozzle and squirted the liquid from one end of the refrigerated case to the other, and the smell of gasoline filled the lab. In seconds all six canisters were dripping with it.

By then the doctor was pleading with Bolan to stop. He was struggling in the twisted-and-tied lab coat. It got him two full inches closer to the action by the time Bolan lit a match and ignited the fuel in each container.

The doctor screamed. The surface of each canister shimmered under liquid flame.

The canisters each had a stainless-steel internal temperature gauges. Bolan watched one.

"What? What does it say?" the doctor pleaded.

"Seven degrees Celsius and rising fast. I guess the experiment is about over."

The bioterrorism researcher said nothing for a moment.

"I'm dead anyway," he finally allowed.

Bolan was pleased as the digits on the displays topped one hundred degrees Celsius. The pestilence stored in the cryogenic cells was being cooked. When the temperature in all the canisters was over 150, he knew they were more than sterilized.

More important, the chambers were ruined. Bolan knew they had been expensive and difficult to come by—one of the former regime's prized possessions. The chambers would be almost impossible to replace. Getting more tissues with which to breed bioweapons in Iraq just got harder.

This was turning out to be a productive evening.

Now, time for the pièce de résistance.

20

Bolan thought this would be a nice night for a pleasure cruise. He returned to the hotel district fronting the Tigris River, then drove upriver to the commercial riverfront. With the Lada tucked against a dock house he took his pack and strolled onto the abandoned wharf. This was the biggest shipping and fishing port in the city of Baghdad, but in the black night it was silent and still, and the heat that never seemed to fully dissipate even in the deep of night brought out the full flavor of the dead fish and fish parts that were splattered everywhere.

They made the great old waterway smell bad, too. It looked as if the wharf were the scene of a bizarre, supernatural shower of fish parts. Stiff, waxy heads from creatures that found their way into Iraqi nets just twelve hours ago, and mummified dollops of rot that had been decaying for days in the hot sun.

Bolan found his transport waiting where it was supposed to be. The purchase had been arranged by Hatim, who paid more to purchase the dingy craft and its coughing old engine than both were worth when new on the black market. There was a half inch of water on the bottom where a deteriorating tar patch covered a gash in the aluminum hull. Bolan wondered if the thing would be up to the task of floating him downriver.

Just one more factor in this exercise that was unpredictable. This was by far the riskiest phase in his strategy of harassment, with far too many elements out of Bolan's control. He knew he was taking a gamble. The possible payoff made it worth the risk.

But he was putting his trust in Kurtzman's skills and Hatim's loyalty to the American cause. Bear wouldn't let him down. Hatim—he just didn't know for sure. He was also depending too much on technology he could not directly control. That deepened his misgivings.

And there was his own physical state. He was worn down.

But there was no choice but to proceed at full speed.

He rowed into the deep water of the half-mile-wide Tigris, then allowed the current to carry him while he prepped the electronics Kurtzman had appropriated for him just for this probe.

What looked like a toy submarine was, in fact, a toy-size underwater reconnaissance robot, crammed with enough electronics and sensors to drive its price tag into the six figures. Kurtzman had been clear to distinguish the unit as a micro AUV, or autonomous underwater vehicle, not the same as the unmanned underwater vehicle, which in military applications was usually a larger probe and typically controlled remotely.

The decades-old development of small underwater devices for reconnaissance was given a boost by twenty-first century miniaturization technology, some of it coming out of MAV, or micro air vehicle, development. But designing effective spy flies was challenged considerably by the need to make the devices lightweight and powerful enough to deliver themselves through the air to their target and stay there long enough to get good intelligence. AUVs had years of small underwater maneuverability systems development to build upon.

Bolan's sonar-sensing micro AUV was about eighteen-inches long, tapered at the front, not quite eight inches in circumference at its widest point. Two small rear props were enclosed in tapered, screened canopies. Combined with the lines of the hull, the canopies made the AUV's profile completely smooth. It was capable of slithering through thick weeds without snagging.

The batteries and the motor made it quick when it needed to be, but capable of operating independently for several hours on a single charge at normal scanning speeds. The computer sys-

tem made it autonomous for most operations. When provided
with a task it would map its own route, adjust the route dynamically to accommodate terrain and obstacles, even adjust its depth
or make repeated passes when it decided it needed to get clearer
scans.

The AUV relayed information back to the tablet PC that could
serve as its control board. The PC was in a mil-spec waterproof
diver's housing, the screen glowing dimly when Bolan booted
it and slipped the dangling umbilical over the side. He powered
up the submersible and watched the diagnostics scroll past on
the PC. When he got the okay, he set the submersible on the
water.

The thing was so heavy he assumed it would float like a
brick, but it bobbed alongside the rowboat on its nylon tow line.

With a single connection he slaved the tablet PC to the heavy
global phone that Kurtzman had provided him. It was one of
Stony Man Farm's last-resort communications devices. The
hardware specialists working with Kurtzman and Hermann
Schwarz at the Farm had thrown everything but the kitchen sink
into the unit so that it would be able to make use of just about
any commercial and some military mobile phone, radio, and
satellite data transfer systems on the planet.

"It would have been a hell of a lot easier just to take a dozen
cell phones and radios and PDAs and wrap 'em all up in electrical tape," Gadgets Schwarz had said proudly, "but it wouldn't
have fit in your pocket."

The unit was surprisingly compact considering its capabilities, but it was still a bulky box of electronics. Gadgets had to
have been thinking of clown pockets. Bolan didn't care as long
as it worked.

"Am I coming through, Striker?" Kurtzman asked in the headset Bolan slipped on.

"Loud and clear, Bear."

"How are you, Striker?" Barbara Price asked.

Bolan was not too surprised to hear her voice. Kurtzman and
Price were very close. He would have trouble keeping regular
communication with Bolan a secret from her—and she would

not like being out of the loop, even if being included made her complicit in some very politically dangerous activities. "I'm fine," Bolan said. "ETA in fifteen minutes."

"How's the game planning coming along?" she persisted.

"Right on schedule."

"Striker," Price said, "you haven't slept more than a few hours in days. Are you sharp enough for this?"

Bolan didn't answer at once. Price knew him. They had their own special relationship.

But she was also the Stony Man mission controller, responsible for ordering the Able Team and Phoenix Force commandos into dangerous missions on a regular basis. If she was questioning his state of alertness, there was a good reason for it.

Was he overtired? He didn't feel like it. Regardless, there was no way this probe could be delayed. It was a now-or-never opportunity.

"I'm sharp," Bolan said. "How's my RC boat? What's it picking up?"

"We're seeing everything she sees. We've got a river bottom and fish. A few undiscovered archaeological sites from the dawn of human civilization. A few old tires."

"Those are big things. We're looking for small."

"We'll see whatever the Iraqis have," Kurtzman assured Bolan. "Sound sensors, motion detectors, mines, nets, you name it. As long as it's in the water, we'll see it."

"The big unknown is their onboard security system," Price said.

"The Iraqis aren't keeping up with the state-of-the-art," Bolan responded. "I've seen evidence of that."

"Pretty insubstantial evidence."

"If I'm spotted, I'll pull out."

"That's when your strategy falls completely apart. You think you're going to sneak out the same way you sneaked in. I don't see how this probe can stay soft, Striker."

"I don't intend for it to," Bolan stated flatly. "Is that our target, Bear?"

The shape of the large boat emerged from the top of the

notepad PC window, highlighted and rendered with fine details by the high-resolution display.

The rendering was actually a combination of old and dynamic information. The image of the craft had been digitally extracted from the many files of photo and thermal satellite data collected after the nature of the vessel was revealed to the U.S. by their spy, Hatim. Eventually the National Reconnaissance Office developed an RF signature for the boat—all that communications equipment was tough to hide in such an underdeveloped part of the world, especially when it was realized one of the signals came from a Singapore-sourced military tracking device. The Iraqis had to have intended for it to be used to locate the vessel if it was ever seized. The Iraqis didn't know their proprietary, low-power signal could be picked up by U.S. intelligence. It had been watched every minute—but it had not moved once in months.

When the Iraqis used the craft, they came to it. It was some sort of a Ba'ath secret meeting place, possibly designed to serve as a mobile government seat if the various bunkers and safe houses were unsafe.

Hatim had heard rumors about its true purpose: it was supposed to have been an escape vehicle for the Glorious Leader if the people of Iraq rose up against him. If the mobs closed in, the U.S. would likely shut down air traffic and the only quick way out of Iraq would be a lightning-fast flight down the Tigris. The boat that had never left anchor under the vigilance of the United States was said to be capable of reaching speeds of 50 mph or more.

Secret and expensive. Undoubtedly it had taken an enormous chunk from of Iraq's strained military budget to procure it and equip it and, undoubtedly, arm it. Taking away this toy would make some higher-ups very angry—and more vulnerable.

Bolan couldn't see the craft, but this stretch of the Tigris was outside Baghdad far enough to be isolated. The river was all black. The brightest things to see were the glow of the PC and the feeble stars shimmering above the haze.

"Close enough," Kurtzman said.

Bolan dropped anchor close to shore with the bottom just three feet under his hull. He entered the tepid Tigris River and strapped on a full-face scuba mask, powering up the water-proofed microphone mounted at his chin and the lipstick video pickup on top of the mask.

Bolan was thankful that Kurtzman had dredged up the CIA reports on Hatim prior to sending Bolan in. He had found mention of the secret Iraqi escape yacht and added the extensive selection of underwater gear to the shopping list he gave to Kurtzman. As long as Bolan had a car to transport it all, why not go in heavy?

The equipment package included the MK 25, the standard closed-circuit oxygen underwater breathing apparatus, or UBA, used by U.S. Navy combat swimmers. The MK 25 MOD 0 variant was for warm-water use, offering no thermal protection while enabling the most user mobility. Bolan had carefully gone through the predive checklist twice, checking the oxygen bottle pressure and inspecting the soda lime canister packing.

The rebreather directed the diver's exhalations through the material in the soda lime canister, which absorbed the carbon dioxide and sent the air back into the breathing channel. Because the air circulation was completely contained, no bubbles rose from the unit to advertise the diver's presence.

The full-face mask was not standard, but required. Bolan would need constant communication to get past the type of security he assumed would surround the former president's escape boat.

Bolan's underwater weapon was a Heckler & Koch P-11, firing a fin-stabilized tungsten dart. The cartridge allowed for five shots before reloading, and at the relatively shallow depths Bolan expected work in, less than three meters below the surface, the darts had an effective range of more than fifteen meters. It was usable out of the water as well.

"Here I go. I'm setting my escort free," Bolan radioed. He detached the cable from the nose of the tiny submersible and the AUV sped away, like an excited dog the moment he was released from the leash. Bolan moved below the surface and swam after it at a leisurely pace.

This part he didn't like—letting a piece of hardware make his security decisions for him. It didn't help that the thing was smaller than some of the catfish it was startling out of the bottom muck. On the other hand, he considered, this was an action that would have been unthinkable without the AUV—his human eyes never could have found tiny sensors or monofilament trip wires staged in the murky black water.

"Hold up, Striker," Kurtzman radioed. "We've got one."

Bolan stopped dead in the water.

Aaron Kurtzman watched the display windows scroll data from the various submersible sensors as it closed in warily on the object that floated ominously in the darkness, tethered to the river floor so that it hovered just beneath the surface of the water. A pair of secondary tension lines tied to the main line stretched out upriver to keep the floating object from moving too much with the whims of the current.

Kurtzman signaled the submersible to move closer to the intersection of the three lines, finding them to be galvanized steel cables looped through a single steel plate. The primary cable passed through the steel plate, then through a sort of vise that tied off a long section of loose cable.

"What's it for?" Price asked, making out the digitally rendered shape on Kurtzman's screen.

"To adjust the mine's depth as the river depth changes with the seasons," Kurtzman explained. "They must do it manually."

"That sounds like fun work." Price imagined divers going in every month for the painstaking and dangerous process of adjusting the level of the lethal floating balls. Talk about job stress.

The mines themselves were small, spiked devices. They were near enough to the surface that even a small craft could have actuated one of those spikes. The submersible was ordered to deviate enough to find the next mine, which materialized almost immediately out of the murk, only ten feet from the first. The next was a few feet closer to the ship and just five feet away. The mines were placed without pattern, making a surface water approach a dangerous undertaking.

But it was easy enough for Bolan to swim between the gap in the cables when Kurtzman gave him the go-ahead. The extremely low visibility would have made finding the gap a hit-or-miss proposition if not for the submersible, which was mounted in the rear with an infrared beacon that showed up in the infrared pickup that flipped down over his scuba mask. Bolan simply swam close behind his underwater guide dog.

Then Kurtzman ordered him to halt once more.

"We've got monofilament netting now, Striker," Kurtzman said.

"Just find me a way under it," Bolan replied.

"Looking now. Here we go. Follow the submersible in."

Bolan approached more cautiously, creeping into the river grass that grew no more than six inches high. The monofilament could be immensely dangerous—virtually invisible, possibly razor-sharp and barbed. A strong, careful diver could get tangled up in the stuff in just a few seconds—and never get free.

The Iraqis used floating fence poles to hold the netting. One end of each pole was secured to an anchor to keep the fence upright, and the level nature of the river bottom in this place made it easy to get bottom-to-top coverage. Bolan wondered if the submersible had truly located a way in.

When he had almost reached the infrared light, he stopped and flipped on his dive light, keeping the setting dim, and the fence appeared an arm's length ahead of him in the blackness. It seemed flimsy, rippling softly with the flow of water, but the dozens of tangled and snagged fish corpses attested to its capability to snatch and hold prey. Bolan had no intention of being caught in this spiderweb.

The gap beneath the reinforced bottom hem of the netting and the riverbed was a foot and a half high, just slightly wider than his shoulders. With the rebreather apparatus he didn't think he would make it through.

"Stony, my gear and I are going to have to go through one at a time."

"Hold on, Striker," Kurtzman said. "I've got an idea."

The submersible's tiny rear-mounted props spun to life, tilting slightly to maneuver the submersible until it hung in the gap just inches below the netting. Two flat metal fingers popped out of the top of the toylike hull. Bolan had not even known they were there. The submersible rose at a rate of just an inch a second, maneuvering slightly until the bottom hem of the net touched between the two steel fingers, which clamped the netting. Now with a firm grasp on it, the submersible rose with the monofilament barrier and left a gap wide enough for Bolan to slither through easily. He played it safe and hugged the slimy riverbed until he was well clear of the netting.

Behind him, the submersible lowered the net, retracted its mechanical claws and swam away unscathed.

The river was much more shallow, but now the seafloor rose rapidly. He went two paces uphill.

"Striker, don't move!" Kurtzman froze Bolan in his tracks. The soldier's eyes scanned the darkness, seeing no sign of the danger.

The submersible was just inches from where he crouched, and it rose to the height of his head and drifted forward, the gentle turning of its screws so soft he could only hear it when it was nearly grazing him. With the flashlight off again he saw only its glimmering infrared signal easing away into the murk. But it didn't go far. It was just sitting there, looking at—something.

"WHAT IS THAT THING?" Price asked.

"I've never seen anything like it," Kurtzman admitted. "The housing looks like a piece of ceramic piping." He tapped the vague image on his screen. "This is some sort of electronics gizmo, but I'll be damned if I know what it does."

"Talk to me," Bolan demanded on the radio feed.

"We've got something up there, but we don't know what it is," Kurtzman admitted. "The database isn't pulling up anything that matches the configuration we see."

"It's not like the Iraqis to be innovative," Bolan observed. "Describe it to me."

Kurtzman described the unusual conglomeration of components, all bolted and wired together and mounted on a steel post about three feet off the bottom of the river, with just a foot of water above it.

"What do you think?" Kurtzman asked.

"I think we need Cowboy," Bolan said. "And I'm running out of time, so we need him fast."

COWBOY KISSINGER'S forehead rolled over his eyes in intense concentration.

"Am I seeing a sewer pipe?" he asked.

"Yeah. Covered with a screen," Kurtzman said. "Then there's this weird cutout at the elbow in the pipe. Looks like it's positioned so the natural river flow sends water in the front end, passes over whatever the gizmo is that's attached at the elbow, turns another right angle and exits the pipe."

"Visual sensors? Thermal sensors? Anything like that in the area?"

"Not that we've found," Price said.

"Time's not a luxury we have here, Cowboy," Mack Bolan growled from the bottom of a river on the opposite side of the planet.

"Understood, Striker," Cowboy said. "Bear, let's swing up behind this thing and take a closer look at the electronics."

Kurtzman gave the submersible orders to circle the odd device then come up behind it. He paused the AUV with its nose just inches from the cutout and flipped on a miniature headlight. Kissinger's face moved closer, until he almost touched the screen with his nose. "I see words printed on the electronics, in English, I think. Change the angle a little so I can see down more."

Kissinger watched the incremental shifting of the image as the back end of the submersible rose, aiming the video pickup and the light source down into the opening at the elbow of the ceramic pipe.

There were serial numbers, upside down from his perspective. They told him nothing.

The imprinted logo that came into view was from a multinational electric parts supplier that made everything from home thermostats to space shuttle control components. The next word that crept into view was *sensor.* The final words appeared halfway and then were covered in shadow again.

"I need a sharper angle," Kissinger said quickly, feeling the urgency build.

"I don't know if I can do much better," Kurtzman answered as he tapped in a command. The angle of the video image seemed to increase a half degree, but no more.

"Now down, just a hair," Kissinger said.

"Yeah," Kurtzman said, and told the submersible to descend a half inch, which brought the bottom half off the next word into view.

"That's as good as it gets," Kurtzman said before more complaints came his way.

"At least flip it right side up."

The image of the backward, upside-down partial letters turned 180 degrees.

"I still can't make it out," Price said as if to herself. "*I, U, K, B, I, I, I, Y.* It can't be a word."

"That's an *R*, not a *K*," Kissinger said.

"Any of those *I*s could be *T*s," Kissinger added.

"Makes no more sense."

"Must be a serial number," Kurtzman said.

A low grumble of a voice said from the speakers, "I'm waiting."

Kissinger knew it wasn't a serial number. It was something. A word with meaning. If he couldn't come up with an answer, Bolan just might decide to risk going through anyway. He had to come up with an answer. And the answer was lurking at the edge of his thoughts—he could feel it.

"How many freaking kinds of sensors are there anyway?" he demanded, angry with himself.

"Thermal, pressure, acoustical?" Kurtzman suggested, shaking his head as he realized none of those made sense.

"EMI, RFI," Price added. "Speed, electric conductivity—"

"Turbidity!" Kissinger exploded. "Striker, don't move!"

"I'm not going anywhere," Bolan said.

"Striker, listen to me," Kissinger said distinctly. "Do not move."

21

Mack Bolan, crouched alone on the floor of the Tigris River, said into his mask mike, "Okay, Cowboy, I read you loud and clear. I'm a statue."

And he was. Stock-still. Muscles relaxed, but his body as motionless as the sunken granite carving of a long-forgotten Babylonian despot.

The submersible wasn't moving either. Her penlight-sized headlamp faded and her tiny motors spun just enough to compensate for the light current and keep her right where she was.

It was like being in a photograph. Bolan wondered what had Kissinger spooked. The voices were buzzing in his earpiece.

"I have no idea what you're talking about," said the voice of Aaron Kurtzman.

"A turbidity sensor measures the level of sediment suspended in a water sample," Kissinger said.

"Yeah, I think saw an ad for a new dishwasher that does that to figure out how long to keep washing the dishes. I'm not seeing the connection," Kurtzman said.

Bolan saw it. "I'm kneeling in silt, Bear," he reported. "The water is less than six feet deep. I take one step, and I'm going to raise a cloud of muck and that sensor can't possibly miss it."

"You've got to hand it to the Iraqis," Price observed after a second of silence. "They created a secure perimeter with old plumbing and cheap appliance parts."

"Let's save the accolades," Bolan answered. "I need to get past these things."

"We can send the submersible ahead. Maybe it'll find a gap."

"No, it won't—not one I can get to without setting this one off," Bolan said.

"The submersible could disable the sensor," Kurtzman suggested.

"That might be enough in itself to raise an alarm," Bolan said. "Besides, if I swim or walk in the silt clouds won't settle—they'll get carried in the current to the next sensor too. I need to get in without touching the ground. Can the submersible tow me?"

There was silence. For a moment Bolan wondered if he had lost his com link. "Are you kidding, Striker?" Kissinger asked finally.

"It's little but it maneuvers pretty well. All I need is for a tow of maybe thirty, forty feet. I'll inflate my vests to neutral buoyancy."

"I guess it could be done. The AUV's got some kick," Kurtzman said. "We might burn out the motors halfway there."

"Let's give it a try," Bolan said. "Bear, bring it around."

"You got it," Kurtzman replied, but the misgiving was there in his voice. Bolan carefully actuated the manual discharge on the oxygen tank's life vest valve, bleeding air into the inflatable compartments until they were tugging at his body weight. He felt the minutes wasting away as he achieved buoyancy and lifted himself from the muck with agonizing slowness. Even these gradual movements sent billows of silt into the blackness. Bolan increased the feeble glow of his dive light just enough to watch the silt dissipate in the current, curling around the post with the improvised sensor.

Bolan was as limp as a corpse, letting his vest lift him until he floated so close to the surface he could have raised his arm and touched atmosphere.

On his instructions Kurtzman ordered the submersible to extend its grappling claws and swing around beneath him. Bolan unfastened one of the rebreather pack straps and placed it between the pinchers, which closed on it. Then the submersible powered up.

For a moment Bolan hung in the water motionless, despite the tugging on his pack, then felt himself begin to move.

He felt like a balloon cartoon character getting towed by a convertible in a Thanksgiving parade, but so what. It was working.

He floated beyond the sensor.

The submersible changed its heading and another improvised dirty water watcher was bypassed.

Bolan's dive light gave him almost zero visibility, and he was alarmed when he saw the bottom coming at him. "Get me closer to the surface, Bear," he said.

The submersible's quick maneuverability was long gone with its oversize tow, and Bolan straightened himself as the murky surface of the muddy Tigris bottom rose up, threatening to crash into him. Then he saw another sensor, not five feet away, lingering at the very edge of his shadowy visibility.

The water depth was less than three feet. If he even brushed the mud, there would be a silt cloud that would undoubtedly envelop the sensor.

It seemed like the riverbed was no more than an inch away when Bolan felt the pull of the little submersible begin to lift him. It wouldn't be enough. The incline of the riverbed was too steep and coming too fast....

Then the riverbed fell away from under him so steeply it was like drifting over the side of a cliff.

"Stop, Bear. I'm in the dredge channel."

The tiny screws on the submersible halted and Bolan drifted to a stop within a few feet. The pinchers released his strap and the AUV zipped away into the blackness for a reconnoiter.

"Looks like the way is clear all the way to the hull," Kurtzman reported back momentarily.

"But there could still be sensors all over that boat hull," Price insisted.

"I'm aware of that. I'll take it from here."

Bolan went in for the probe.

OLLA MEHMOODA was nervous. Something was going down in the capital, and the rumors were confusing. From what he understood the damage was minimal compared to what his worst fears could conjure, which made the rumors stranger. The entire resistance network was in some sort of clandestine high-alert status.

So far things were quiet out here at the Big Boat. That's what they called it, since the damn thing didn't even have a name. The security detail was never supposed to even discuss their duties outside their own ranks.

Mehmooda didn't know why they couldn't talk about it, or why the Big Boat didn't have a name, or even what the Big Boat was for. He was just supposed to guard it.

There had to be something valuable inside—he'd never been inside except into the few rooms for use by the guard detail. There had been numerous visits by the Ba'ath VIPs in the months he'd been here.

He wasn't worried about the danger. He knew how extensively the place was guarded above and below water.

So what was there to be nervous about?

This job wouldn't be nearly as tedious and nerve-racking if he didn't have to stand here in the pitch-black all night every night. Even if they let him smoke a cigarette once in a while it would make this job bearable.

"Olla." His name came through a crackle of static from the radio on his belt. He grabbed it.

"Yes?"

"Check the aft port side. We've got a couple of signals in the water."

Not again. "Doing it now."

The stupid hull sensors were always picking up readings, even though they all knew that the only thing that was going to get this close to the Big Boat was marine life.

He flashed on his light and shone it into the water. Something slender and white ducked beneath the surface.

"It is a fish," he radioed.

"Both of them? We've got two signals."

"I just see one," Mehmooda replied irritably. "I think if one was a fish then the other one was a fish."

"Keep an eye on it."

"I will."

Morons. Do they think an intruder, even if he could sneak this close to the boat, would somehow manage to bring in a fish to serve as a decoy?

Then he thought about it. He had seen the fish for just an eye blink, but it had looked very linear. It was just a little thing, no bigger than his forearm. And it had dived when he turned his light on.

It had to be a fish.

There was a little splash just a few feet below him. He leaned over and flipped on the light.

The little fish was looking at him with an electronic eye.

Then came the big fish. It shot out of the water, fixed Mehmooda with steely cold eyes and snatched him over the deck rail with a single powerful yank.

Then there was nothing but water and chaos. Mehmooda fought like a thrashing alley cat, but the water made his movements feeble, and the hands that were around his throat were too strong. They were iron clamps. They were inescapable. His flashlight was somehow still working and Olla Mehmooda waved it, hoping to see something, anything, that might be used to save him.

He saw the little fish, motionless in the water like no real fish ever was, watching him die with its one tiny electronic eye.

BOLAN LEFT THE DEAD GUARD and slithered on deck, making quick work of equipping himself from the waterproof pack.

The boat was living up to Hatim's description. Although painted to look like a derelict, it was actually some sort of a high-end work boat. The rusty-looking deck plates were solid. The outer hull, he had noticed from below the waterline, was clean as if it had been scraped this week.

He found Guard Number Two at the front end of the vessel. Number Two wasn't demonstrating the same restlessness as the man at the rear, just lazily pacing the foredeck and watching the skies.

Bolan rushed in. Number Two heard the padding footsteps when they were almost on him. The Executioner slammed the gun stock against his forehead and Guard Number Two slumped to the deck.

The radio on Number Two's belt squawked, and a few seconds later squawked again. Bolan was moving. Leisure time was over.

A light came on in one of the deckhouses, showing Bolan a pair of armed guards coming out of the interior doorway. He reached the door as they opened it, and swept them down with a burst of 5.56 mm tumblers. They never knew what hit them.

He leaped the bodies and went into the door, thundering down the brief ramp into a security room. The guard saw Bolan and slammed his fist onto the glass covering of a red emergency button even as Bolan eviscerated him with autofire.

Too late. As the guard dropped to the deck, the security control board sprung to life with lights and alarm messages. Bolan ran into the adjoining corridor to face a pair of sleepy-looking guards emerging from their quarters. One of them was holstering a handgun. He turned the handgun on the warrior, but Bolan took the gunner down with a brief burst of fire, and his companion fell beside him. Bolan found that one of the 9 mm rounds had grazed the first gunner and plowed into the second below the ribs. The man's eyes were rolling into the top of his head.

"How many on board?" Bolan demanded.

A long, final exhalation was the only answer he got.

Bolan raced through the boat, kicking in doors, arriving last at the engine room, and determining he was alone.

Back on the bridge he found the entire vessel blazing with light, automatically activated by the alarm. He turned off the lights except for the dim lights in the bridge and searched for weapon controls. There was a touch-pad screen for the remote operation of the 20 mm guns mounted fore and aft, but when he flipped them on he found the multilingual display demanding his password.

Bolan saw lights on the river. A pair of 20-foot fiberglass craft mounted with belt-fed machine guns raced toward him, crisscrossing each other. The radio began squawking on the bridge controls.

Bolan had more or less expected a reception such as this. He kept one eye on the approaching boats as he found the drive controls and started up the engine. No password lockout here. The power plant thrummed to life without hesitation, and the sound was like a steady earthquake. Bolan had not had time to check it out when he was hurrying through the engine room. Whatever drove this boat, it was big.

Bolan tried the rudder and throttle controls. Everything seemed to be in working order.

The machine-gun boats were coming to a halt and turning broadside to him, flashing their spotlights on the deckhouse. Bolan grimaced. They weren't coming any closer, locked out by the ring of mines. They knew just where it was, and they kept their distance.

Then he saw the lights of an aircraft, a mile beyond the boats and coming fast over the river. How was he going to deal with it?

There was no time to dial up Kurtzman and get him to work hacking into the weapons system. Those 20 mm guns would take out the helicopter and would have enough range for the boats as well. But that would take way too long. So how—?

The Executioner grimaced at the idea that popped into his head, and with the quick flip of a bank of switches he activated the anchor winches.

The ship would be free-floating in seconds.

Bolan jumped out of the deckhouse and put a surprised expression on his face for the benefit of the boat gunners as he observed the helicopter. Someone shouted through a bullhorn from one of the boats but Bolan ignored it, thumbing a 40 mm round into the breech of the M-203 grenade launcher mounted under his M-16 A-2 assault rifle. As he squinted into the spotlights estimating his target distance, he heard the helicopter coming up fast behind them.

Bolan triggered the M-203 and watched the HE grenade zip away into the darkness. The round smacked the water and blew with a curiously subdued glimmer of light.

The HE burst was followed by a mine explosion, then another, then another, and the geysers of water burst into the night sky. The steady glare of the spotlights transformed into wild swinging disco lights as the boats rocked in the agitated water.

But Bolan's eyes were on the aircraft, fascinated. The helicopter was deluged by a wall of water from beneath. The helicopter wobbled, the pilot frantically fighting for control.

Now the gunship was within the range of the M-203. Bolan triggered another grenade, and the 40 mm round cracked against the side of the aircraft, engulfed it in flame and dropped it like a rock into the Tigris River. Another quartet of mines detonated where it fell and chewed the flaming wreckage into scraps.

One of the machine-gun boats had been swamped and was sinking beneath the murky water. Two men were swimming for the second boat when Bolan began turning the Tigris into watery perdition. He sent a trio of HE rounds flying at the machine-gun boat in rapid succession, placing them carefully about ten feet apart and blowing the subsurface mines one on top of another.

Before the airborne cascade of water had fallen Bolan was back on the bridge, flipping on the hull lighting and discovering that the big boat had drifted dangerously sideways during its brief moments of release. Its aft end was seconds away from plowing into the rise in the river floor. He put power to the screws and the Tigris behind him became a muddy froth. The front end sped at the wall of rain still falling on the boiling water.

The huge Iraqi boat was gaining more speed than Bolan would have thought possible, and he didn't have time to second-guess his steering as he maneuvered the boat through the new-made gap in the circle of mines. He was beyond it in seconds.

To his surprise, the second machine-gun boat was in front of him. Bolan twisted the wheel. The big boat responded immediately, aiming directly at the boat. There were just two men on board, and the driver brought his engines to full speed and steered for safety. The little boat maneuvered itself deftly out of Bolan's path, only to find itself lifted out of the water by the heavy wake.

Bolan steered the boat through a wide, sweeping U-turn and found the second boat now belly up. Two figures were clinging to the floating wreck and shaking their fists at him.

They should have been saying thank you. They got off pretty easy.

Bolan brought the engines to top speed, finding himself careening over the black waters at 50 mph.

He'd be back in Baghdad in no time.

22

The old cameraman yawned. "Any day now."

"You think this is really going to happen?" asked the reporter, a young Swede who was usually too dapper, too well-groomed for the old cameraman to take seriously.

"I've seen stranger stuff. And Gotts said it was a reliable source."

The old cameraman knew more than he was telling. He and Gotts Sigus were old drinking buddies. He knew who this source was—it was the American woman who called herself Bee.

Bee had given the Scandinavian news agency some of its best tips. Whoever she was, she was involved with some heavy, heavy stuff, and when it suited her purposes she was not above making use of a little international publicity.

They got the call from Gotts at three in the morning on the encrypted global sat phone.

"He's going to land it right outside your freaking hotel!" Gotts had almost shouted. The cameraman had not heard his old pal so excited since, well, the 1970s at least.

"The former president's escape boat? I didn't know he had an escape boat."

"Nobody did!" Gotts enthused. "Just think of what it means— the thing is a symbol. He and his sons were ready to run in the face of a revolt. It's a great fucking story, and if this guy really does crash it right there in front of your fucking hotel, it'll be fucking great! The Americans will eat this up!"

The cameraman tried to calm his old friend before he had a heart attack. "If it happens we'll get it, Gotts, I swear."

The cameraman got excited himself as he was searching for a shot. In the end he decided there was no better, safer view of the action than from his own hotel window—if this thing came down he could never publicly film it without having his equipment confiscated on the spot.

The reporter had his doubts from the start. Now, as the long, quiet minutes passed, and Baghdad slept uneventfully, the old cameraman was beginning to wonder, too.

Had Bee let them down?

Her tips were always good. Hell, some of them turned into magnificent scoops. Be a shame to ruin her perfect score.

He heard the hum, far off.

In any European or American city there would have been the lull of street noise to mask it, but in Baghdad, with its crumbling infrastructure, there was almost no nighttime traffic. The hum became a rumble.

"There it is." The old cameraman grinned as he manipulated the display on the rear of the camera. The monitor showed him the Tigris River almost a mile away, a maximum-zoom shot he had framed and focused an hour ago. He began recording and gave the reporter the hand signal to keep his mouth shut.

The reporter came to look over his shoulder and they both saw the big boat speed into the frame.

And it just kept coming.

That's no boat—it's a fucking yacht, the cameraman thought, pulling back a little and moving the camera along to follow it. The camera's servomotors were controlled by a CPU that could be taught a series of motions, and the cameraman had spent his idle time in the last few hours composing the perfect scan of the Tigris.

But the programmed scan's speed wasn't cutting it. The boat was going like a bat out of hell. The cameraman took manual control of the speed and backed up his zoom even further, keeping the boat in the frame and adding enough of the surrounding scenery to give the shot perspective.

It wasn't slowing.

The old cameraman silently swore, something vulgar in Swedish. Was he going to bring the thing on shore at full speed? He'd tear it apart.

If anything, the big boat seemed to put on an extra burst of speed, then the prow pointed at the shore. A landing ramp was there, but it couldn't accommodate a boat with half the length of this monster.

The cameraman tried to keep his mouth shut as the huge ship plowed into the ramp, its front end collapsing and shattering. The immense inertia propelled the entire bulk out of the water, flattening the bottom and spraying fiberglass shards around the open park. The riverside recreational area, once landscaped by the government to give visitors in the hotel district a false impression of its public works commitment, was plowed in two by tons of composite and steel.

Then there was quiet, except for the whooping of sirens coming through the city.

"Look!" the reporter whispered in spite of himself.

A man moved on the deck of the boat. He jogged to the rail and collapsed to the ground, then rose to his feet and fled the scene.

The camera caught it all on tape, as clear as day. Every light on board the big boat was still on. The engines and generator were probably shot, but the lines from the batteries had to have survived. The cameraman was grinning ear to ear. This was perfect. The man had vanished into blackness, but he was zooming in tight on the remains of the boat, getting wonderful details of the deck and upper levels. Aside from the shattered glass everywhere the top deck looked good as new.

His lens found a body wedged tight under the front end rail, and he got a tight zoom shot of the man's face and the Republican Guard designation on his uniform. There was another body in the deckhouse. He couldn't see the face this time, but he found the same insignia on the corpse's bloodied chest.

"Choppers," the reporter whispered.

The cameraman reluctantly pulled himself from the window.

It wouldn't do to be seen filming the mess below. As it was, the Iraqis would probably be pounding on the door soon to demand their videotape.

The cameraman plugged the camera into the global phone modem and began sending data. He paced, cursing the data transfer's snail pace while the reporter spied through the curtains, watching the crisis-control efforts in the park.

The sky was lightening when the process was completed. The old cameraman held his breath as he disconnected the camera and made a voice call to Stockholm.

Gotts answered the line with, "It's perfect. It's fucking beautiful."

The cameraman grinned. "But is it going on the air?"

"As we speak. First we run an exclusive. CNN will have it in an hour. We'll release it to every network on the planet by the time you're at the hotel lunch buffet."

"That'll give me an appetite."

Almost whistling for joy, the cameraman did a fast-erase on the videotape. He finished just seconds before the commotion started in the hall. There was a knock on their door. They opened it to find the dour man who served as the media relations representative for Iraq.

"What's up?" the reporter asked.

"I must confiscate all media."

The reporter from the Arabic news network was standing in the open door of the adjoining room, protesting loudly. "We were just on our way to get tape—you can't hide this!"

"Tapes and disks, please!" the media relations man insisted.

The Swedish cameraman, looking puzzled, put his blank tapes in the hands of the Iraqi, who then left in a hurry.

"These guys are total assholes," the Saudi reporter grumbled.

"Hey, what's all the fuss about, anyway?" the cameraman asked.

The Saudi looked at him as if he were out of his mind. "You couldn't have slept through it?"

"Slept through what?"

The old Swedish cameraman and the sharp-as-a-tack Saudi

reporter had shared a meal or two in their time in Baghdad. It was a sort of competitive, brotherly friendship.

The Saudi smiled suddenly. "You got tape out?"

"Now, how could I have done that?" the old cameraman asked, his smile spreading from ear to ear.

The Saudi nodded with satisfaction. "I cannot wait to see it."

"You'll just have to wait your turn."

23

The Lada was gone, towed off by thieves. It didn't matter now.

Dawn was coming fast. Last night's safe house couldn't be called safe any longer.

Bolan went in search of a temporary home, and every step was harder than the last.

Barbara Price had been right. Bolan was exhausted. He had marshaled his body's resources, but the bruising impact of the crash, even cushioned in a nest of life vests, had brought the pain of all his recent wounds and burns and bruises to the surface. Suddenly he was drained of energy, distracted by agony and muddled by exhaustion.

He was vulnerable; he was in danger.

Fighting to stay focused, he forced his legs to carry him a mile from the crash site, then another mile. The gray dawn was exposing him to passersby. He needed cover, and he needed it now.

There was a fish-processing shed coming up. The stench was muted and the fish scraps were skeletal. It hadn't been used in a while.

He inspected his surroundings. There were a few concrete housing projects a quarter mile away, and some early-morning traffic on the road, but as far as he could tell he was unseen.

He ducked into the shed. The stench was an attack. The interior was stripped bare except for a single table with one end collapsed. No hiding place here.

But the floor was raised at least a few feet from the sloping

riverbank. Bolan used his combat knife to poke at the pressboard
floor planks and jimmied one up. The nails screeched. The second one came up more easily. Bolan stepped inside, pulled in
his pack and yanked the boards back into place as best he could.

Then he was unconscious.

JAWDAT TRIED to put the drink down on the table, but it slipped
from his fingers and spilled on its side. The air filled with the
pungency of vodka.

Jawdat did not notice. He simply stared at the thing in front
of him, seeing nothing else.

The thing came closer, and smiled.

Jawdat felt his stomach knot. He couldn't speak. He was not
even sure that what he was seeing was even real or some sort of
a vengeful phantom.

Because it looked like it had come straight out of the grave.

"I've been busy." It nodded at the television.

Jawdat glanced at the muted TV. CNN Europe was showing
the footage of the boat crash for the thousandth time.

"You did that?"

"And the whorehouse. And the biological research lab. And
the front gate of your compound."

"You couldn't have done all that alone!"

"I did," the Executioner said, his voice like gravel, then added,
"It wasn't easy."

Jawdat nodded dumbly, staring at the bruised, scarred, bleeding man that stood in front of him. He looked like he'd been
caught in a rock slide.

But the American didn't look weakened or beaten by the or-
deal. His eyes burned with determination and the submachine
gun in his hands was as steady as a steel girder.

"You should have seen me before I had my beauty sleep,"
Mack Bolan said.

"Why did you do these things?"

"To send a message to your coconspirators. Seems they
haven't fully appreciated one of their most valuable assets.
There's a certain Iraqi who wants to make it known that he will

not be underrated any longer. I left messages to that effect at several of my stops last night."

"Who is this man?" Jawdat demanded.

"You, of course."

Jawdat barked. "Preposterous."

"I know. But in case you haven't noticed, the men who sail this screwed-up ship are all paranoid lunatics."

"But they won't believe a stupid scheme like that!" Jawdat roared.

"But they will not discount it. They're that paranoid. You know it, Jawdat—you're one of them."

Jawdat sat there, wide-eyed and stunned. "I'll have you killed."

"The press releases go out in one hour to every news agency on the planet."

Jawdat's eyes flickered from side to side. "How do we stop it!"

"I make a phone call. Every hour for the next twenty-four hours. If I make that call, it stops the e-mail from going."

"I'll be dead," Jawdat stated matter-of-factly.

"Eventually. First you'll be questioned. Knowing you and yours, the questioning could take months. But you know how to keep it from happening, Jawdat. Just a little cooperation, a little intelligence, and I make it all go away."

Jawdat, a former general of the Republican Guard, murderer of thousands, sobbed once.

Then he said, "All right."

Arlington, Virginia

Brigadier General Edwin Juvenal, U.S. Army, had waited for days for the shoe to drop.

When he sent a small, hand-selected group of soldiers to erase the problem of the Iraqi troublemaker Khalid al-Jabir, he never considered the possibility that they would be identified. It seemed impossible that they could be detained. Getting killed in the process was an absurd notion that never crossed his mind.

After all, these men were the best, and they had been doing dirty work for Juvenal for years.

Juvenal had always had a knack for getting the system to provide him with a personal staff of hardmen. He always selected soldiers with special skills and a special lack of conscience.

But now they were dead, and the dead men would be linked to him, and sooner or later somebody would come around asking him about it. The most unnerving thing was that it hadn't happened yet.

It finally came at 2:12 a.m., according to the clock radio at his bedside. Agnes Juvenal had long ago become accustomed to middle-of-the-night phone calls for her husband, but that didn't mean she had to stop complaining about it. He waited out her belligerent sighing and shifting before putting the receiver to his ear.

"Juvenal." He turned the name into a command.

"General Juvenal, I hope I woke you up."

"Who is this?"

"Who doesn't matter, but where should be of interest. I'm driving south out of Baghdad. I expect to reach Karbala within a couple of hours. From there I'm going out into no-man's-land, a place in the desert about twenty miles southeast of al-Suba."

Juvenal was sweating, jaw clenched. It was about to come down on him, the whole house of cards, but somehow he managed to keep the strain out of his voice. "You present a boring travelog, mister, and your choice of vacation destinations leaves a lot to be desired."

"I expect to have your men by nightfall, General."

"My men?"

"The Seven Scorpions. At least the four of them who are still alive."

"You've got really bad taste in jokes, pal," Juvenal said. "Those were good men. Their memory deserves a little more respect."

"The men themselves deserve to come home. It's up to you to arrange transportation."

Juvenal's anger got the better of him. "Just who the fuck do you think you are, and where do you get off making these kind of accusations? I'm a United States Army brigadier general, and I don't have to listen to this crap."

"*Crap* is the key word here, General," said the voice on the other end of the line. "You're shoveling more manure than I want to chew on, so let's cut through the bullshit. I've got the goods on you, and I'm about to make them public. Why don't you go check your e-mail and I'll call you back in ten."

The line went dead.

What did that son of a bitch mean by "goods"?

Juvenal stomped into his study and booted his PC, downloading his e-mail. How would that SOB have his personal e-mail address? How'd he get his home phone number, for that matter?

The general's broadband connection was quick, but it still spent an endless two minutes downloading the video attachment.

When Juvenal saw the face of that terrorist Khalid al-Jabir, he just about started overturning furniture.

On the video the Iraqi was battered and bruised, and spilling his guts about the Seven Scorpions. The video had to have been taken in the hours before al-Jabir died in the melting Ford Excursion in a lonely Pennsylvania field.

Al-Jabir said to the camera, "They said they were ordered in by an Army officer named Juvenal. They were to meet an Iraqi contact to get a document or agreement or something, I do not remember. They said they thought it was very irregular, but they were sworn to secrecy. They claimed they never knew it was a traitor selling out Iraq they were to meet."

Juvenal didn't hear the rest of it, not really. The use of his name was damning enough. But his attention was riveted again when the Arab started naming the prisoners who still survived. "They are Al Long, Sandwell Foley, George Bolson, Ricardo Leone. Leone is having pneumonia on and off, and who knows if he is still alive."

"The U.S. government DOD documents claim that all of them were killed in an exchange of gunfire on the ground in Iraq," said a voice from offscreen. "How and when did the others actually die?"

The offscreen voice was the same one Juvenal had just heard on the phone. The same guy was working both sides of the ocean on this one. How many people, and who, were backing him up?

"There was no gunfight," the Arab explained. "They strolled right into an ambush of five hundred Republican Guard soldiers. They were surrounded before they knew what hit them. They had no choice but to surrender."

"So? How did they die—the other three?"

"They were questioned."

"You mean they were tortured?"

"Yeah, that is what I mean. Every day for months. All of them. In the beginning they were praying for a rescue, but pretty soon they were begging for death."

"Why did they think there would be a rescue attempt?"

The Arab shrugged on the video. "They talked to Juvenal about it."

Juvenal felt like he was going to throw up.

"When?" asked the offscreen voice.

"During the standoff at the ambush. Before they surrendered. They were in radio contact with the man himself, and he promised them a quick extraction or a diplomatic solution. But the extraction never happened. After Iraq made its strategic withdrawal from Kuwait and we presented our demands to the interlopers—"

"You mean after we spoiled your pirate raid and kicked you out like mongrel dogs."

"Yes. There was negotiation afterward. The fate of these particular prisoners was never discussed."

"The U.S. never brought it up?"

"No."

"And the Hussein regime wasn't going to offer this information in the interests of humanity. It wasn't in their nature."

"Yes." Al-Jabir couldn't look defiant. He was simply beaten and defeated.

The narrator said, "So many lies and misinformation surround the fall of Hussein's regime. How do you know that what you have told me is true?"

Al-Jabir shrugged. "I have interviewed the prisoners myself. I was to know personal information, and I was to undertake blackmail or ransoming if certain other of our plans failed. I can tell you the name of Mr. Foley's first girlfriend. I know where Mr. Leone buried his dog that died when he was six years old."

The video clip ended.

Juvenal stared at the frozen image of the Arab, then played back the sections of the video where the offscreen interrogator spoke. The voice wasn't anyone he knew—he had never heard it except for the phone call. Who the hell was he?

Speak of the devil—Juvenal snatched up the phone midring.

"How did you like my documentary?" the caller asked.

"I want your name, rank and serial number," Juvenal demanded. "I want to know the name of your CO."

"I haven't had a CO in a lot of years.

"What branch are you? CIA?"

"I work independently."

"Bullshit."

"Ready to toe the line, General?"

"You have nothing on me, son. That video doesn't prove a thing. It's just the word of some dead Arab con man."

"I'll have video of the prisoners themselves in a couple of hours."

"Show that to me then."

"By then it might be too late for you to meet my demands."

"Which are?" Juvenal was incredulous.

"We need an extraction."

"No way in hell."

"Did I tell you I was taping all this, General? I'll add your comments to the video when I start the broadcast e-mail program I have set up on my PC in the States."

"That's illegal wiretapping!"

"Not quite as morally repugnant as your crimes, General."

"You don't have evidence of that!" Juvenal shouted.

"I think the only fair thing to do is let the public decide your guilt or innocence. These recordings will help."

"If I bring those men out of Iraq, I'm just as screwed."

"If you bring those men back, I'll refrain from releasing these tapes to the media. You'll be able to come up with some sort of a spin that'll cover your ass. At least enough to save your pension."

"Give me time to think about it."

"You've already had thirteen years to think about it. Give me your answer now or I go over your head."

"Fuck you!" General Juvenal slammed down the phone.

Almost instantly Juvenal regretted it. He should have played ball, at least for a little while so he could come up with a plan of action. It was too late now. He sat morosely in his silk robe with a tumbler of Scotch for almost an hour.

There had to be a way out of this. But he'd been pondering this for days.

The phone rang at his elbow. It wasn't even 4:00 a.m. It had to be his nemesis in Iraq. Now he could try some stall tactics.

But the call wasn't from Iraq. He heard, "Please hold for General Wheatland."

Wheatland? Wheatland was the top man, the Army Chief of Staff. Then Juvenal knew his nemesis in Iraq hadn't been bluffing. He had gone up the Army chain of command.

"Edwin?" asked the voice of the highest-ranking man in the Army.

"Yes, General," Juvenal answered smartly. But he wasn't feeling too smart.

"I want you in my office. Five minutes ago. I think you know why."

"Yes, General."

Juvenal stared at the floor. His career was over, and he couldn't think of any damned way of weaseling his way out of this. If it wasn't for that stupid fuck in Iraq, this never would have come back to haunt him. He'd worried briefly when the U.S. went into Iraq in 2003, but in all the chaos his secret remained buried. Now it was a different story.

Yeah, he'd go to Wheatland. He'd take what was coming to him. But first he was going to do what he could about putting a name on that fuck in Iraq.

Juvenal had friends. At NRO, at Justice, at Homeland. Quickly he made a few calls and gave his NRO contact access to his home PC and his phone line.

"Trace the calls and that e-mail and find out where they came from," he told them. "I want to know who he works for. He's not working alone, I know that. I want to know who's signing his fucking paychecks."

His friends in high places promised to get right on it.

While that was happening, Juvenal dressed and was out the door by 4:30 a.m. He felt like a prisoner on his way to the gallows.

25

Stony Man Farm, Virginia

Nobody knew the aircraft was en route until the vast network of security systems began buzzing the alarm. Buck Greene, the chief of security grew even more concerned when he identified the approaching aircraft by its transponder code. That particular small jet was a frequent visitor to the Farm. Why was it coming in now without radioing ahead? This was *not* standard procedure.

He took the radio from the operator and raised the jet himself. After an exchange of identifying code words, the security chief ended up speaking to the big Fed himself.

"Is everything all right, sir?"

"No, in fact, nothing is all right! Get me on the damn ground! And get me Aaron and Barbara. I want them waiting when I get there."

"Yes, sir."

Greene had never witnessed Hal Brognola on a rampage, but he had heard rumors. More like legends, actually. The tales always seemed to end with a moral, like an Aesop's Fable: When Hal Brognola is really, *really* angry, a body needed to be somewhere else.

It was advice Greene intended to take to heart.

THE JET HIT the ground abruptly and stopped short of the regular passenger debarking point. A powerful-looking figure stormed out and stomped down the roll-away steps. Hal Brognola climbed into the waiting jeep and rode the short distance to the farmhouse in silence.

"You want to explain this to me?" he demanded as he stormed into the War Room and dropped a brief printed report on the table. Kurtzman slid the page across the wide conference table and nodded. "It looks like our intercepts protocols worked perfectly."

"Huh?"

"The safeguards we've put in place to alert us if there are inquiries being made about Farm activities. Inquiries made within the Justice Department are designed to channel to you."

"I know that—"

"They worked. An inquiry was made and you got it, within seconds, too, according to the time codes. So we were protected and the probe was stalled."

"I'm not asking about the safeguards, I'm asking about the nature of the investigation. Why do I know nothing about this?"

"You didn't ask?" Kurtzman suggested.

"I shouldn't have to ask when you start meddling with the effing Pentagon!" Brognola snapped. "I'm supposed to be the Farm's liaison. How am I supposed to deal with a situation like this when I have no clue it's even going on?"

"It's not sanctioned," Price said. "It's Mack."

"Oh, shit. Of course it is. I had this pegged as cleanup somehow from the mess Phoenix was dealing with in India. I guess I didn't think it through." He sighed, long and heavy. "So what's our connection?"

Before Price could get a word out Kurtzman said, "I'm the one who uncovered it in the first place and requested Striker insert himself in it."

"Which means what, exactly? What is *it?*"

"Intervene in the al-Jabir prison break. From there I asked him to continue following the trail. I heard from him less than an hour ago, and he thinks he's got the real goods this time."

Brognola's bushy eyebrows raised, like a face-only shrug.

"He's almost found the prisoners," Kurtzman elucidated.

"The prisoners from the federal pen? Al-Jabir?"

Kurtzman and Price looked at each other. "The American prisoners of war," Price said. "In Iraq."

Something profound happened to Brognola, as if he had just learned someone close to him had died. He lost his bluster, and every taut muscle in his face slackened.

"Are you telling me," he said, "that there are American prisoners of war inside Iraq right now?"

"Yes," Kurtzman replied.

"Were they just captured?"

"No. They're from Desert Storm."

Brognola looked and felt ten years older. But mostly he looked and felt immensely—sad.

Price had come into the meeting thinking she was going to butt heads with the big Fed in a huge way. Now she wanted to reach across the table and take his hand. Neither she nor Kurtzman could remember seeing him affected like this by a mission—and this little family had seen the worst humanity had to offer.

"Okay," Brognola said finally. "Okay, then, tell me this. Who's this Brigadier General Juvenal? What's his involvement?"

Kurtzman had thought Brognola would have all the details, but now realized the man from Justice knew very little. "Juvenal's the one who left them there."

"Left them there?"

"As in abandoned. Sent them in on unofficial business and wrote them off as dead when they were captured."

"He knew they were alive and in Iraqi custody?"

"Yes. He knew about the planned jailbreak, too. He sent in his hit squad to take out al-Jabir so the thing would stay under wraps."

"Son of a bitch." Brognola shook his head slowly. "That son of a bitch."

He reached across the table and his hand was shaking. His face was animated again, but it was the clenched tension of rage.

Brognola wasn't one of the great moralists, or one of the

great ideologues. He didn't have the dogma of justice that he knew drove Mack Bolan on and on. He was a politician, he played the games of compromise and bureaucratic manipulation. But he was a man with an ideal.

It was an American ideal that transcended America. It was a moral code that he could never have put into words. It was a knowledge of right and wrong and loyalty and patriotism.

According to Hal Brognola's code of justice, this thing was wrong in every possible way.

A man who was selfish enough to condemn the soldiers that trusted him to a living hell just to keep his own reputation untarnished—that was selfishness to an unthinkable degree.

But as he sat there, silent, the big Fed came to the conclusion that there was a subtle aspect of this thing that made it even more despicable: Juvenal was a United States Army brigadier general. He *was* the United States of America in his capacity as a trusted leader.

By perpetrating this horrific deed he made the U.S. itself guilty of it.

"If this is true, then he's a traitor." Brognola had wadded up the printout without knowing it. "I want to know it all. Every detail. I want the evidence on Juvenal."

"We've got it," Price replied. "Phone conversations. Solid links between the men and materiel used to assassinate al-Jabir."

"And in a few hours, Striker will have the testimony of the men themselves," Kurtzman added.

"Good," Brognola said fiercely. "Then we can fry the bastard."

26

East of al-Suba, Iraq

Bolan found the path in the arid hills, a faint stretch of side-by-side tire tracks. Jawdat said it was one of two ways to get through the hills to the old forgotten prison, but the easier, southerly route was patrolled by coalition forces and would take at best a half day to get to.

The trail kept disappearing on expanses of flat rock. Bolan always found it again by virtue of oil stains, and eventually found he could not possibly get lost since the path followed the only vehicle-accessible trail through the hills.

It had been chosen just for this reason—although when the tiny prison was founded, in the nineteenth century, the prisoners had come in on carts pulled by horse or camel. The jail was meant to hold enemies of the Ottoman sultan, at a time when he still wielded nominal control in Iraq. The sultan wanted the British and the French interlopers out of Iraq, but the trade potential kept the British and French coming.

Some of the key figures in the trade invasion had ended up in this remote valley. The bones of hundreds of French and British corpses were still scattered in a pit at one end of the valley where the dead were dumped.

But it was too isolated and was ultimately abandoned. Only a small clique of men connected to General Jawdat were even aware of it.

Jawdat's driving directions were based entirely on natural landmarks, and Bolan stopped when he found the outcropping that meant he was a quarter mile from the valley.

Jawdat had tossed the jeep in as a part of the bargain. Bolan managed to tuck it behind a spill of boulders, then he scaled the nearest high peak to have a look.

He had made better time than expected, and he was not surprised to see guards still packing up. This was not a temporary move. They were clearing out for good on Jawdat's orders. The guard detail was told that the prisoners would be collected in a day or two for relocation. The security of this facility, he told them, had been compromised, according to fresh intelligence. Any guards who remained behind would be taken into custody by coalition forces if they weren't killed in the battle for the territory.

That had to have motivated them. They were moving fast, literally running in and out of the mud brick huts with armfuls of clothing, boxes of food and collapsible plastic jugs of water.

Bolan saw the place cleaned out, and soon all that remained of the guards was the dust of their receding vehicles, which headed south, on Jawdat's orders.

It appeared that the coercion of Jawdat had been effective, but the Iraqi was desperate and unpredictable. He might have put an ambush in place for Bolan.

The Executioner waited and watched.

JAWDAT BLINKED his eyes open. They felt like they had gum in them. His head swam, and he knew he was still very drunk. Was there somebody in the room?

"Stand up, General."

"Who is it?" he asked irritably.

"Tereq."

"Radhi? What are you doing here?"

"I am arresting you, General."

Jawdat struggled to his feet. General Radhi Tereq was an acquaintance, sometimes even an ally. He had been a chief of al-Hadi, Iraq's Project 858, an intelligence agency that monitored communications within the country and, when possible, outside it.

"I do not understand this. Arresting me for what?" Jawdat demanded.

"Conspiracy. You are a traitor, General."

"Nonsense!" Jawdat found himself surrounded by the soldiers who filed in behind Tereq. They cuffed his wrists in front of him. Jawdat stared at the bracelets. "I am not a traitor, Tereq."

"I did not want to believe it myself, General," Tereq said. "But we have surveillance on you. We watched you conversing with an unknown American. The man matches the description of the man who perpetrated major crimes against Iraq in the past twenty-four hours." Tereq leaned close. "You even gave the man one of your cars and let him drive away from this house. I think it is obvious he was working for you."

Jawdat grimaced. "No, he was blackmailing me."

Tereq bleated a short, harsh laugh. "I do not believe it, of course. But if it is true, I cannot wait to find out what this American has on you that made blackmail possible in the first place."

"I will tell you everything."

"You certainly will."

Jawdat had a mental image of his immediate future. He would be tortured. He had conducted these tortures and even participated in them, many, many times. Eventually he would die, but that would be a long time coming.

His intoxicated mind struggled for clarity as they led him through his house. He fought the need to vomit.

Then he had an idea.

He stopped resisting the nausea and gagged noisily. In the front hall he stumbled and spit bile down the front of his shirt. He collapsed on his knees and willed himself to bring up the contents of his stomach.

The soldiers fell back from him. Tereq was clearly disgusted.

Jawdat sat up, spit out the last of the rancid stuff that now soaked his shirtfront and grabbed underneath the spindly table that stood inside the front door. Even with his hands cuffed he was still able to yank out the .25-caliber revolver hidden there, and he targeted Tereq.

He fired a shot, but the slime on his hands made his finger slip from the trigger and spoil his aim.

It didn't matter. The consequences were just what he wanted.

"Do not fire!" Tereq ordered his men, but the fusillade was already plowing into the prisoner.

Saleh Jawdat did not feel the pain, only the pressure of the bullets and the weakness that was pulling him into blackness.

He was a disgrace. He was humiliated. He was dying without ever having achieved what he had wished to achieve. It had been a waste of a life. But ending it now was better than the alternative.

RADHI TEREQ STORMED into the Project 858 intelligence center, shouting for his secretary and record keeper. "Where is the transcription from the videotape?"

"We have a first draft, but the quality was poor and we are still trying to clean it up," his secretary explained.

"Well, for now it is all we have to work with. Give me the draft and find out why we have not tracked down that jeep!"

A languages assistant hurried forward with a few sheets of printed paper and took flight as soon as Tereq snatched the pages. He flopped into the nearest desk chair without even heading for his office, then leaped up again not a minute later. His assistant rushed up without being summoned.

"This page gets top priority. I want to know exactly what is said here, and I want it in five minutes."

The assistant fled and Tereq grabbed a phone, glancing at the wall clock. Time was running out.

BOLAN WOULD HAVE preferred to wait until dusk, when he could scope the place out with night vision, but he didn't have the luxury of time. It was beginning to look like the transport wasn't going to be forthcoming until he could transmit video of the actual, living prisoners.

That would do the trick. The bureaucrats would bow to that kind of pressure. Bolan stopped long enough to detach the retransmitting module for the phone and position it on the peak, where it he hoped it would keep his communications uninterrupted even from within the rock walls of the valley.

When he drove into the valley there was no reaction except for the sudden flight of scraggly birds feeding on the trash pile.

He circled the collection of buildings, which were mostly made of mud-mortared rock. One structure, the long, low building that housed the prisoners, was concrete. That's where the prisoners would be.

If they were really here at all.

He scanned the walls of the valley and saw no sign of hiding places. He was alone.

He searched the mud-and-rock structures first, finding nothing but trash and a mind-numbing stench.

The smell from the prison was worse.

Three .44 Magnum rounds finally cracked the lock on the iron door, and when he pulled it open he was assaulted with a wall of heat and stench that he had to swim through. Inside was darkness.

Bolan circled the building and shot out the second door lock, then wedged it open, too. The breeze in the valley was a mere trickle, but it instantly began drawing out the torpid air inside, and it illuminated most of the interior. Bolan stepped inside.

He was in a narrow aisle between two rows of iron bars set in a waist-high concrete barrier. Behind each set of bars was a single large cell filled with huddled human beings.

All Bolan could see were bones. Spines sticking out like the ridges on the backs of lizards. Rib cages and skulls. These men had no flesh, only pasty, flaccid epidermis draped over crooked skeletons.

But they were alive. There had to be twenty, thirty people here, and yet he felt alone, like the only man in a room of coma patients.

Somebody spoke in Arabic.

"Who speaks English?" he asked.

All the prisoners were blinking in the sunlight but one man nearby tried to look at him, then squeezed his eyes shut again and buried them in his arm. "Are you an American?" he asked in disbelief. His accent was right out of the Bronx.

"Yes. I'm arranging for transport out of here. I'm looking for the Seven Scorpions."

"I'm one of them. Christ, have we finally beat the Iraqis?"

"We can catch up later. Right now I've got to get a message back home. I need evidence that I've found you guys."

The man tried to look at him again. "Doesn't sound to me as if you've got a ride waiting outside."

"No. Not exactly." Bolan had already activated the lipstick video pickup on his headpiece. He had tied it into the Stony Man communications unit and said into the mike, "You getting this, Bear?"

"We're getting every damn second of it, Striker."

But that was not Aaron Kurtzman. It was the man from Justice himself. Bear's secret project had blown its cover.

"Hal," Bolan said testily, "tell me you're behind us on this."

"Don't insult me, Striker. I'm already in contact with the President. He's got aircraft en route and he'll order them in as soon as he's convinced we've got Americans that need rescuing."

Bolan considered that. "Hal, I have a message for the President."

"Yes?"

"Tell him this. I'm recording this personally. I can send the data anywhere from where I'm standing. If he doesn't save these men, I'll use it. Make no bones about it—I *will* blackmail the President. I'll expose myself if I have to. I'll create a storm of negative publicity that will shoot down his presidency. I know I can do it, and I will."

There was a moment of expectant silence hanging in the vast distance between the two men, who had battled for and against each other for years.

"Striker," Brognola said finally, "if the President doesn't save those men, I'll help you do it."

Washington, D.C.

"YOUR CALL from the Justice Department."

The President of the United States almost looked startled.

"Clear out, please, gentlemen," he said to the finance and education aides. "We'll finish later."

His Homeland Security chief and the head of the Joint Chiefs almost bowled over the aides on their way in. The head of the Joint Chiefs was carrying personnel file printouts, complete with color photographs.

They didn't sit. The three of them huddled shoulder to shoulder at the video display mounted in one of the Oval Office bookshelves. The test pattern was replaced with a static-blurred video image.

Then they saw what might have been, once, a human being.

"Sergeant Al Long, United States Army, serial number—" The man hacked and drank from a canteen. Finally he managed to rattle off his serial number.

The head of the Joint Chiefs was holding up a photo from a personnel file. It was the same face, allowing for fifteen years and near starvation.

"I didn't want to believe it," the President said.

There was another man now. His voice was more clear, but he was just as wasted, as if he had not eaten in months.

"Sergeant George Bolson," he said, and provided his serial number. He had been a scrawny figure of a soldier before Desert Storm, but he still looked skeletal compared to his old self in the personnel photo.

The third soldier was more difficult to identify. He had no eyes. His sockets were twin sunken scars. A white, pulsing triangle of flesh showed where a patch of his scalp had been ripped off and healed over.

"You are Captain Sandwell Foley," said a voice behind the video pickup. The eyeless man nodded. "All these men were tortured, but Captain Foley had it worse than the others. His tongue and eyes were cut out."

"Could be him," the head of the Joint Chiefs said, looking from the old personnel photo to screen.

"It's him," the President declared.

"Who is that behind the camera?" asked the head of the Joint Chiefs. "What's he doing there, anyway?"

The President didn't even acknowledge the question. On-screen the camera moved from the Americans. They saw more men huddled in straw, and then the camera came to another man lying in the far corner of the dark cell. A flashlight came on to illuminate the figure.

The President pursed his lips. The head of Homeland put the back of his hand to his mouth.

"Lieutenant Ricardo Leone," continued the narrator matter-of-factly, "died fifty-seven days ago. The Iraqis refused to remove the body."

The video mercilessly stayed on the corpse.

"This good enough, Mr. President?" the narrator asked.

The President had been repulsed by the cadaver, but the sudden bitterness in the speaker's voice was like a backhand to the face. He walked away from the video a few paces and looked back at it, chagrined.

"More than enough," he said to the faceless warrior who could not hear him.

27

Juvenal shot to his feet. Before him stood the highest-ranking officer in the United States Army and, alongside him, the Air Force Chief of Staff who currently headed the Joint Chiefs of Staff.

There were no pretty words; there was no preamble.

"Brigadier General Juvenal," said the Army Chief of Staff formally, "the President has just ordered an immediate combined-forces operation into central Iraq, the purpose of which is to rescue three American special forces soldiers who were under your command during Desert Storm."

"What?" Juvenal said. The performance didn't fool anybody, and he knew it.

"Don't even think of playing the denial game, Juvenal. I am ordering you to cooperate in every possible way in the extraction effort. If there's anything you can do to make this happen, I want you to do it. Right now that is our only priority. Understand?"

"I understand, General."

"The accounting will come later," the head of the Joint Chiefs added.

Juvenal had no doubts that it would.

He was still standing at attention as they walked out, but Wheatland glared over his shoulder and said, "Juvenal, you'd better hope they come out alive."

Juvenal walked dismally through the long hallways of the

Pentagon to the stateside command center for the operation. It was so impromptu it didn't even have a name. He was rushed to a debriefing that was just commencing, including brief clips from the video that had been transmitted from the hellhole prison.

Juvenal found himself more interested in the unseen man behind the camera than in his soldiers. It was the same son of a bitch who had harassed him on the phone.

"Who is that?" asked one of the other command coordinators.

"Unknown," said the Army lieutenant colonel who was conducting the briefing. "We know only that he is the American who tracked down the prisoners."

"Are you implying he reached the prisoners on his own?"

"That's need-to-know information," said the lieutenant colonel. It was evident he had no clue.

He wasn't military. He wasn't a spook. The more he thought about it, the more it looked to Juvenal like the guy was some sort of lone wolf mercenary.

The pieces of the puzzle fell into place. Of course. The SOB was ex-special ops or something like that. Somehow he got wind of this and decided to make himself into a freaking hero. Just think of the payoff. He could write a book, sell the film rights. This escapade was going to make that asshole into a millionaire.

While Juvenal went down in flames.

No fucking way.

"General Juvenal, sir, I understand you have some background on this situation. Anything you know that will help the extraction?"

Juvenal stifled a grin, managed to turn it into a stern frown. "Those are my men," he said, trying to sound bleak. "I inserted them in Iraq in Desert Storm. The man behind the camera was their contact. He reported their deaths to me when the mission ended."

The briefing room shared a stunned silence.

"He's a traitor and a murderer," Juvenal said. "I want him arrested."

There was an excited buzz as the briefing broke up. Juvenal felt a small swell of confidence. He was still working on the details, but he knew this much—going down would be easier if that son of a bitch went down, too.

Iraq

MOST OF THEM could walk. The others Bolan lifted and carried out of the prison, settling them in the fresher straw in the mud brick dwellings of the former wardens. All of them were thirsty and starving, and made quick work of the boxes of food Bolan had raided from Jawdat's kitchen. It was too rich for them, even starting with just a spoonful, and they became sick on it. But soon they were ready to try again.

Weak and malnourished, none failed to revive visibly with water and cleaner, cooler air. When he was sure there was nothing more he could do for them, he made another phone call.

This time he wasn't calling the United States.

Outside Ramstein Air Base, Germany

THE PRETTY BLOND WOMAN lifted one of the headphone cups and let go. It slapped against her husband's head. He grabbed his ear, wincing, and dragged off the headset.

"Phone's for you." She smiled.

"You could have tapped me on the shoulder. Who is it?"

She shrugged and he took the phone. "Hello?"

"Samuels?"

"Yes?"

"You know who this is?"

Master Sergeant John Samuels, USAF, knew the voice. "Yeah. You're Belasko. We met in Azerbaijan. I'd kinda like to forget that mission."

"You did me a favor."

"Yeah."

"I need another favor."

"Okay, what is it?"

"I need you to store some video data on your personal PC. It must *not* be stored on government equipment. It will be routed through a U.S. server, but it must not be physically stored inside the United States."

Samuels was a producer for Armed Forces broadcasting. His first meeting with this man who called himself Belasko, who implied at the time that he was CIA, had been in a village filled with victims of a chemical attack.

Taping the victims of the attack had been the most gruesome experience of Samuels's life. All those bodies...

"How much data we talking about."

"Twenty, thirty MEGs."

"No problem."

"Burn me a few DVD copies, then wipe it from your hard drive."

Samuels's interest was piqued. "Is this security stuff? Can I look at it?"

"There's no reason you can't," Bolan said. "But I don't know why you would want to."

"Oh. You're still one of the good guys, right?" Samuels said. "There's nothing illegal here, is there?"

"If you think there is, turn it in," Bolan replied without hesitation.

Samuels gave him the IP and password for his home server and the video started FTPing in.

It was done surprisingly fast, and then, as promised, Samuels recorded it onto DVDs and trashed the hard drive copy with the best permanent erase software he had.

But not before he took a look at the contents. It wasn't as shocking as the video from Azerbaijan. But almost.

28

The good news was that the president *did* sanction a rescue mission. The pickup would come, guaranteed.

The bad news was that the President sanctioned the rescue mission, which meant it had the attention of half the DOD.

"Have they at least formed the committees to determine the best feasible extraction procedure?" Bolan demanded acidly.

"It's not as bad as that," Price replied, voice neutral.

"Tell whoever is in charge to come soon or don't bother. We're sitting ducks. Jawdat could change his mind or tell all. Then we're dead."

Bolan signed off. He couldn't muster the elation of the prisoners. They were in a party mood, convinced they were about to be airlifted to safety. They were talking excitedly. Americans and Iraqis and Kuwaitis. Bolan learned from their conversations that they had all been here since Desert Storm. In 1993 that one dismal building had become home to sixty-seven men. There were twenty-six left. Today was the first time any of them had been outside the cell since their torture sessions ended.

"Stony Base to Striker." It was Price again on the headset. He was keeping the line to Stony open. There was something about her voice that told him it was time to stop celebrating.

"Striker here."

"The Iraqis are on their way."

"ETA?"

"Looks like helicopters are fifteen minutes out."

"Stony, these men don't have the strength to throw rocks, let alone fire weapons. That means they've got me. Just me."

"You're pretty capable, Striker."

"I'm not going to be able to defend this bunch against enemy aircraft or a squad of rebel Iraqis!"

Bolan heard someone behind him and found the captain, Foley. His eyeless face was turned to Bolan and he gestured. It wasn't sign language, but Bolan understood.

"You overheard. Then you know I haven't done you a hell of a lot of good showing up here. We're about to be annihilated."

The captain pointed up in the air. Bolan looked around until his gaze settled on the only thing of interest—a small ledge on a cliff that had served as a watch post a hundred years ago.

"Long," Bolan shouted. "We've got Iraqis on the way. Foley's trying to tell me something. Is there a defensible cave up on the cliff?"

Long limped to him and strained to look at the cliff.

"No. There's nothing there. Just a rock wall. They used it to defend this valley in some old-time fighting."

Foley was shaking his head vigorously. He pointed into the air, spun his finger, then brought it directly down like a fluttering leaf. Then he pointed at the floor beneath the ledge.

"What you trying to tell us, Captain?"

The mute blinded man repeated the gesture. Bolan looked at the ground below the ledge, trying to figure out what was special about it. It was just a flat acre of land.

The only flat acre of land in the valley.

"That's where the helicopters will land," he stated. Foley took the warrior's shoulder and nodded vigorously, then he stabbed his finger at the cliff wall.

Now Bolan understood. "And that's the perfect place to get the drop on them," he said.

The twisted scar of Foley's mouth became a wide smile.

BOLAN HUSTLED the prisoners into the mud-brick hovels, then drove back the way he came, finding a steep incline that took him ten feet up to a more gradual rise in the cliff side wall. When

he hit the brakes he was on top of the cliff, looking down. A
steep, narrow pass took the jeep onto the ledge, no bigger than
a VIP box in a Broadway theater. He covered the jeep from front
to back with big, flat stones from the low rock wall on the ledge.
The wall had been built more than 150 years ago to shield the
ledge.

The jeep, the rocks and the cliff wall all seemed to meld together. Even the black tires were so dust-covered they matched
the desert. Bolan heard the thrum of helicopter rotors and he
crawled partway under the jeep.

Two bulbous Russian-made transport choppers rumbled overhead and descended one after another into the valley. Bolan
peered through the gaps in the low rock wall, wondering if the
choppers would even land. Maybe they would just deposit their
troops anywhere and take off.

They headed for the only level surface in the rugged terrain
of the valley, just below Bolan.

He could have spit on them.

As it was, he might have to resort to spitting. He was running
low on ammo. But he had tactics in mind to conserve what am-
munition remained.

The troop transports settled and opened, disgorging some
twenty soldiers each. They fanned out, forming a line like a riot-
control police unit marching on the silent, deserted-looking
buildings.

Pigs to the slaughter.

Bolan struck. Slaughter it would be, and he didn't have to
think twice. From the guard wall he hoisted a flat slab of dense
shale rock that weighed more than fifty pounds. He lifted it
overhead and jettisoned the rock into open space.

One of the soldiers saw him and shouted. All the men turned.
They raised their guns to fire, and then the rock inserted itself
in the rotation of the nearest set of spinning rotors.

The effect was catastrophic. Rotor blades shattered, flying in
all directions. Eight of the Iraqis flopped to the ground, killed
instantly by the flying metal, one of the bodies halved with meat-
slicer precision. Another guard found himself staring at an empty

arm socket. It happened so fast he couldn't come to terms with it and ended up walking in circles for several seconds before the blood loss dropped him.

He was one of the lucky ones. The unlucky victims were contending with massive deep-tissue wounds, some mute with shock and some screaming.

Bolan had expected the first rotor destruction to result almost immediately in the second rotor's destruction, but somehow that hadn't happened. There was a series of shouts and shots that dropped Bolan behind the cover of his wall. He heard the whine of the second chopper increase even as the first chopper's motor spun out of control. Bolan grabbed another rock, stood, but took cover again as a series of shots smacked into the wall inches below him.

He heard the helicopter take to the air, and the cover shots stopped to avoid hitting the helicopter. Bolan rose and pushed the next stone away from the cliff and saw the panicking helicopter rise up to meet it.

Bolan dived to the earth as his projectile met the rotors just below the level of his ledge. The stone wall imploded as if a cannonball had hit it, and rained down on him.

He felt fresh pain explode from several parts of his body, then heard the thump of the old Soviet helicopter returning to the valley floor.

He wriggled wormlike through the rock debris. A stab of pain below his left arm advertised a cracked or broken rib, but the rest of the injuries were simply bruises. He already had more bruises than he could count. He crawled on all fours onto the wrecked pile of rock and peered over the ledge, finding the Iraqi troops in disarray.

Half were dead or severely injured. Both aircraft were scrap heaps.

A shout. An Iraqi was pointing at the mud-brick buildings. One of the damn fool prisoners was standing there, watching the goings-on.

The Iraqi soldiers, those who still lived, now had somewhere to direct their anger.

Bolan cursed savagely. He hadn't gone through all this just to watch the prisoners get wiped out in front of his eyes. He yanked the M-16 A-2/M-203 from the jeep, chose autofire and triggered it into the knot of men marching on the prisoners. Three dropped before the burst ended.

The retaliation was instantaneous, and Bolan crouched on top of the rock pile to ride out the onslaught of rounds from below, then crept forward enough to pick off two more Iraqis as they were running for cover. The others got the message—the safest place was directly beneath the madman sniper.

At least, that was what Bolan had intended them to think.

He was out of 40 mm HE grenades, but he still had a few of the five-gallon incendiary variety. From the rear of the jeep he dragged out the plastic gasoline cans and lit the rags stuffed in their caps. He scooted the first can to the ledge and gave it a nudge, sending it spiraling earthward with bullets flying around it.

The gunfire halted and the gunners tried to run, but the gas can crashed close by and the fiery fingers lashed out at them. They were burning. They were screaming. Others were fleeing from the flames that swept across the earth.

The Executioner twisted, then put the weight and strength of his entire body behind the second gas can. It spun like a Frisbee, arcing out over the valley for an incredible distance and coming down in the path of the fleeing soldiers. Those who had been farthest from the fires were suddenly at the forefront of a fresh conflagration. They became burning, dancing puppets.

They were dead men who just didn't know it yet, and Bolan wasn't going to waste bullets on them.

He triggered the M-16 A-2 into the oddballs who had managed somehow to avoid the bodily harm of Bolan's hell on earth. Two of them dropped, and the third was returning fire when Bolan took him in the chest with a 5.56 mm shocker that stopped his heart.

But now the M-16 A-2/M-203 was just as dead. Bolan's assault rifle rounds were used up.

He dropped it, yanked out the .44 Magnum Desert Eagle, then

sighted on an Iraqi who thought the warrior was now unarmed and helpless. The gun blasted once, twice, three times, and the Iraqi gunner fell over with half his skull gone.

Bolan heard the thrum of another rotor and found a tiny bug-like speck rushing over the hills from the north, coming right at him. He witnessed a flash of light from under its belly. Rockets.

Bolan ran, up and out the narrow passage, then along the cliff top for three long strides before the rocket arrived.

It couldn't find him. The projectile wasn't designed for man-sized targets. It focused its attention on the only machinery in its range of vision. General Jawdat's jeep exploded and went over the edge, raining more flaming metal on the scattered Iraqis.

Bolan kept running. The gunship kept coming. And if the fly-by-wire rockets had trouble homing in on a target as small as a human being, well, at close range they would work just fine. Better yet, a few short trigger pulls on the machine guns and there would be nothing left of Mack Bolan except scraps for the vultures.

Bolan was feeling it again—the sense of utter depletion. He had pushed too hard, slept too little, suffered too many injuries. He was a walking train wreck, and the resources his body needed to heal all those cuts, scrapes, bruises and burns were as substantial as if he had a single major wound he was trying to overcome.

He was slowing. His legs would not carry him faster. The angry buzzing of the gunship was closing in like an angry hornet. The drop-off from the cliff top to the trail was a hundred feet away and Bolan clawed at the air, cursed the soil, sucked in the oven-hot air, and it didn't make a difference. He was incredibly fit, but he was drained beyond his deepest well of resources and he wasn't going to make it.

But he sure as hell wasn't going to die while running for cover. He brought himself to a halt, turned and raised the Desert Eagle defiantly at the hideous black insect that closed in on him.

The Iraqi pilots couldn't quite believe what they were seeing.

There was a man there, who had to be one of the escaped prisoners they were ordered to look for. He was a scarecrow, a bloodied, ragged, dirty stick figure. He was panting like a marathon runner. He was wavering on his feet like a drunk.

And he was threatening the Soviet gunship, one of the world's deadliest technological creations, with a handgun.

The pilot grinned. The copilot smiled sardonically and waved.

The scarecrow grimaced, as if he, too, saw something amusing in the situation.

Then, just for their amusement, he tucked the handgun into a hip holster and pointed his finger at them, thumb up, like a pistol.

The pilot laughed out loud.

The scarecrow fired his finger and mouthed the word "Bang."

And the Iraqi gunship exploded.

"WHAT THE FUCK is he doing?" the gunner cried.

"Distracting them, dammit!" the pilot shot back. "Take 'em out before they see us!"

"With him standing right there?"

"Just fucking fire!"

The rocket tore away from the U.S. Apache gunship with a plume of white fire. The radar jam that the Iraqis had attributed to equipment failure couldn't hide the rocket signature and the radar on the Iraqi gunship squealed an alarm for an eighth of a second—then the alarm stopped dead, along with every other system on the gunship and her crew.

BOLAN FOUND HIMSELF running again, fleeing the ball of fire. The gunship crashed atop the cliff, where her munitions and fuel ignited uncontrollably.

He came to the edge of the trail. He saw his shadow below in the brilliance of the wall of fire about to engulf him, and he dived into open space. He fell, twisted, met the steep decline and rolled like a log down a mountain.

He came to halt on his back, looking up at the tongues of fire licking the sky, licking the rock, trying to reach him. Then their life force faded and the tongues retreated.

MACK BOLAN DID NOT move. The sky was blue now, clear and clean. It could have been the skies over the Blue Ridge Mountains. Or Oahu or Anchorage. It could have been the blue skies of Pittsfield, Massachusetts.

The War Everlasting had consisted of a thousand battles, but rarely had the Executioner been pushed so hard, bludgeoned and bruised and battered as he had this time.

But he pushed himself. Maybe, as strange as it seemed, he had become too personally invested in what had started out as a favor for Aaron Kurtzman.

The reason? The nature of the crime struck a powerful chord in Bolan. He had seen war. He knew men who were captured by the enemy.

It was to a nation's shame that it failed to bring back its prisoners of war. But for a man of power to deliberately abandon his nation's soldiers to the enemy was so dishonorable to those men that it was a personal affront to Bolan.

That was why he fought and struggled to keep going despite the pleas of his body to rest.

All governments had corrupt elements, but this crime made the U.S. seem—what? Unclean? Yes. Unclean. Bolan the patriot had been incapable of permitting the stain to linger uncleansed.

He rolled to his feet as the thrum of U.S. transport choppers and gunship chaperons filled the desiccated Iraqi valley.

He was paying for his compulsion now, and he'd be paying for weeks. He couldn't find a place on his body that didn't hurt.

"Sir!"

A pair of Army field medics was racing at him. They tried to grab his arms and sit him down to await a stretcher. He shrugged them off and limped among the devastation he had made of the Iraqi transport choppers. The rock was burned black. Twisted corpses issued a sickly gray smoke.

"The prisoners," he said.

LONG WAS WAITING outside the transport chopper. He was insisting on being the last of the prisoners to be boarded.

"There's going to be hell to pay, Sergeant," Bolan said.

"Sir?"

"Juvenal is going to face the consequences of his actions. You'll have the pleasure of testifying at his court-martial."

Sergeant Long looked at the ground, then at Bolan. "Sir, we won't testify against General Juvenal."

Bolan said nothing.

"He was our commanding officer, sir," Long explained. "We were sworn to secrecy. The mission we were on was a good one."

"The mission has nothing to do with the fact that you were left here to rot for more than a decade just so he could avoid disciplinary action."

"We knew going in that this was hit or miss. We agreed from the start to follow orders, and even after we ended up in this stinking jail we swore that we wouldn't betray the cause that got us here."

Bolan shook his head. "Long, even that cause was a sham. Juvenal was more interested in his career than a negotiated peace. The oath you took was just a tool of his manipulation."

"Sir," Long said with finality, "I'm sorry, but the oath is made. We won't stab General Juvenal in the back."

Long followed the last of the gaunt prisoners into the waiting medevac Chinook.

"Sir! Mr. Cooper!" A pair of MPs was jogging from the Black Hawk UH-60M parked nearby. "You need to come with us, sir."

Bolan said nothing, did nothing. The MPs got nervous. Behind Bolan the hatch closed on the Chinook and the big chopper took to the air. In seconds the flurry of rotors filled the valley with a deafening miasma of echoes, and then the aircraft was gone. Only the Black Hawk remained.

"I know you're the one who found these guys and all, sir. I don't know what Washington's problem is, but I'm afraid we have to take you into custody, sir."

One MP took one arm. One MP took another.

"Would you grunts get a move on!" barked the UH-60M pilot. "We got a hundred berserk Iraqis gonna come down on us in about one minute!"

The Executioner was guided to the open entrance to the Black

Hawk. The MPs jumped up, and Bolan plodded after them. The MPs grasped him by the armpits and lifted him inside.

One MP jogged up front to pound the cockpit wall. "We're good to go!" he shouted.

The rotors whined and the landing wheels left the valley floor. Bolan straightened abruptly and floored his handler with an elbow to the gut. The second MP cursed and grabbed for his wrist. Bolan cracked the man in the chin and lifted his assault rifle from his shoulder in one sweep.

The ground was eight feet away when Bolan stepped off and plummeted to the rock, rolling, rising to his feet and running for cover behind the wreckage of the nearest Iraqi helicopter.

The MPs and the pilot shouted back and forth while the Black Hawk hung motionless. Bolan fired the MP's assault rifle, stitching the helicopter's body panels. That was all the argument the pilot needed. The Black Hawk ascended fast and shot out of the valley.

29

The valley filled to overflowing with a blessed silence.

Bolan felt disillusioned. Defeated. He had done what he set out to do, and he felt like he had accomplished nothing. Achieved nothing.

The U.S. rescue team had put plastic handcuffs on the surviving Iraqi rebels. A box cutter was supplied so they could free themselves later. The box cutter was on a rock a hundred feet from the survivors, and one of them had managed to crawl halfway there when Bolan confiscated it.

The Iraqi muttered at him unpleasantly. When Bolan appropriated all the water bottles, too, the muttering turned vehement.

Bolan left the valley. Within a couple of miles he took cover in a shallow depression in a stunted cliff wall and waited.

By dusk the Iraqi patrols had ended and the desert was silent. The air became cool. Bolan started walking.

He had water, he had a replacement M-16 with a nearly full clip, and he had his handguns. He would head southeast and eventually run into one of the dry riverbeds that would lead him south. He would find a hole to sleep in tomorrow at dawn and be in friendlier country by the morning of the next day. He could get a flight or a car in al-Lifiyah—on the Saudi Arabian side of the border.

Every step hurt like hell, but he would probably survive.

Bolan pulled out his phone and flipped on the power. The lights came on and he heard Kurtzman say half of the word

"Hello" before Hal Brognola came on the line and bellowed, "Striker, where the hell are you?"

"Still in Iraq. I declined the U.S. government's offer of free lodging in the military lockup. Seems I've rubbed somebody the wrong way. Probably our friend Juvenal."

"That rat bastard," Brognola exploded. "They had him assisting in the rescue. He must've issued the order to have you arrested."

"How come *he's* not locked up, Hal?"

"He is by now. The question is how long he'll stay there. He's a D.C. insider, Striker, Army or not. He's connected, and he's going to call in every favor he's owed. It'll be tough to nail him and make it stick."

"The charges are serious," Bolan countered, but it was a half-hearted argument.

"You know the game," Brognola said.

"I know the game," Bolan agreed. "I know about the pariah syndrome, too, Hal. No amount of political leverage can overcome a good negative-publicity blitz."

"No way, Striker. You're not using Stony Man files to publicize Juvenal's shortcomings."

"I wouldn't dream of it, Hal," Bolan said. Brognola's next words were lost when the soldier cut the connection.

He dialed another number from memory.

"Samuels," Bolan said. "It's me."

"Hey, Belasko Productions, the man himself," said the German-based airman. "Let me guess. You just finished filming your latest laugh-riot comedy flick and you want me to make copies for all your friends."

"You're almost right," Bolan said. Then he told the airman what he needed done.

"The networks will never air all this stuff, man," Samuels said.

"They'll air enough of it to show the world what really happened. Can you distribute it without being fingered?"

"Yeah, sure. I'll upload the video to a newsgroup from the Internet vending machine at the hypermarket in Frankfurt," Samuels explained offhandedly. "Then all I have to do is send anonymous e-mails telling the news networks where to find it. The video will be there for anybody and everybody to see."

"Fine. Do it."

"Hey, that was you, wasn't it, man?" the airman asked. "You're the guy behind the camera? You were actually in Iraq to get those guys."

"Yeah."

"That took some real balls, man."

"Samuels, you want to know something funny—that's the one part of me doesn't hurt at this moment."

"Got the shit kicked out of ya, huh?"

"Yeah."

"But you kicked some ass, too."

"I guess I did."

"And now nobody appreciates all your hard work?"

Bolan smiled. This smart-ass kid was putting things into a pretty good perspective. "Think I'll come to Ramstein and buy you a beer."

"A beer? You're gonna owe me like fifty beers. And after watching that damn movie of yours, I feel like drinking them all in one night."

Bolan felt satisfied when he hung up. The well-connected General Juvenal was about to become world famous, and the most shunned man in Washington, D.C. His career was over. His friends would suddenly forget they knew him. He might even get a fair trial.

If it happened, it would be justice.

Justice was the least, and the most, that he could ever hope for.

His body was tiring, aching, slowing, but mentally he felt better than he had in days. He pushed on through the night with the Saudi border just a hundred miles away.

Epilogue

He emerged from the blackness slowly. He remembered nothing, then he remembered everything.

He should be dead. They shot him. He *made* them shoot him.

When he opened his eyes, he was face-to-face with Radhi Tereq.

"Good morning, General Jawdat."

Jawdat tried to speak, but his mouth wouldn't work. It felt as if it were caked shut with dried mud.

"Do not be alarmed. You are fine," the intelligence officer said, wearing a plastic smile. "You were shot a number of times, but we pulled you through. You are in al-Azimiyah getting the best medical care."

There was a covert prison hospital located near al-Azimiyah, one of the five Baghdad palaces. This facility specialized in fostering the recuperation of those prisoners who were viewed as valuable information sources. Jawdat had himself attended interrogations here.

"We've suffered some great setbacks in recent days," Tereq said. "The American prisoners you were holding in the mountains escaped the country. They suffered not a single casualty, while we lost several aircraft and many men. We're anxious to learn what you know about the man who spearheaded the operation. No one believes that one American could have caused so much mayhem and destruction without help. But you're coming along well. In a few days you will be well enough to tell us about it."

Jawdat knew what that meant and he tried to say something. Anything. He would beg Tereq to free him, or kill him. Any option was better than torture by the pain artisans of Baghdad. Tereq observed his struggles dispassionately.

"Not yet, General. You need a few more days to get well. Then we'll take the brace off."

Oh. They had clamped his jaw shut. It was standard practice when it was feared a prisoner might chew off his own tongue to make questioning impractical. The big metal brace locked around his skull and a large wad of gauze was in the mouth to keep his tongue from moving around and being swallowed. The apparatus had a quick-release knob on top, in case the prisoner vomited while wearing it. Jawdat tried to move his arms and found them shackled to a belt around his waist. When he struggled to move his arms the pain in his chest sprang to life.

"Don't overdo it," Tereq advised as he turned away. "Rest. Get your strength back."

To Jawdat's mind there came an unbidden memory of being at this hospital years ago with one of the American prisoners of war. Jawdat himself had done the questioning. The American prisoners were his pet project, and very few people besides himself, the president, and a handful of top-level advisers had known about their existence. Now, because of his involvement with the Americans, he was about to face the same torture they suffered.

The hideous irony struck him as funny, somehow. He chuckled, and the sound came out as a grotesque gargle.

Tereq was waiting for the guard to unlock the door to the room, and he looked at Jawdat curiously. "I hope you do not go mad on me, General," he said. "That would spoil everything."

The gargle stopped. Tereq departed.

Jawdat wished he could go mad. That would make the rest of his life more bearable. But he was perfectly sane, and strong-willed, and despite himself he was going to last a long time here in the clandestine hospital at al-Azimiyah.

And what about the American with the steely eyes—he had engineered the events that labeled Jawdat a traitor. Now that American dog was free.

There was no justice in the world.

James Axler
Outlanders®

MASK OF THE SPHINX

Harnessing the secrets of selective mutation, the psionic abilities of its nobility and benevolent rule of a fair queen, the city-kingdom of Aten remains insular, but safe. Now, Aten faces a desperate fight for survival—a battle that will lure Kane and his companions into the conflict, where a deadly alliance with the Imperator to hunt out the dark forces of treason could put the Cerberus warriors one step closer to their goal of saving humanity...or damn them, and their dreams, to the desert dust.

Available August 2004 at your favorite retail outlet.

Or order your copy now by sending your name, address, zip or postal code, along with a check or money order (please do not send cash) for $6.50 for each book ordered ($7.99 in Canada), plus 75¢ postage and handling ($1.00 in Canada), payable to Gold Eagle Books, to:

In the U.S.	In Canada
Gold Eagle Books	Gold Eagle Books
3010 Walden Avenue	P.O. Box 636
P.O. Box 9077	Fort Erie, Ontario
Buffalo, NY 14269-9077	L2A 5X3

Please specify book title with your order.
Canadian residents add applicable federal and provincial taxes.

GOUT30

DEATH LANDS®

Separation

*Available June 2004
at your favorite retail outlet.*

JAMES AXLER

DEATH LANDS

Separation

The group makes its way to a remote island in hopes of finding brief sanctuary. Instead, they are captured by an isolated tribe of descendants of African slaves from pre–Civil War days. When they declare Mildred Wyeth "free" from her white masters, it is a twist of fate that ultimately leads the battle-hardened medic to question where her true loyalties lie. Will she side with Ryan, J. B. Dix and those with whom she has forged a bond of trust and friendship...or with the people of her own blood?

GOLD EAGLE®

GDL66

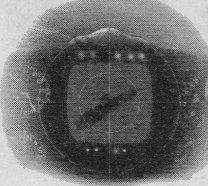